MORE PRAISE FOR THOMAS TESSIER!

"Thomas Tessier is one of those writers who can find the unexpected poetry and subtlety in horror."
—Peter Straub

"Vastly talented...Tessier is a masterful practitioner of the art of dark fiction."
—*Publishers Weekly*

"Thomas Tessier is horror fiction's best kept secret."
—*Washington Post*

"Tessier is a vastly talented writer, who uses not just words, but always just the right word, to tantalize his readers."
—*Rocky Mountain News*

"A master of quiet terror."
—*Anniston Star*

"Tessier is one of the most capable and conscientious writers to grace the contemporary field."
—*The Magazine of Fantasy and Science Fiction*

"Tessier knows how to write a crackling good story."
—*The Tribune* (San Diego)

"Thomas Tessier is one of the genre's living masters. His novels and stories combine the visceral satisfactions of first-rate popular fiction with the aesthetic satisfaction of literary fiction at its best."
—Bill Sheehan, author of *At the Foot of the Story Tree*

"One of the very best writers of horror fiction of this generation."
—*Shadowings: The Reader's Guide to Horror Fiction*

VANISHED

"The local nightlife, down in the south end. Take a look. You might be surprised."

"Okay, I will," I told her impatiently. "But, Jenny, who am I supposed to focus on—town hall, the police, the Jaycees?"

"Yes," she answered immediately. "All of them. Start where you want, but they're the ones. They control things. Believe me. Even the churches. *Especially* the churches."

"Right, okay."

"You've seen the churches?" she asked.

"The ones around the green. I'm staying at the Birch Inn."

"Right, they're five of them there," Jenny said. "Did you notice anything odd or strange about them?"

"I wasn't looking. The odd and strange finds me all by itself."

"I'll tell you something else. Some people have disappeared here. In Lauck County. Schramburg. *Winship.*"

"What do you mean, disappeared?"

"Disappeared," she stated flatly. "No searches, no official investigations, no news reports. They just disappeared...."

Other *Leisure* books by Thomas Tessier:

RAPTURE
FINISHING TOUCHES

WICKED THINGS

THOMAS TESSIER

LEISURE BOOKS NEW YORK CITY

For my sister, Carol, and
in memory of Franklyn Tessier
and Harry Oemcke.

A LEISURE BOOK®

June 2007

Published by

Dorchester Publishing Co., Inc.
200 Madison Avenue
New York, NY 10016

ISBN-10: 0-8439-5560-0
ISBN-13: 978-0-8439-5560-6

The name "Leisure Books" and the stylized "L" with design are trademarks of Dorchester Publishing Co., Inc.

Printed in the United States of America.

Visit us on the web at www.dorchesterpub.com.

WICKED THINGS

WICKED THINGS

Chapter One

"So, what have you got for me this time?" I asked.

Steve McAuliffe smiled. "Some mysterious so-called accidental deaths, a few nasty dismemberments. That kind of thing."

"All in one case?"

"That's what I want you to find out."

"Sounds like fun. Where?"

"A town called Winship, in Lauck County. It's way the fuck upstate, out in the middle of nowhere. The next nearest town is Schramburg, and that's more than twenty miles away."

I didn't know upstate at all; it was just a big blank nowhereland to me. But I knew it would be a long drive. That was okay—I'd rather drive than fly anywhere. We were sitting in Steve's second-floor corner office.

He runs an organization that goes by the clumsy name of the Insurance Industry Consulting Group. Some big companies kick in to help fund it, and he has a big mainframe that sometimes spits out very interesting information. Computers are starting to make a difference in this business. A woman is murdered. Her husband is not charged but the police have reason to suspect him. If she happened to be insured for $100,000 nobody would think twice about it, but if there were six or seven different policies on her, each in that amount, with companies scattered across the land, then the picture would begin to look very different. Steve's powerful little team deals with such cases, and they never lack work.

I am a freelance insurance investigator. For a while I was a cop, but I gave it up. Too much boring paperwork and too many long hours spent hanging around the courthouse for petty bullshit cases. Then I was a private eye: working divorce cases, tracing bad fathers who skipped out on child support payments, looking for runaway teens. But the emotional wear and tear began to take a toll, and I often had to fight just to collect my expense money, so I was ready for a change when I landed my first insurance case. It was painless, elegant, and entertaining, and the company paid promptly.

"Upstate, okay," I said. "Tell me more."

"We're concerned about nineteen claims in the last two years. Call it sixteen—I don't want you to waste time on the three dismemberments. Sixteen accidental deaths."

"Ouch."

"Exactly."

"How many companies are involved?"

"Sixteen."

"How many local agents?"

"Right," Steve said with a smile of appreciation. "Three of the policies were bought by the parties concerned, but the sixteen we're dealing with came through one independent agent. A guy by the name of Joseph Bellman."

"Sixteen companies, sixteen claims, and one agent."

"Right."

All the major insurance companies have their own trained investigators, but in a case like this it simply isn't practical to have sixteen different people out there, each one looking into his own little claim. The total payout on all the claims is more than enough, however, to justify sending in one man who will try to save everybody's money. Someone like me, Jack Carlson.

"Mr. Bellman sure spreads his business around."

"Yes, he does."

"Steve, you want me to look into sixteen different cases, talk to all the major people involved in each one?"

"No, no, that'd be too much," he replied with a wave of his hand. "Look through the files, pick two or three that grab you the most and see what you find with them."

"Okay."

"I trust your instincts, Jack. The companies

are under growing pressure to pay up on these claims, and if you tell me everything feels okay, they'll do so. If you think something's wrong, then we'll back you all the way and we'll see where it all leads. You might start with Bellman. He's the central guy in this."

"Oh, I intend to start with him."

"Too many cases, too much money."

"Has anybody been there ahead of me?"

"Three companies not affiliated with us sent their own people in, but they had no luck. They decided Bellman looked okay, the claims were not outrageous, so they paid off and closed their books on it."

"Sounds a bit like Hopeville," I said.

"I had the same thought."

A couple of years ago Steve's people noticed that there had been a remarkable flurry of personal injury claims from the small town of Hopeville, down south, and he sent me to see what was going on there. It was a backwoods hamlet, desperately poor, and the people were very unfriendly. But there were an awful lot of shiny, brand-new Jeeps and pickups around the place. That was because close to half the adult male population of Hopeville had recently suffered an accident and collected the insurance on it. Most of the time it was a hand or a foot that got blown off in an unlikely hunting mishap. A small price to pay for a new Cadillac or truck. There wasn't much that could be done about it, except to put the word out in the industry. The folks in Hopeville are probably still poor, but they've got some pretty toys to help them while away the time.

"What's the total payout at risk here?" I asked.

"Two point four."

I liked that. I get a small retainer up front, and of course my expenses are covered, but in the final accounting I'm paid on a percentage basis, so the more I save the insurers, the more I get to take home. On the downside, if I don't save them anything, all I come away with is that dinky retainer. Sixteen cases, with two point four million dollars at stake. A lot of incentive.

"That's a nice number."

"Don't get excited," Steve said. "This doesn't sound easy."

"I know, but this guy Bellman has put up a lot of arrows and they're all pointing right at him. What's the story with the beneficiaries?"

"Just family members, spouses. Routine, nothing at all out of the ordinary there, or so it would seem."

"What about the local cops?"

"Not much help, but they haven't been a hindrance. They say a couple of the deaths might look a bit funny at a distance, but aren't really, and they haven't come up with anything. You know how it is."

"If it looks like an accident, write it up as an accident."

"Exactly. And I'll tell you right now, Jack,

most of these cases do look like relatively simple, unfortunate accidents."

"But the probability is off."

"Way off."

"What have you found out about Bellman?"

"Not much. The State Insurance Commissioner's office has no record of any complaints against him. Ditto the police and civil courts. Seems like he was just an ordinary small-town insurance agent selling all the usual policies. Until the last two years, when people started dropping like flies on his turf."

"What would he get out of it?" I wondered aloud.

"That's your job, to find out," Steve said. "Remember?"

"Oh yeah. You said there were some dismemberments?"

"A few, yes." Steve shrugged. "They might not be connected in any way, but I've got a brief outline of those cases for you too, in case you do happen to come across anything relevant to them. Any significant claim that comes via Bellman is suspect now. Otherwise, don't bother spending much time on them."

I nodded. There was a green folder on Steve's desk, bulging with papers. "Is that my homework?"

"Yes. Sorry it's so big. I've thinned it down as much I can, but with sixteen different claims, well . . ."

"That's okay. What about the other three?"

"You'll find a short summary of them in there for information, but they have been settled already. If you did manage to tie them into a fraud case, and any money is eventually recovered, I know that the companies involved would be happy to cut you in for your share."

"I won't hold my breath on that."

Steve laughed. "Yeah, recovery's always a breeze."

"You want this done right away, right?"

"A couple of the parties are now threatening legal action to force payment. So, the sooner the better. As in now. Any problem?"

"No, none at all," I said. "Today's Thursday. I'll make sure Bellman is going to be around next week. Assuming he is, I'll drive up over the weekend and get going first thing on Monday morning."

"Great. Oh, and here's our usual paperwork."

"Right."

Steve and I each signed their standard hire agreement. I put my copy in my briefcase, along with the big fat file and my retainer check.

"You have the number of my direct line here."

"Sure do."

"And my home number?"

"Yep, but I shouldn't need to bother you there."

"Don't worry about it, call any time you need to."

"Thanks, Steve."

"Take care of yourself up there, it's a long way from anywhere."

I smiled and nodded. "I always do."

Later that afternoon I was back in my little office at home. It was originally the dining room, but from the day I moved in it has been my workspace. Now it's pretty cluttered, with a desk, some filing cabinets, a couple of chairs, and a growing library of reference books on shelves along the wall and stacked up on the floor in various places—they were edging toward the living room.

I looked through the file Steve had given me, just skimming. I didn't find anything that jumped up off the page at me. A good deal of it was vaguely familiar, since even accidental deaths and dismemberments tend to follow certain well-worn paths. You don't have to know anything about insurance to appreciate the beauty of a hunting accident. It has a classic simplicity. *I was climbing over a barbed wire fence, my sleeve got snagged, I fell forward, the shotgun got pulled around and blowed my left hand off.* Or, *Unbeknowst to me, I stepped in a gopher hole and twisted my ankle real bad, and when I hit the ground, boom, the shotgun went off, and the next thing I knew, my other foot was disattached.* It's funny, but these accidents seldom seem to happen when you have four guys sitting around together in a duck blind.

To get away with this kind of thing, all you really have to do is endure the pain and stick to your story. It's also a very good idea to have a friend nearby in the woods, not so close that he actually sees what happens, but to get you to the hospital so you don't inadvertently bleed to death.

The three cases that had already been paid off were hunting accidents like that, except that the people involved had died and it was their heads that had been disattached. Other people were in the area, but no one had actually seen the fatal accidents happen. I looked at one of the dismemberment cases, out of curiosity. A guy named Marcie Lebeau was cutting up some logs. A wood chip hit him in the eye, since he wasn't wearing goggles. He jumped, and the chain saw lopped off his hand—his left hand—at the wrist. He wrote that he would have taken the loose hand to the hospital to see if it could be reattached, but he passed out, and when his wife found him a few minutes later, the dog had made off with the hand and it couldn't be found. I kind of wanted to believe that one. Sometimes companies will stall on a claim like that just because the claimant is usually right-handed and the hand that is lost is usually the left one.

The file showed sixteen supposedly accidental deaths in less than two years. Some poor souls are so hard-pressed that they'll commit suicide and try to make it look like an accident so that their families will be left financially better off, though most companies specifically exclude sui-

11

cides that occur in the first two years of the policy. I hate those cases. And then there's murder, sometimes staged as an accident, that most appealing of crimes—as long as it happens to someone else.

Seven men and nine women. All very ordinary, at first glance. A car crash on an icy road. A gas explosion. Two electrocutions. Not much so far. One man blew himself away with dynamite while working in his own garnet mine. Another man potted his wife while cleaning his rifle (*"I would have swore on the Bible that the gun was empty"*). A drowning, a fall, and so on, to the inevitable hunting accident (*"I still don't believe it was Floyd, not a deer, but I guess it was"*).

I checked the atlas. Lauck County had a population of about fifty thousand people, of which some eleven thousand were in Winship. Obviously a rural area, and more accidents like these *do* happen in rural areas—relative, that is, to the population sample. The probability was off in Winship, though, not simply because the number of accidents was too large for that population base and time span, but rather because there were sixteen claims on sixteen different companies. That looked all wrong, downright suspicious, as if the agent were deliberately trying to avoid attracting attention.

Most independent agents steer their business to a handful of major insurance companies, depending on the rates offered and the coverage required—home, life, auto, medical, etc. But sixteen different companies for the same basic life/accidental death policy? Uh-unh. I still could not see how Joseph Bellman might profit from any of this. You can find one evil person to join you in a plot to kill another person and then split the insurance money—but sixteen? Still, it all came back to Joseph Bellman, he was the man at the center, and I was looking forward to meeting him.

"Hello, Bellman Insurance," a sweet young voice answered.

"Hello. May I speak with Mr. Bellman's secretary?"

"I'm Chris Innes, Mr. Bellman's assistant. May I help you?"

"Yes, I'd like to make an appointment to meet with him."

"He's in right now, if you want to speak to him."

"No, that's all right. I have to go out in a minute."

"Okay. Did you want to come in here to our office or would you like Mr. Bellman to visit you at your home?"

"I'll come in to the office."

"Okay. And when would suit you?"

"Is he free Monday?"

"Morning or afternoon?" She quickly added, "He's also available for evening appointments, if that would be more convenient for you."

"Morning would suit me."

"Ten o'clock all right, or something later?"

"Ten's fine."

"And your name?"

"Jack Carlson."

"Thank you, Mr. Carlson, we'll see you Monday morning at ten."

"Looking forward to it."

I hung up. She had a nice voice. Untroubled.

Chapter Two

Upstate has always been pretty much a blank to me. I know there are some scattered towns and small cities, mountains and lakes and a lot of rolling countryside. Dairy farms, apple orchards, potato fields as well. A good place for hiking, camping, fishing, swimming, and skiing, if you like that kind of thing. I was up there one time when I was a kid, spent a week with an aunt and uncle and their two boys, my cousins Ricky and Jimmy. They'd rented a cottage on a lake, and I was invited along. The lake was slimy, the cottage was a dump, the mosquitoes and horseflies tormented us, and my aunt and uncle bickered about everything. That was upstate to me, thank you so much.

I left on Saturday morning, to give myself plenty of time for what promised to be a drive of between four and five hours. I would need to find a decent place to stay, and my plan for Sunday was to get to know my way around Winship and the immediate area, and perhaps even to take a look at a couple of the accident sites. I had the map open on the passenger seat beside me. Once I hit the Northwestern Turnpike it was smooth sailing for a couple hours. Eventually, the pike swung away from where I wanted to go and I had to use county roads, which were narrow, winding, and often not in great repair. My progress slowed considerably as I tried to pick the right turns to make. I'm one of those people who has a car compass mounted over the dash, so I knew I was driving more or less in the right direction, but the few signs I saw didn't mention Winship.

After a while I had no clear idea where I was. What good is it to know that you're traveling in a northwesterly direction if you've already strayed beyond the point where northwest is right? I was fairly sure I had drifted into Lauck County, but I had yet to find any of the pinprick villages shown on the map.

It was the kind of area some people would call God's country, but they could have it. I see a pretty lake, and I can also see the big, ugly old snapping turtle hiding somewhere beneath the surface, ready to rip a chunk off my big toe. I see a forest, or a mountainside thick with dark trees, and I can imagine running into animals I would prefer never to see anywhere but on television. I see a lovely landscape, unspoiled by any human trace, rolling gently to the horizon, and I know that if I went for a walk there I would get lost—hell, I was driving and I was lost.

I saw few houses, and they all looked empty, uninhabited. Summer people, probably, who had packed up and left the week before, right after Labor Day. I suddenly realized that I couldn't remember the last car I'd seen on the road—it might have been half an hour ago. I felt as if I were in some vacant place where you could meander up and down and around and back forever.

I would come to a fork in the road every so often. If there were a signpost, it invariably meant nothing to me. I stayed with my compass since there was nothing else to do. For some time the road climbed very gradually, but then I found myself over the top and on a steep descent. Three miles down, through a tight tunnel of trees—it was like driving into a mineshaft. The bright sun disappeared, and I had visions of eventually running into a swamp before I could hit the brakes.

But then I was back in the daylight and the road leveled off as it merged with a slightly larger one, and just ahead was a gas station. Life. People. I parked at the pump, filled the tank and then went inside to pay. A young woman in blue jeans and a maroon sweatshirt sat behind the counter.

"Can you tell me how far it is to Winship?"

"You're there," she answered with a bright smile. "Stay on this road, you go around the bend just ahead a little ways, and you'll see the whole valley and the town right in front of you."

"Ah, great. Thank you."

"You're welcome."

I started to leave, but then stopped and turned back to her. "If you needed a room in Winship for a couple of nights, where would you go?"

"Oh, you've got several choices," she said eagerly. "You'll see a few motels on this road as you head into town and there are a couple more down in the south end. They're all okay places, they're clean, and it's off-season now, so the rates just went down. But if you want the best place, that'd be the Birch Inn."

"Oh? Where's that?"

"Right in the center of town, on Church Street. It's a big old country inn, you know? Real quaint and classy. The rooms at the front face the green, which is pretty, and the rooms at the back look out on the river, and that's nice too."

"Sounds better than a motel," I said.

"Their restaurant is really good too. The off-season just started, so the rates'll be lower and you won't have any trouble getting a room."

"The Birch Inn. Thanks."

"You're welcome. Have a nice stay."

Winship was right where she said it would be, and the view as I came around the bend was quite attractive—some residential neighborhoods stretching up and down both sides of the river, and nestling in the middle of it all a clutch of white church spires, some taller buildings, and the elegant arches of two iron bridges. On this side of the river the steep mountain loomed nearby, but on the far side the land inclined gently, and I could see several terraced plots and greenhouses.

Then an official sign confirmed it: WELCOME TO WINSHIP.

I drove slowly, glancing around at the houses and stores. I soon realized that the place was different. I had seen a lot of small, isolated towns along the road that day, and they all had a tired, ramshackle look about them, as if they were caught in some interminable rustic paralysis. Peeling paint, unmowed grass, old appliances junked in the yard, sagging porches, dead cars, trucks, and tractors—all the usual signs of sweet surrender and neglect.

But Winship, in contrast, was postcard-bright and tidy, a prosperous-looking community of trim lawns and crisp white homes. I found myself thinking of Norman Rockwell's paintings, but there was a little roughness around the edges in most of his work, and everything in Winship had a smoothed-out look. Even the kids that I saw were neatly dressed, hair combed and brushed in place. I had expected something rundown and backwoods, the kind of town that sleeps for nine months of the year and wakes up only for the summer visitors. Wrong again.

Downtown, it was more of the same. The commercial district was only a couple of square blocks, but it looked lively enough. No empty storefronts or FOR RENT signs in the windows. The city green was right out of a textbook, with a fountain, a gray stone war memorial, and some benches beneath the maple trees. It was surrounded by churches, the town hall, the courthouse, the public library, and a number of beautiful old colonial houses that had been converted for professional use. It took me a second turn around the green to find the Birch Inn, since the only sign was a small brass plate mounted beside the door—hard to see from the street. But I liked the look of the place at once—wide stairs up to a long veranda that had several cushioned wicker chairs, so you could sit comfortably with a drink in hand and observe life's slow parade. I thought that I might even do that before I left.

Inside, the lobby was delightful, with lustrous old wood and soft lights, cool and soothing. It was indeed the off-season, and the older gentleman at the reception desk offered me a choice of rooms on the second or third floor. I took the one on the corner of the second floor, overlooking the green and the city center.

"Can I get something to eat from room service?" I asked. It was past three in the afternoon, and I hadn't stopped for lunch.

"Yes, of course. There's a menu in your room, but if you know what you want I'll take your order now and save some time."

"Club sandwich and a bottle of beer?"

"Club sandwich and . . . any particular brand of beer?" Before I could answer, he continued. "May I recommend Five Towns? They make a very nice lager, a strong ale, and a dark beer. You can't go wrong with any of them. It's a local brew, very fresh."

"There's a brewery here?"

"Oh, yes, for decades, going back even before prohibition. Or as the saying goes, before, *during*, and after," he added with a sly smile.

"Well, let's try it then," I said. "Make it a lager."

"Very good, sir."

I felt much better a little later, sitting back on the bed, a stomach full of food and the rest of the beer in my hand. The kinks in my body were gone and I didn't want to move. The room was pleasant and the furniture was more comfortable-old than precious-old. Most of the time when I'm out on the road for a job I have no choice but to stay overnight at a chain motel. I can't knock them—they're handy, clean, and cheap, and at the end of a long day it's good to know you'll get all the basic comforts—but the Birch Inn was a welcome change.

I looked at the label on the brown bottle: *Five Towns Lager, South River Road, Winship*. There was a simple decorative motif, a shield emblazoned with an ornate cross. They weren't the first brewery to use an image like that. I did like the beer; it had a bit of a hoppy edge. A bit of text on the back label informed me that Winship was formerly known as Five Towns, deriving from the five original villages that grew up there in settlement times.

Late afternoon, a balmy Saturday in September. I had opened the window, and a soft breeze filtered into the room. I felt comfortable, a little drowsy. So far, Winship looked like a nice town in a nice setting. The kind of place I might even bring Jacqui for a romantic long weekend, if we were still together. I might even bring Maggie here, but we're no longer married and not on speaking terms. I was still just on the right side of forty, but on the wrong side of life.

I heard children singing. I couldn't tell where the sound came from, but it had to be choir practice at one of the nearby churches. Clear young voices. But they weren't singing any hymns that I knew. I went to the window and listened carefully. It was difficult to make out any words, but they didn't sound like English or Latin. French? Perhaps they were going over some wordless choral harmonies, though it didn't sound exactly like that either. Whatever it was, it was lovely. A shimmering, ethereal sound, like something out of Debussy. I put the bottle on the table, stretched out, and the voices soon faded away. I fell asleep.

It was just after six in the evening when I awoke. I washed my face, put on a jacket, and went outside for a walk. It was the dinner hour, but there were quite a few people about. Perhaps it was the lingering summer weather. The winters had to be long and brutal there, so every moment of sun and warmth counted. The sun had just moved down behind the hill across the river, and the sky was pale and luminous, with faint pink shadings off to the west. I was on the street behind the hotel. It ran along the river and was closed to vehicles for a couple of blocks, thus creating a pleasant promenade. When I came to an outdoor café I sat down and ordered a cup of coffee.

Some canoeists and kayakers were there, drinking beer and talking animatedly. I was struck by how attractive it seemed just then, everything—the time of day, the season, the setting of a neat little town in a pretty, rural valley, the café perched on the river, the light in the sky, and the people around me. It felt almost European, maybe Swiss or Austrian, in its picturesque tidiness. But that was probably because I had come to Winship with such low expectations.

By the time I finished my coffee and lit a rare cigarette, I noticed that the sky appeared brighter. That didn't make sense. It should have been getting darker. The rosiness was gone, but the pale white glow was somehow more vivid. Was it an illusion? But no, I was sure my eyes weren't fooling me. I turned to the people at the next table, an elderly couple.

"Excuse me," I said. "Is it my imagination, or does the sky seem to be getting a little brighter now?"

"It's not your imagination," the woman replied with a kindly smile. "It's often like this in the summer and fall. You're not from around here."

"No, I'm just passing through." I looked up at the sky once more. It seemed to be glowing with a high and clear white light. "What causes it?"

"The farther north you go," the man answered this time, "the more likely you are to see unusual atmospheric effects. Look out later, when it's dark, and you may see the aurora."

"At this time of the year?"

"Yeah, sure," he told me. "All year round."

"Especially in this valley," his wife added.

"Why is that?"

"Just the location," the man said with a shrug. "We're very fortunate. We don't have too much industry and development here, or in the surrounding area, so you can see the sky more clearly at night."

That didn't sound very convincing to me, but I let it go.

I had a late dinner in the hotel restaurant, a cozy room at the back of the inn, with more of that fine old woodwork. The sound system unobtrusively played Telemann, Vivaldi, and other baroque composers. The food was as good as promised. I had brook trout with wild rice and assorted vegetables—all local produce, according to the menu. Customers came, ate, and left, replaced by more of the same. They were older, and they had the marbled, smug look of a provincial upper set.

After dinner I went into the next room, the hotel bar, for a quick nightcap. It had the look and feel of a tavern. I tried the Five Towns dark ale but it was a little too sweet and heavy for me, so I washed it away with a mug of lager, which was even tastier coming from the keg.

The moment I stepped into my room I saw the faint flickering in the dark. I left the light switched off and went to the window. The sky was alive with glimmerings of color—red, purple, and a transparent whiteness—which appeared briefly and dissolved, and then blossomed again elsewhere a second or two later. The colors flowed in and out of each other against the black backdrop of the night. It was remarkable; the streetlights below were not strong enough to diminish the display. I stood there watching the sky for some time.

Chapter Three

The kids woke me. It was Sunday morning, and the unseen choir was in action again. I didn't mind at all. I was starting to like the sound of it, although I still had no idea what it was they were singing. Besides, it was after nine o'clock, time to be up and about.

I showered, dressed, ate a light breakfast, and then went out for another walk. The green was full of people emerging from the various churches around it, and the bells were ringing loudly, as if in competition. It was evidently something of a social event. The children horsed around underfoot while the adults gathered in small circles and chatted among themselves. I carefully threaded my way through the well-dressed crowd.

Main Street runs north and south from the green. It took me five minutes to locate Bellman's office. It was in a spruced-up lane just off South Main. Bellman had the second floor of a two-story brick building that had recently been given a fresh coat of colonial white paint. The ground floor was occupied by a hospice chapter. I didn't expect to find anyone there on Sunday morning, and the entry door was indeed locked.

But I was satisfied with my first look at Bellman's place of business. It wasn't shabby, it wasn't plush modern. It was the kind of place where a man might work who pulled down a decent but not extravagant annual income, I thought. But people can begin to get ideas in any setting.

I went back to the hotel by way of the river walk. The café was packed with churchgoers who had moved on to brunch. It was a brilliant, sunny morning, and they all looked festive and lively. It occurred to me that it had never been like this anywhere I'd lived. There was something seductive and corny about Winship. It had the clean-cut look of an ideal American community, the kind that probably never existed outside of a scriptwriter's mind. It made you want to smirk—but at the same time it conjured up thoughts and images that reached some other part of you and almost made you want to belong.

Back in my room at the inn, I picked up the slender telephone directory (it covered all of Lauck County) and looked up Joseph Bellman. I found his office number in Horseshoe Lane, and beneath that was a residential listing on Whipoorwill Road. I bought a local map at the front desk on my way out.

It wasn't far from downtown. A quiet neighborhood of modest ranch houses where the hills
started to rise on the west side of the river. When
I spotted the right number on a mailbox, I drove
ahead another quarter of a mile or so, then
turned back. I stopped just before I got to it
again, opened my road atlas and the town map
and made like I was lost. I had a good view of
the house. I just wanted to see where he lived.
Every little bit helps.

It was a slate-blue ranch, and judging by the
yard plantings it had been there quite a while. It
wasn't one of those long expensive places that
snake around country clubs, but merely a middle-
class six-roomer. A family room with a wood-
stove had been tacked on the side, and maybe
something else had been added on out back, but
overall it was nothing special.

He had about a half-acre cleared, and I didn't
know how much of the surrounding woods were
his. It was a lazy man's yard, not really too far
gone but in need of more attention. There were a
couple of apple trees choked with suckers, and
some bare spots in the crabgrass. Stuff you mean
to get around to.

Two cars in the driveway, both American.
One a '75 Mercury Montego, which surely doubled as the family and work car; the other a station wagon, maybe five years old, which was for
the wife to toodle around in. They had two kids,
according to the note in Steve's file, not yet
teenagers.

An antenna on the roof. No obvious signs, no hint of greed or excess about the place. He was even then probably stretching out on the sofa, ready for the football games on TV. How was the reception, so far from anywhere?

I found myself hoping that this fellow had not gone and done something wrong, that he had a perfectly convincing explanation I could take back to Steve with me. Maybe he was just eccentric and was trying to set a record for the number of companies he did business with, and his clients had an astonishing run of very bad luck. Unlikely, but certainly not out of the question. I hated to think about his family and what they would go through if their little domestic world came crashing down around them, thanks to dear old Dad. I had seen enough for the time being. I put the map away and drove back to the inn.

I had lunch and then sat on the veranda for a while. It was nice, but it soon crossed over onto the boring side. I took another drive around the city, trying to get my bearings and recognize my way. I spent the rest of the afternoon and evening in my room, reading the file over and over, until I was thoroughly familiar with the details of every case.

I missed the white sky at dusk, but when I looked out before going to bed I saw the northern lights again. No choir, nothing, not even the sound of a car on the street. Winship was pretty quiet on a Sunday night.

* * *

I was right; she was blond. Nice smile, intelligent eyes, good shape. I don't care for blond jokes. There are plenty of bright blondes around—I know, because I meet them and I never get anywhere with them. Chris Innes, according to the nameplate on her desk. Innes—was that Scottish? I wondered if her family were among the first settlers in Five Towns. We exchanged smiles and introductions, and I took a seat. She didn't ring her boss; she stepped into his office to tell him I had arrived. The outer room was small and plain, a reception area with a couple of seats, her desk, filing cabinets, and a copier. No frills.

"Mr. Carlson? You can go right in now."

"Thanks."

He came around to the front of his desk to greet me. A little on the short side, a little overfed, beige suit and matching necktie on a white shirt, and the work smile of instant bonhomie.

"Mr. Carlson? I'm Joe Bellman."

"Hi, how are you?"

"Fine, thanks, and you?" We shook hands. He had the hearty salesman's grip. "Come in, sit down."

"Thank you."

There was nothing special about his office. The knotty pine paneling was inexpensive, as was the off-white industrial carpeting. An oak desk and cracked brown leather chairs that could have been picked up at a bankruptcy sale. His phone was overloaded with buttons, as if he sometimes juggled half a dozen calls at the same time. He had several civic plaques and certificates on the wall, family photos on the desk. Joe Jaycee, at your service. It's a wonderful life, if it is.

"Carlson . . . ," he meditated aloud as he took his seat across the desk from me. "I know a lot of the people in town, but I'm darned if I can think of any Carlsons. Are you from Winship?"

"No."

"But, Lauck County."

"No, I'm not from around here." Like the lady told me.

"Oh, really?" A slight tremor in the voice. "Where are you . . . ?"

"The Insurance Industry Consulting Group," I said. "I've been retained by them to investigate sixteen cases of accidental death. For which claims have been filed on sixteen different companies."

"Oh really. Heh. Nice work, if you can get it."

That was pure instinct, the words popping out automatically. But Bellman's skin dialed down a few notches to the shade of greenish-white you associate with incipient nausea. Just guessing, but it seemed the dumb fuck had anywhere from one to sixteen somethings to hide.

"On policies issued through this office. By you."

He did his best to hold the anxiety in check and gut it out. He nodded stiffly and rearranged pens and things on his desk, as if this had suddenly become a colossal waste of his time. He no longer bothered looking me in the eye with that implacable salesman's stare.

"I don't understand what the problem is," he said, switching to a gruff tone. "I've had other investigators in here the last few months. I cooperated with them. They looked into their claims, they talked to the people involved, and they've all since paid the benefits. As they should."

"And I hope we can clean the slate," I told him. "But there are still some questions and details I'd like to—"

"Fine, fine," he cut in. "You go ahead. But I can't in all conscience tell these people to wait indefinitely. Some of them, they're poor folks, widows, with their houses on the line. And I can't just tell them not to take legal action. I know what these people are going through—first a terrible family tragedy, then this. It's not fair. They're friends and neighbors to me. What am I supposed to do?"

Joe didn't know how to give good gruff, at least not to me. There was a lot of wind, but it kept turning petulant. I saw the way he wiped sweat from his forehead, trying to make it look like he was simply smoothing his hair back. His cool steady gaze, the hallmark of a born marketing man, was gone, and he kept shaking his head slowly and sadly, as if this were a matter of such regret—which, no doubt, it was, to him.

"These policies are all pretty much the same," I said.

"Yes." Impatiently.

"Life, full and partial disability, the loss of a limb or an eye, and so on."

"That's right." As if to prove a point. Almost made me want to like him.

"Well, can you tell me," I asked, "why you put these sixteen policies out to sixteen different companies? I mean, they're all the same."

"Yes?" he said with a blank look. "What's the problem?"

"I'm just asking you why."

"Look, I'm an independent insurance agent." He then pointed to the familiar eagle-topped IIA logo on a brochure. "It happens to be in the best interests of both my client and myself to get the best terms I can in each case, and I do that by dealing with a lot of companies, all over the country. That's the market."

"Okay. I'd like to look at your files."

"No."

"Just the files on these cases," I explained.

"No," he repeated. "I'll produce them in court if I have to, but I'm not opening them up for just anybody who comes along on a fishing trip. They contain a lot of confidential personal information."

That was kind of a dumb attitude. I didn't expect to find anything of interest in his files, it was just a tossed-out request. If he was willing to show them in court, why not to me? And if there was something awkward in there, all he had to do was say sure, come back tomorrow, and clean the file between now and then. But maybe he was being obstinate over this minor point simply to convince himself that he really could tough it out. Never give an inch.

"If you could—"

"I'm sorry, but I've got work to do, and then I have a lunch to attend." He thought he was in command now. "I suggest you go see the police, and the doctors involved. Then, if you still have any questions, give me a call."

I let him show me out. Give him time to think, and stew. I had other things to do, and then I would come back to him. In the few seconds it took to step into the front office, he had worked up a fresh infusion of strength.

"Chris, this man is an investigator for some of the companies that are stalling on some of those outstanding claims," he told her. "If he contacts you, you don't have to talk to him about anything, and you are not to discuss anything that has to do with this agency."

"Yes, sir," she said, casting a glance at me.

"I'm staying at the Birch Inn," I told him. "If you give it some thought and decide you want to talk more about this, call me, leave a message. One way or another, I'll get back to you."

Joe got it, but tried to ignore me, speaking instead to his secretary. "If this man comes here when I'm out, all you have to do is tell him to leave. If he refuses to go, call the police. Understand?"

"Yes."

I left, feeling upbeat and encouraged. I didn't

have anything, nothing at all. But Joe hadn't reacted well. It's like playing chess against somebody whose hand shakes a little when they move a piece. The tiniest wobble tells.

Chapter Four

Detective Ted Miller was glad to meet me. I knew he was; he told me so. But his manner was out of sync. One minute the air was quite chilly, the next he seemed merely bored. He would like to help me—if he could. Miller was an angular middle-aged man with graying hair. He had a habit of rubbing his naked upper lip with his thumbnail, still grooming a mustache that had been removed. He spoke slowly, grudgingly, as if he had to pay for each word.

We were sitting in his nondescript office on the first floor of the Winship Police Department, a stone building that looked like a scaled-down Norman castle. It was located discreetly on a side street not far from the green and the courthouse. Det. Miller had written up nine of the accidental deaths. One of his colleagues, Det. Brandt, had covered the other seven, but he was home with a bug.

"So, what's the problem?" Miller asked after I explained who I was and why I was there.

"Maybe none. I just want to know how and why these people died."

"All of them?"

"Yes."

"Well, okay."

Okay, I thought. "Can you let me read through your reports? I'd like to see the file for each case."

"Okay," Miller said after a pause. "I can show them to you, but you can't take them away."

"No, of course not."

"And if you want a copy of anything, whatever company you're working for will have to send a written request. I can give you the forms. There's a whole other procedure for that."

"I know." So far, so good. "Now, you—"

"Don't get your hopes up, though," Miller added. "You won't find anything worth picking at."

"You sound pretty sure."

He shrugged. "I know those cases."

"Nothing at all odd or suspicious?"

"Nope."

"Not even one of them?"

"Not really. Donnie Burnette, for instance. He crashed his car last winter, up on Sawyer Hill— that's the worst road in the county. We have a dozen accidents a year there. The snow melted some that day, then turned to ice that night. He decided to come into town and have a couple of beers, hit a sheet of ice and flew right into a big pine tree. It crushed the left side of his body and pinned him there, and by the time somebody else came along he was dead from loss of blood and shock."

"Yes," I said.

"Well? What else could it be?"

"Was that road sanded?"

"Plowed and sanded, after the snow fell a few days earlier. But not that particular day, no. You know what, you get some sun, the snow melts a little, some water runs across the road in places and it freezes when night comes. But you can't sand everywhere, every night, just before the drinkers go to town."

Reasonable. I didn't want to debate the Burnette case. Miller could use that one as an example, because it looked so much like a road accident, plain and simple. It was probably the least suspicious of all the cases I had in my folder.

"What about Joseph Bellman?"

"What about him?" Miller echoed. "Never been in any kind of trouble. He grew up here, he has a family, seems like a hardworking, ordinary guy."

"I know he works hard," I said. "I can tell that just from the number of claims he's put in all over the country. You don't think that's a little strange?"

"What, exactly?"

"Bellman wrote up sixteen different policies,

which were all basically the same policy, for sixteen different companies."

"Yeah, I heard that. What's wrong with that?"

"It's not typical behavior," I said. "It looks like he was deliberately trying to avoid unwanted attention."

"You ask him about that?"

"Yes."

Miller grunted. "What did he say?"

"That he's just trying to get the best deal for his clients and build up his trade and make useful contacts by dealing with lots of insurance companies, rather than just a few."

"Anything wrong with that?"

"No," I said. "But it doesn't hold up. Bellman works in a geographical area with a population base that isn't going to grow rapidly or change suddenly. There's an upper limit to the amount of business he can generate, and spreading it around all over the country will not increase it."

"But is there anything wrong in doing that?"

"Not in itself, no. But—"

"Look," Miller said abruptly, "the only thing I really know about insurance is that it's a legal racket. Now, I've looked at some of those cases, I handled them myself, and I did everything by the book. And I'm telling you I didn't find anything fishy in any one of them."

"Okay," I said calmly. I could tell he wasn't finished.

"I'm ready to cooperate with you, but we

won't get very far unless you have new evidence to present. Otherwise, these cases are closed."

"I understand. As soon as I have something, you'll see it. But for now, I wanted you to know that in my professional opinion Joe Bellman's actions are cause for suspicion."

Miller shrugged. "That's what you're going on, is it?"

"Part of it."

"Well, you just remember that there's some folks here who're hurting, and they'll continue to hurt until you make up your mind about their claims."

I didn't care for that, coming from him. Bellman could fuss and fume on his own behalf and that of his clients, but Det. Miller was a cop. He knew that what I was doing was only proper, not an act of personal meanness.

"I'll be as quick as I can."

"Good. You do that."

"Well, can I get started on those files?"

"I'll have Joyce pull them for you sometime this afternoon," Miller said. "They should be ready tomorrow morning."

Doctor Gow was also prepared to help me, sort of. I stopped by his office, which was located in a handsome old federal building on a quiet street a short walk from the green. He was not exactly thrilled, but he agreed to see me at 5:30 that afternoon, when he had treated the last of his scheduled patients. Gow had a regular family practice, but he also served as the official medical examiner for Winship and the surrounding area.

I had some time to pass in the afternoon, so I followed the map to Sawyer Hill Road. It was long and steep, and it had some wicked curves—worse than the road I'd come down on my way into Winship. I found the tree that young Mr. Donnie Burnette had plowed himself into last March. The scars and scrape marks were still clearly visible. It all looked right—the flat area in the turn where ice might form, spinning a vehicle around and flinging it off the road. But there was an element of luck involved, bad luck, in Donnie's case. A few feet either way, and he might have walked away from it with nothing more than a few cuts and bruises.

I also drove by the home of the late George L. Winthrop. He was the man who had somehow blown himself up while working in his garnet mine. His place was up in the hills, a rambling farmhouse with some outbuildings. There was nobody home. I walked around, saw a couple of dirt roads disappearing into the woods. No dogs, no sign of life. I didn't like being there. The darkness of the surrounding trees, the empty buildings, the still air, the close sky that hung like a dull sheet metal lid—I got a bad feeling. I didn't care for any of it, so I left.

I got to Gow's office on time, but there were still a couple of ailing citizens ahead of me. It was quarter past six when the last one hobbled away. Gow came out to the waiting room to greet me, shake my hand, and apologize for the delay. He was sixtyish, tall and a bit stooped. He reminded me of a doctor my parents took me to for a while when I was kid. Gow led me past the consulting rooms, to his office, a small, cluttered, boxy little room. He even had the same kind of ancient furniture my old doc had in his office way back when.

We chatted about the cases in general for a few minutes. He had pronounced the verdict of accidental death in each of the sixteen, and he showed no hint of doubt about any of them. He was calm, sure of himself, and although he had the air of a tired man there was a lively, penetrating intelligence in his eyes.

"Have you seen the police files?" he asked me.

"No, but I'm going to look at them tomorrow."

Gow nodded. "You'll find copies of my reports in there. If you still have any questions after you've read them, just give me a call and I'll try to answer them for you."

"Thanks. I will."

"Which ones are you worrying about?"

"All of them."

"Oh. But why?"

I told him about Bellman's habit of steering his policies to many different companies, which in itself was enough to justify closer attention. Gow made a face to show that he wasn't impressed, but at least he didn't say so out loud.

"About George Winthrop . . ."

"Yes?"

"How badly was his body damaged in that explosion?"

"The damn fool. It was bad, very bad." Gow smiled, as if he seemed to enjoy the recollection. "The police had to scoop up the pieces and they didn't like that, I can tell you."

"But there was no problem identifying him," I said.

"Oh no, no, not at all. His head was intact. It was burned and blistered some, and it wasn't attached to his shoulders, but you could make out his face easy enough. There's no question, it was George Winthrop. Matter of fact, he still had his cigar stub stuck in his teeth."

"Is that right?"

"You'll see. The police took pictures."

We touched on some of the other cases, but they were more of the same—a few simple facts, the verdict plain as day. Dr. Gow wasn't bothered. He seemed ready to sit there for as long as it took to satisfy me, although I was obviously keeping him later than he probably would have preferred. I thanked him and then headed back to the Birch Inn.

I didn't have much to show for my first day at work, but I'd made some of the necessary contacts and had seen a little more of the relevant territory. Most of all, I had come away from my meeting in Horseshoe Lane with a strong impression that something was not right about Joe Bellman.

But the day wasn't over yet. The phone rang barely a minute after I got to my room.

"Hi," she said. "It's Chris Innes."

"Chris? Oh, yeah." Bellman's secretary. "Chris—"

"Right, we met today."

"Yes."

"Remember that drink you offered me?" She was breathless or nervous, or both. "Well, I'm free after all, if you'd still like to get together tonight."

"Sure." I played along with her, since that was apparently what I was meant to do. "There's a nice little bar here in the hotel."

"No," she said too quickly. "There's a place I like called Doran's. It's on North Main, a couple of miles up on the way out of town."

"I'll find it. What time?"

"Ten?"

"Sure. Does your—"

"See you then."

Click, and she was gone. Chris Innes. She obviously wanted to talk to me about her boss, but why the charade about my having offered to take her out for a drink? As if she were afraid that someone might be listening to us, and she wanted our date to seem quite innocent. But she could have called from a pay phone, and who would be eavesdropping on me at the hotel? Then again, Chris was emphatic about not coming to the hotel for a drink.

I didn't get beyond that point when the phone

rang again. It was another one of my new acquaintances.

"Hello?"

"Mr. Carlson? Hi. It's Joe Bellman."

"Yes?" Indeed. "What's up, Joe?"

"I just thought I'd give you a call to see if you've thought some more about what we were discussing this morning."

I nearly laughed. "I've been on it all day."

"Yeah, well, do you have any news for me?"

"You mean about the claims?"

"Uh, yeah."

"No," I told him. "I've got a lot more to do before I reach the point where I can make my recommendations."

"Oh. Okay." He said nothing for a moment, and I could hear the evening news on the TV at his end. "Okay."

"Anything else, Joe?"

"Oh, no." Almost wistful, then more silence from him. It's curious how a person can sound lost on the phone without speaking a word. "Carlson?"

"Yes?"

"Can you stop by my office tomorrow evening?"

"Tomorrow evening?"

"I'm pretty busy during the day," he explained, "and I'll be out for most of the afternoon. So the evening would better for me. If that suits you."

"Okay."

"It's just that I've been thinking," he went on, sounding as if he had to drag the words out, "and I feel maybe you and I got off on the wrong foot today."

"Yes."

"So I thought we ought to talk some more. . . ."

"Sure. What time tomorrow evening?"

"Around seven?"

"Seven's fine with me," I said.

"Right."

"You'll be there, Joe?"

"What? Yes, of course I'll be there," he said, clearly making an effort to sound eager. "I want to talk to you."

It wasn't completely convincing, but it wasn't totally false either. It was the voice of fear and uncertainty. Joe had tried the aggressive approach that morning, but now his second thoughts had apparently led him to this show of reasonableness and cooperation. It's hard to know what to do when you find yourself the main target of an investigation. Innocent or guilty, you have no attractive options.

"Well, good," I said. "Anything else?"

"Uh . . . no."

"See you tomorrow, Joe."

"Right."

"Thanks for calling."

I had no idea what was actually going on, but it seemed kind of screwy. Chris sounded as if she could conceivably be involved in some harebrained scheme to set me up. But Joe didn't. He was in some other place, vacant, lonely, adrift. He had lost all the starch he'd mustered up that morning. I didn't know what she was up to, but I wanted to think he was starting to crack.

Not that it was me, personally. But other investigators had already been there, and although their companies eventually paid the claims, it could be that my arrival was enough to convince Joe that it would never end, that there would be more and more investigations, that he would never get away with it.

Whatever *it* was.

You have to consider the possibility that in some way you're being set up. It's happened before and it has never worked. But you always think the next time, *this time*, you just might step in quicksand. Or catch a bullet.

Were they working separately or together? Either way, they weren't clever enough to sucker me. So I told myself. Besides, if you let it worry you too much you'll just end up sitting there in your hotel room, shrinking into yourself while the night spins by all around you.

If I wanted to do that, I could do it at home.

Chapter Five

It was still fairly mild outside when I left the hotel, but there was a touch of chill in the air. No stars were visible in the night sky. The pleasant breeze was now turning gusty, leaves swirled and hissed in the trees, and it felt like rain. As I was getting into my car, I heard the choir again. I was tempted to follow the sound, because it seemed odd to have children out at that time of night—and on a school night at that. But I had a date.

Doran's was easy to find, and since I got there early I took a minute to cruise around the block. It was an old neighborhood, working class, and now showing distinct signs of wear, but as tidy as the rest of Winship. Doran's looked like a corner saloon that dated back to the thirties. I parked up the street from it, sat, and watched. A couple of people went in, one left. Nothing unusual. A quiet Monday night. At ten o'clock I went inside the bar.

Chris was already there, and she greeted me as if I were an old friend, giving me a big smile and a rush of silly chatter. But she was obviously nervous and had already fortified herself with most of a vodka tonic. I bought a fresh one for her and a draft lager for myself, and we moved from the bar to a plain wooden booth along the opposite wall.

"Nice place," I said, glancing around at the brass fixtures, the golden oak woodwork, the black-and-white tile floor, and the tin ceiling. "I like it."

"Yeah, it's neat, isn't it?"

"Do you live around here?"

"In the neighborhood," she said, nodding.

"Does your boss know you're meeting me?"

"God, no. He'd be very upset."

"Why?"

"Well, you know the answer to that," she said. "You heard him this morning. You're here to investigate him and he doesn't want me to give you the time of day, much less discuss any of his confidential business."

She was pretty, with a lot of fair hair tumbling down across the collar and shoulders of her tweed jacket. She appeared to be calming her nerves, though her eyes were still edgy.

"But you *are* going to."

"What?"

"Discuss his business with me."

"Oh, no." A frown, eyes avoiding me. "I couldn't do that."

Okay, she wanted to make me work for it.

"Why not?"

"Because it *is* confidential. It wouldn't be right."

"Then why did you want to see me?" I asked.

"To tell you about him. Joe."

"Okay, go ahead."

"Well, he's a good person," she said. "I mean, he's honest, he works hard, he's fair. And he never bothers me. You know, the way some bosses will bother women who work for them."

I nodded. "And he's got a wife and kids."

"That's right, and they're a religious family," Chris added. "Joe's on the church committee to organize fundraisers and stage various events throughout the year. He's very civic-minded."

"Uh-huh." I gazed at her; it wasn't hard to do. "So what is all that supposed to mean? That he's a good citizen?"

"Yes," Chris said, but falteringly. "I guess it's just that I wanted you to know what kind of person Joe is, seen by somebody who works with him every day. I don't know exactly what it is you think he's done, but I can't believe he'd do anything wrong. And I think I would know."

"How long have you worked for him?"

"Over a year now."

"So you helped process those policies and claims."

"Well, typing, Xeroxing, and mailing. That kind of work, yes."

There were eight or nine other customers in the place. None of them had shown any interest in us so far. They were mostly an older crowd and they had the look of regulars—each one planted on his or her own personal bar stool. I was still nursing my beer, but Chris was ready for another vodka, so I went and got it.

"Anything else?" I asked when I returned.

"No, thanks," she said, taking the drink.

"I mean, anything else you want to say about Joe?"

"Oh, right. Well, I've told you what I think of him. Maybe if you told me why you're so suspicious of him . . ."

"A lot of claims with a lot of different companies."

"You know, he's told me about that a million times."

"Really?"

"Yeah, he's always saying contacts are so important," Chris explained. "The more contacts you make, the better off you'll be down the road. People move on and move up, and the person you do business with now in some small company may eventually become the marketing director of one of the giants."

"Uh-huh."

"That makes sense, doesn't it?"

"I guess so."

"Another thing," Chris continued. "He doesn't stand to make a dollar on those claims. In fact, he's really going to lose all the commission he would earn if those people were still alive and paying their premiums."

"That's true, I guess."

"Yes, so . . ." She smiled hopefully and arched her eyebrows, waiting for me to nod my head and admit that I was on a wild goose chase.

"Still," I said. "Sixteen is a lot of accidental deaths."

"Well, I know."

"Chris."

"Yes?"

"What was all that nonsense on the phone?"

"What nonsense?"

"About me asking you out for a drink. That routine you went through when you called me."

"Oh, yeah. I'm sorry. I just wanted it to sound like we were in a date type situation, not as if we were meeting to talk about my boss and his business. In case somebody was listening in."

"Who would be listening in?"

"I don't know."

"Where did you call from?"

"My apartment."

"So why would you think your line is tapped?"

"I don't, really." She hesitated, but then went on. "Sometimes I pick up the telephone and hear clicks. And so does Jenny—she shares the apartment with me. Doesn't that mean the line is tapped? If you hear clicks?"

"Maybe, and maybe not," I said. "But there would have to be a reason why somebody would tap your phone, something they wanted or expected to hear, and you or your roommate ought to be able to figure what that could be, since it has to do with either you or her."

"We've thought about it, and talked about it, but neither of us could come up with anything that would explain it."

"Jealous boyfriend, or ex-boyfriend?"

" 'Fraid not."

"Have you told the police, or the phone company?"

"The phone company, yeah. They said they would send a man out to check, and I guess they did, because they called a few days later and said that our line was clear. No problem, nothing wrong."

"Then it probably is okay."

"I guess."

"Why didn't you want to meet me at the Birch Inn?"

"I like this place more," she answered promptly. "Well, that and the fact that Joe's sister Connie works in the restaurant there. If she saw me with you, or any stranger, Joe would hear about it pretty quick."

"You know, you sound kind of afraid."

"No," she said, with no punch. "I'm not."

"Of something, or someone."

"No."

"Anybody ever come in to the office to see Joe—somebody who didn't have any obvious insurance business to discuss?"

Chris shrugged. "He has friends and acquaintances who sometimes stop by and say hello if they're in the area."

"Anybody you didn't like? Who seemed odd or wrong to you?"

She gave a short laugh with an edge of . . . bitterness? "I've had to shoo away a couple of his friends. Married men, that kind of thing. But nobody who gave me any trouble or cause for concern, if that's what you mean."

"And Joe has never tried anything with you?"

"I told you, no."

"Come on, Chris. . . ."

"I mean it," she insisted. "No, he hasn't."

"Okay. So, how come no boyfriend?"

"Is this part of your investigation too?" Sarcastic, but with a smile.

"Nope, just me being curious," I replied.

"There were a couple of them, but they didn't work out." She shrugged. "Maybe I'm just too fussy."

"You have reason to be."

"Why, thank you."

We talked a while longer, but it went back and around in the same circles. She stood by her boss. She even liked Bellman's wife and kids. All very well and commendable, but I couldn't attach great significance to her testimony. I hadn't learned much. Maybe I hadn't learned anything at all. On the other hand, it was better than sitting and drinking alone. I kind of liked Chris.

"Could you drop me off on your way?" she

asked when we were about to leave Doran's. It was raining steadily.

"Sure. Did you walk here?"

"No, Jenny gave me a ride. She's a nurse, late shift at the hospital. I figured I'd just walk home, but this rain . . ."

"No problem at all."

Chris was subdued for the duration of the short drive to her place, speaking only to tell me which streets to take.

"Just ahead on the right."

"The white one?"

"That's it."

I stopped the car in front of an old duplex and put it in park, the engine idling. Chris looked tired and wan, as if she didn't want to move, but then she sat up and reached for the door handle.

"Thanks."

"Thank you for calling," I said, "and talking to me."

"I get the feeling you're not married."

"You're right. It's been a while since I was."

"Want to come up for a nightcap?"

I'd already been considering how to answer this invitation if it came. It was not a good idea to mess around with any woman connected with a case you're working. All it takes is one false charge of impropriety, and you're shot for that job; your credibility goes right down the toilet. But I wasn't picking up anything remotely like that kind of vibe from Chris. She seemed lonely.

Maybe she was tired of having those nightcaps by herself.

"Sounds good to me."

I followed her up the stairs and into her apartment. She turned some lights on and then led me into the kitchen, telling me to help myself to a beer from the fridge. Chris poured herself a vodka, straight up. I thought we were going to sit down in the living room, but she took me directly into her bedroom instead. There was a warm glow from the bedside lamp. She set her drink down and then stepped close to me.

"Does your hand ever get cold?" she asked.

Threw me for a second. "What?"

"When you're holding a bottle of cold beer like that."

"Oh. I guess it does, a little."

"Let me see." She took the beer from my hand and put it on the table. Then she took my hand and slid it up under the ivory turtleneck sweater she was wearing. She pressed the palm of my hand to her skin—she didn't flinch or give a start, but her eyes widened and she smiled. "Oooh, it does get cold." Then she moved my hand higher, up over her breast. I could feel her nipple responding at once. "You just keep it right there and it'll warm up in no time." She put both of her hands on my hips, her fingers moving and pressing firmly. "There's something else I wanted to ask you, Mister Man." Her voice was soft, almost drowsy.

"And what would that be?" I put my other

hand on her hip and started doing the same thing she was doing.

"Sometimes I get the feeling that what I need more than anything else in the whole world, right then and there at that moment, is a really good fuck. Is it just me, or do you sometimes get that feeling too?"

"Yes, I do."

Chris took my hand out from under her sweater and pressed it to her cheek. "Oh, yeah, it's *much* warmer now." She took my index and middle fingers in her mouth, sucking them, licking them with her tongue. Then she stopped for a second, still holding my hand to her mouth. "I'm sorry—did you answer my question?"

Then we were on her bed with the answer, first-timers with each other, anxiously pulling each other's clothes off, bathing in each other's flesh, devouring each other, and Chris was screaming, "Fuck me harder, harder, *harder!*" and I did and it was easy and sweet and fast for both of us.

It had been a while for me too.

I must have drifted off; next thing I knew she was gently shaking my arm and telling me it would be better if I didn't stay. No problem. We did a little more kissy stuff then, before I stood up and started to dress. Chris sat cross-legged on the bed. She was wearing a T-shirt and blue bikini briefs.

"Jack? How long are you going to be in town?"

"Not sure, I'll see how it goes." I quickly added, "Can I call you here, would that be okay?"

She smiled. "Sure. I'm in the book. I-n-n-e-s comma C."

"I know your name."

"You'd better!" Then she got serious again. "Jack, if he did something wrong, you won't just be bringing him down, you'll be destroying his family too, a wife and kids. You know that."

"Chris, if he did something wrong," I said, buttoning my shirt, "he did it to himself and to his family as well."

"I know," she said, her voice small and quiet. "Please be careful."

"I will."

"Jack, I mean *very* careful."

"Of Joe Bellman? Is he dangerous?"

"No. I don't think so."

"Well, then, who?"

"I don't know."

I was tucking in my shirt, and I stopped. "Chris, what is that you are not telling me? I know there's something."

"No." She made a brief, empty gesture with her hand. "I don't know, really, it's not any one thing. It's this whole town. Just be careful."

"Okay. I'll call you. If not tomorrow night, Wednesday."

"Jack,"—looking up at me, soulful eyes—"I don't want you to feel, you know, that you *have* to call. I won't be—"

"Oh, I'll call," I said, cutting her off. "Because I want to."

She smiled, and this time it was the first relaxed, happy, natural smile I'd seen on her face. It made her look even better.

The rain had passed, the streets were deserted, and most of the houses were dark. I checked my watch and saw that it was just after two in the morning. I parked on the street behind the inn. I heard the choir as soon as I stepped out of my car. The sound was low, distant, but there was no mistaking it.

This is crazy, I thought. I had to see if I could find it. The wind and the noise of the trees obscured it some and made it hard to pick up a sense of direction, but I started walking north along the river. It couldn't be a children's choir, not at this hour. Perhaps it was a small factory, some kind of machinery.

I hadn't gone far when the wind let up for a few seconds and the sound was suddenly clearer and closer. And damn it, it still resembled young human voices more than anything else that I could imagine. It was lively and spirited, but it meant nothing to me: a confusion of chanting and droning, interspersed with wild barks and yips. But then the wind came back and I couldn't focus on the sound.

I came to a cemetery and stood at a stone wall that nearly reached my chin. The tombstones inside looked very old; it was probably the first burial ground established in Five Towns, close to the churches and the green. The sound definitely seemed to be coming from somewhere in there, but it was too dark for me to see very far. I moved along the wall until I came to the main gate. It was chained and locked tight. The bizarre voices continued to float around me like an invisible cloud of sound.

Then I saw something. A vague flicker of white somewhere in the dark distance. I saw it again a couple of seconds later, but farther to one side. The wind snapped sharply toward me at that moment, and I was hit by a shower of grit and sand swept up from the gravel path on the other side of the gate. It got me in both eyes. I looked down, blinking, trying to clear my vision.

When I looked up again, I saw a long flowing whiteness that seemed to race through the cemetery, snaking behind and in front of the various monuments. Then the sound stopped and the strange white thing disappeared. I was still wiping tears away; I didn't know what I'd glimpsed.

It had to be kids. Maybe they were running around, trailing old bedsheets after them. Halloween was still more than a month away, but it had to be something like that. I heard a car drive up and stop behind me, and I turned around. Police, two of them. The one on the passenger side side got out and approached me.

"Can I see some identification?"

"Sure."

I took out my wallet and handed him my driver's license. He stared at it, then back at me.

"John Carlson? Is that you?"

"Yes, I'm Jack Carlson."

"What's the problem?"

"Nothing," I said. "I'm staying at the Birch Inn, and I was taking a short walk to get some fresh air when the wind blew some dust in my eyes. That's all."

He continued to give me the cop stare.

"You okay now?"

"Sure, fine."

"Okay, Mr. Carlson." He returned my license.

"Thanks." As he got back into the car, I added, "I thought I heard somebody in the cemetery. It could be teenagers making a little mischief."

He nodded. They drove away slowly. I left.

After breakfast that morning, I walked back up the river and took another look at the graveyard. It didn't have a name at the entrance, but near the front gate there was a large bronze plaque mounted on the stone wall. Somehow I'd missed it the previous night. It was the size and shape of a medieval shield, and it had an ornate cross on it. No letters, no other symbols. Same as the Five Towns beer label.

The gate was open, so I went in and walked around. It was old, but well-tended—the markers were straight and the grass neatly trimmed. The first dates I read were early 19th century, and then I found some that were even older. The cemetery was not large, an acre or so, but it had a narrow front and extended back a fair distance. The ground was roughly level, with only a few dips and rises, and there were some birch trees scattered about.

The farther back I went, the older the tombstones. Soon, it was very difficult to make out even a single letter or numeral on any of them. Blank, weathered faces, anonymous as the dead whose burial sites they marked.

But none of them were tipped over or tilted and there was no grafitti. None of the flowers or plantings had been torn up and thrown around. There was no sign at all of teenage vandalism. I was a little perplexed, wondering what it was that I had actually seen and heard the previous night.

But I had wasted enough time on that little puzzle. I had a file bulging with more important matters to deal with.

Chapter Six

She heard the truck before I did. A look of relief crossed her face as she stood up and went to the front window. I hauled myself out of a sagging armchair and followed her.

"That's Billy," she told me. "I'll go get him."

"All right."

I saw the tail end of a green flatbed disappear down the dirt driveway below the house. I moved around to see if I could spot it again, but all I saw was a swirl of dust where the drive circled around behind an outbuilding. Then Mrs. Winthrop, moving awkwardly in that direction to bring him back.

It had taken me twenty minutes to get her to relax enough to let me inside the door. Her son Billy wasn't home, so she didn't want to talk to me. According to the insurance record, the widow Winthrop was fifty-four, but she looked at least ten years older, chunky, with a face the years had scuffed up pretty thoroughly and a weak hip that accounted for her laborious gait.

Even when we were sitting in her living room she didn't want to discuss her husband's accidental death. She was very nervous, but I didn't think that had anything to do with a sense of guilt. Mary Winthrop was simply used to letting the men in her life take care of business, and she didn't want to say anything stupid that might somehow be twisted around by a clever lawyer and result in her losing the $125,000 she was due. Her last husband, George, had died in the garnet mine explosion, so Billy was the man in charge.

I did want to see Billy. With his father gone, he was a lot closer to inheriting the farm. He wouldn't be the first child to hasten his parent's departure from this vale of tears. But I was also glad to find that he was out when I arrived. I had a chance to hear Mary Winthrop's story with no one else there to influence what she said. Assuming I could get her to talk.

I started by asking her about the farm, and she appeared to relax a tiny bit. There was a lot of land, but much of it was too hilly and rocky to be of any use. George and Billy hayed, kept a bunch of chickens and a few cows, and every year they raised veal calves. Mary took care of the house, all the cooking, and a large vegetable garden. I didn't bother to ask if she canned and froze things for the winter months; she obviously did. I suppose three people could get by like that, an existence with few frills and a lot of hard work. A good simple life, some would even say. But it chilled me. There was something lonely and claustrophobic about it, too much American gothic gloominess.

George and Billy had occasional help from friends, but they generally managed by themselves. In the winter they plowed snow, did some hauling within the county, and otherwise saw to whatever repair work had to be done around the farm.

"Always busy," Mrs. Winthrop said with resignation. "Always something that needs to be done."

I know. It's like that at my own little house, but I didn't think telling her so would cheer her up.

"What about this garnet mine?"

"Well . . ." She hesitated, perhaps fearful that I was again trying to edge her closer to forbidden topics.

"I mean, I've never heard of anybody having a garnet mine in their own backyard," I said. "Does it go down pretty deep, or—well, what's it like?"

"Oh, it's not like a coal mine," she replied with a sheepish smile. "It's just an open rock face back in the hills. We call it the cliff, because it stands twenty or thirty feet high. It's got garnet in it—George has been taking 'em out for ages. But it's hard to get, takes a lot of work, and he never made much money at it. It was more of a hobby, I guess you could call it. Whenever the mood took him, he'd go back there with some tools and chip away at the cliff."

"Did he ever use explosives before?"

It was a perfectly harmless question, but she was apparently troubled by it. "On some stumps, but not on the cliff." But she went on, "I don't know, maybe he did. I couldn't say."

That was when the truck arrived.

I had a minute or two, so I quickly went to the desk in the adjacent dining room. I'd noticed it earlier, in particular the fact that it was covered with papers. The dining room looked as if it hadn't been used for meals since Eisenhower was president. I saw some unpaid bills, a few copies of the local newspaper, and masses of junk mail—maybe it had some entertainment value in a remote place like that.

But I saw nothing of interest until my eye caught a drawing of two men. One of them held the other by the hair from behind, pulling his victim's head back while drawing a long knife across his throat. It was the front cover of a cheaply printed pamphlet that had the straightforward title *Commando Techniques*. It was published by an outfit called Wewelsburg Press in Grand Marais, Michigan. Was this one of Billy's hobbies, mail order combat training, to help while away the long winter nights?

I heard them coming up the front porch stairs, so I quickly stepped back into the living room.

Billy Winthrop marched in and gave me a fierce stare. He was tall and too heavy, but muscular. His mother struggled in behind him.

"Billy, this is . . ." She couldn't remember.

"Jack Carlson," I introduced myself.

Billy nodded once. My outstretched hand apparently did not enter his field of vision, so I withdrew it.

"Did you bring the check?" he asked in a low raspy voice.

I suppressed a smile because he was younger than me and so much bigger. I tried to look sympathetic.

"No, but I—"

"Why not?" His face tightened up a notch.

"I've been hired to look into a number of recent insurance claims—"

"Who hired you?"

"The insurance companies."

"Why?"

Mrs. Winthrop lowered herself into a chair on the other side of the room, but Billy showed no desire to sit down. He was like a tree that had somehow taken root in the living room, so I stood there and explained my business to him at some length. He wasn't happy about it, which came as no surprise.

"What's the matter with my mother's claim?"

"Nothing yet, as far as I know," I told him. "But I do want to ask you a few questions, and then I'd like to see the site for myself. If that's okay with you."

"The site?"

"Yes, the mine. Where the accident occurred."

"Okay," Billy agreed reluctantly. "What do you want to know from me? I wasn't there."

"Where were you, then?"

"In the barn, feedin' the calves. Ma seen me, she was up on the porch. I came out of the barn just a minute or two after the boom went off."

"That's right," Mrs. Winthrop offered. "I was trimming beans for supper. It was late in the afternoon."

"Did you know he was going to be blasting?"

"Sure did," Billy said. "Told him he was crazy."

"Why?"

"I figured it'd blow the garnet to bits, but he hadn't found any in quite a while, so he made up his mind to blow out a hunk of rock and see what was underneath."

"Had he used explosives before?"

"Not on the cliff. Took some stumps out a while back."

"Have you ever used them?"

"Have I ever used what?" His eyes narrowed.

"Explosives."

"No."

Of course not. I asked a few more questions and got the same kind of plain answers. I didn't expect Billy to slip up and say something I wasn't supposed to know. It doesn't happen that way outside of TV. But I did hope to learn something about him, what kind of person he was. In that respect, he did his best to keep me guessing. He was short and to the point; hard to figure. He was a study in body language—he still hadn't moved an inch, as if even just to shift his feet would amount to a concession of some sort.

"Are you going to keep on working the farm?"

"Why not?"

"Sounds like it was a lot of work for two people."

"I'll manage," he said. "I've got a couple of guys who come over now and then and help out when I need them. We may have to cut back a little on one thing or another, but we'll get by okay."

Especially if that check comes through. I was frustrated by his lack of response. I was feeling reckless and I wanted to get some reaction out of him. I knew Billy was thirty years old and single.

"Do you have any marriage plans at this time?"

"What kind of question is that?" he flared.

"I was just curious to know whether you'd given any thought to settling here on the farm and raising a family."

"What the hell's that got to do with anything?"

"It's routine," I said, trying to sound like a bored office worker. "They like to know the situation of family members."

"You can put down that it's none of their damn business," he yelled in my face. "They're dragging their heels for no reason, is what the situation is."

And he gave me more like that, before he abruptly brought it to a halt and fixed me with a silent glare. Billy wasn't exactly crisp with intelligence, but neither was he downright stupid. He had small dark eyes, alert and vaguely predatory, set deep in his fleshy face, suggesting an instinctive canniness that would guide him well enough—but within definite limits.

"Maybe I ought to go look at the mine now."

"Suit yourself."

"Can you show me where it is?"

"I'll tell you where it is," Billy replied with a cold grin, "and you can walk it by yourself. I got work to do."

"I can't drive there?" Probably a dumb question, but I had seen a couple of dirt roads winding up into the hills out in back of the barn.

"You can drive to the first rise, but you may drop a pipe on the way," Billy replied with a grin.

"How far is it?"

"Oh, half a mile or so."

"Is it up one of those dirt roads I saw?"

"No, it's across the fields."

"Where do the dirt roads go?"

"Places where the mine ain't."

"Ah."

So I walked. Billy pointed the way, and then he went into a small cinder block building behind the hay barn, where his truck was parked. It was a long half-mile. The ground climbed slowly in a series of rippling swells. It was covered with field grass, scattered trees, and a few persistent wild-flowers, but it was also strewn with emerging rocks and small boulders. The sky was gray, but the air was mild. The road and the farmhouse soon disappeared behind me.

I passed by a hollow, where the Winthrops had abandoned some trucks, tractors, and other farm machinery over the years. No trade-ins, I guess. It was a monument in rust.

I saw the cows, and they saw me. Ten or twelve of them came lumbering up behind me in a display of bovine curiosity. It must be a hum-drum existence, from barn to pasture and then back again, day after day until the hammer drops. They trailed along closely as I walked, they stopped when I stopped, and they backed away in a confused clutter when I turned and clapped my hands at them.

The cliff was exactly where it was supposed to be, and I was glad. I'd half-suspected that Billy had sent me off in the wrong direction and would later claim it was my own dumb fault if I got lost and didn't find it.

The cliff face was broken in a few places where wedge-shaped openings had been gouged out, and the ground was littered with an accumu-lation of rock chips and shards. It was easy to see where the explosion had occurred—it had thrown out a tongue of dust and chips still visible in the grass four months later, and there were black scorch marks on the inner walls.

Otherwise, there wasn't much to see. I kicked at the debris on the ground, I poked in the crevices of the cliff, but I didn't notice anything that looked remotely like garnet.

I sat down on a convenient rock shelf and allowed myself a cigarette. George Winthrop had three sticks of dynamite, but it was the blasting cap that did him in, or so the theory went. You can't get clumsy with blasting caps. I was not happy. It would be hard to show that George's death was caused by anything other than a simple accident.

Maybe it was because I don't smoke much and my brain was hit by a double jolt of nicotine, but I was just sitting there, and I suddenly went blind for a moment. No, *blind* is the wrong word. My vision shuddered and changed, and all I could see was a wasted monochrome landscape. The trees and hills and grass disappeared, replaced by a kind of lunar heath. The air itself had gone gray, and it was impossible to tell where the horizon was. I looked up and around, and even the cliff behind me was gone. It was as if I were on some high rocky plain, pressed against the sky. I felt so lonely it shocked me and then I had to fight a surge of panic. I put my head down; I was like a kid struggling against dizziness in church. The ground beneath my feet was dead, with no blades of grass—there was only rubble and dust.

I heard gunshots, a tight volley of them.

I looked up and the world was back again. I felt faint, but the moment had passed. I knew the gunfire was real because I could still hear a receding echo of it. I wasn't sure, but I thought it had come from the direction of the farmhouse. I hated the place, the Winthrops, and their miserable land, and I wanted to get away from there as quickly as possible.

I was halfway back, crossing the bottom of a dell, when they appeared on the crest above me. Five men with rifles. They had the sky behind them, so I couldn't make out their faces, but from his size and shape I knew Billy was the one in the middle. They stood there, widely spaced, staring down at me. I had a flash of helpless premonition—they would shoot me there like a pig in a ditch, and throw my body in quicksand or drag it up into the woods and let the animals dispose of it. They could move my car, burn my clothes, and I would disappear completely from this world.

But there's no point in hesitating at a moment like that: if they're going to do it, they'll do it. So I trudged up the hill, stopping when I was more or less level with them. I nodded, and they gazed at me as if I were already dead.

"Well?" Billy finally said. "You find it?"

"Yeah. Thanks."

"Satisfied?"

He didn't introduce me to his playmates, but they all looked like the same kind of mean country hardass he was.

"I'm not finished yet."

"So what's the goddamn problem?" he demanded.

"Oh, I'm not even sure there is one."

I walked past him, and I could almost feel the heat. But he wasn't going to do anything, not when I was beginning to sound so sweet and reasonable about it. He bought it.

"Will you give me a call?"

"Sure," I replied over my shoulder. "In a day or two."

"You do that."

He wanted to sound tough, but there was too much eagerness in his voice. He could already picture that check for $125,000. He would have his mother endorse it and he would put it in the bank. For her. Of course. No problem.

Chapter Seven

"There you are," Det. Miller said.

"Here I am."

"Thought you were coming round this morning."

"No, you said the files would probably be ready by then, and I said fine. You didn't put them away, I hope."

"No, they're waiting for you."

"Good."

"You come up with anything?" he asked.

"Not really. I talked with Dr. Gow, and I took a look at a couple of the accident sites."

"Which ones?"

"Burnette and Winthrop."

Miller nodded. "You met Billy."

I smiled. "Yeah, what about him?"

"What about him?"

"Has he ever been in any trouble?"

"No."

"Not even a bar fight?"

"Not that I ever heard of."

"No? Well, I noticed that he's studying hand-to-hand combat techniques, and he has four buddies who carry guns."

"Lots of folks around here have guns for hunting and killing varmints. You have a situation with them up there?" Miller asked with interest.

"No." I smiled at his choice of words. "Not at all."

He relaxed. "It's probably a good idea to watch your step with them. If they decide to beat you up real good, and there are no witnesses, well . . ."

"I know." There would be nothing the police could do about it. "But you don't think Billy could have rigged up his father's accident? He wouldn't even have to bother with his mother, she'd let him take care of the money."

"Yeah, it crossed my mind right away," Miller said. "But it would damn near be the perfect murder, and I don't think he's got it in him. Billy would screw it up somehow."

"His mother wouldn't say anything even if she knew for sure, and I don't think she has a clue."

"You're probably right about that. But the fact remains, we don't have any evidence," Miller emphasized again. "None."

"Not yet."

He wasn't biting on that one. "You saw the tree where Donnie Burnette racked himself up?" Miller asked, changing the subject.

"Yeah, I did."

"And?"

"And what?"

"What do you think?"

"Bad luck."

"How do you mean?"

"The way he spun right into that tree, and all that open ground on either side of it. Just a matter of inches, and he'd still be alive."

"Probably," Miller allowed. "At least until the next time he got tanked up and hit the skids."

The police reports were not very helpful; they didn't set me off on any new lines of thought or speculation. I wrote down the names and addresses of some of the witnesses, the ones who had first arrived at the scenes and called in the accidents. I wanted to interview them at some point and get their impressions in case they had seen something odd that the police didn't bother to write up. But there were no witnesses who had seen any of the accidents at the moment they had actually occurred.

Dr. Gow's reports were clear and concise, enumerating the assorted injuries in each case and specifying the physical causes of death. I didn't see much room for interpretation or argument.

Slim pickings all around, as Det. Miller had told me it would be. True, he'd had twenty-four hours to clean those files, but I didn't think that had happened. If there was fraud, it had been perpetrated on the other side by Joe Bellman and some of the victims' relatives. Miller struck me as fairly straightforward, a typical cop. He resented my presence. I was an outsider and I was trying to prove that he had failed in some way to do his job. I get that reaction frequently. And as for Dr. Gow, at his age he seemed an improbable coconspirator.

What I didn't like about the police files was the feeling of official complacency. The authorities were handed a whole series of accidental deaths, each one as neat and simple as sirloin on a platter, and they'd taken them at face value. No hints of doubt, no troubled questions, no serious investigations. It happens that way all the time, not just in Winship, but that's no excuse. It's all very well for Miller to say that Billy Winthrop isn't smart enough to pull off the perfect murder. The detective has his instincts, fed by experience and his knowledge of the people involved. But I have mine too. I thought Billy might have sufficient backwoods cunning to try it—it was such a simple "accident" to arrange. Billy had the motive, means, and opportunity, and he was not exactly a reassuring personality. But Miller had merely gone through the motions instead of making a real effort. And that was only one case.

I called Steve collect from a booth in the post office. The lobby was crowded with office juniors who were carrying stacks of mail. They stood in fuzzy ramps of dust that were defined by the late afternoon sun.

"Jack, how's it going?"

"Okay, and you?"

"I was just on my way out of the office."

"I forgot, you're an executive."

"Very funny. How's Winship?"

"Beautiful. They have their own brewery and they make great beer. I'm staying at a place called the Birch Inn."

"The Birch Inn, right."

"But I'm calling from the post office."

"Any particular reason?"

"Just a precaution," I said. "Bellman's sister works at the inn, so I'd rather not risk anybody listening in. I'll phone you when I have news."

"And if I need to talk to you?"

"Call me at the inn, but keep it short, and then I'll go out and call you right back. Or just leave your name if I'm not in."

"Okay. What have you got so far?"

"Nothing definite yet, but I can tell you that Bellman looks bad, acts bad, and smells bad. I'm pretty sure he's got something to hide, and I'm still trying to figure out what it is."

"Is he playing it tough?"

"Not really. He threw me out yesterday, but it wasn't a very convincing performance. He was jumpy as hell."

"Okay, interesting."

"Then he called me last night, sounding kind of down, and he asked if I could meet him again this evening."

"And you're going to?"

"Sure. I wanted to let you know."

"Where are you meeting him?"

"At his office. It's right in the center of town."

"Okay, but watch yourself."

I'd been hearing that a lot lately. "I will, don't worry."

"What else? Did you find anything of interest in the police files? I don't mean the official reports, but the notes."

"I got the names of a few witnesses to talk to, but not much else. Basically, they took each case at face value, the cops and the M.E. They weren't crooked or incompetent, just a little lazy."

"Routine."

"I think so."

Steve growled. As we talked it became clear he was more interested to learn of my secret meeting with Chris Innes and my visit to the Winthrop farm.

"She's Bellman's secretary and her home phone is tapped?"

"She *thinks* it is," I corrected. "But don't get too excited about that. She also gave her boss a glowing testimonial—how he is such a fine family man, honest, a churchgoer, and so on."

"Anything going on between the two of them?"

"No, nothing at all."

"You sound remarkably sure of that."

"I am. She's too lonely. And if she were having an affair with him, she wouldn't have arranged to meet me."

"Not even to see if she could find out what you know?"

"She never really tried."

"Okay, but there's two of you worrying about the telephones. I find that kind of interesting, don't you?"

I smiled. Steve loved to play backseat detective.

"Maybe, but—"

"Keep working on her. She's got to know something about it, even if she doesn't know she knows."

"Oh yeah, I'll be seeing her again."

"And Winthrop—he sounds promising."

"He might be."

"I'll be home all evening, so give me a call later. Even if your meeting with Bellman is a bust, I'd like to know."

"Okay."

It was still overcast outside and the wind was picking up as I left the Birch Inn shortly before seven. The air of lingering summer was gone and the warm colors of the turning leaves were flat and subdued in the gray chill of dusk. There were few people out walking, traffic was light, and the town was quiet.

I reached Horseshoe Lane in a few minutes. There was a soft glow of light in Bellman's window on the upper floor. I climbed the stairs, knocked twice, and went inside. The outer office was cast in gathering darkness. Chris's desk was neatly arranged for the start of work the next morning.

"Hello?"

I caught the smell of powder in the air before I reached the partly open door of Joe's office. He was on the floor beside his desk, and part of his face had been destroyed. I moved a little closer to him. It looked as if a single shot had hit him in the right cheek or eye socket, smashing up through into the brain. No sign of an exit wound, surprisingly little blood. I touched his wrist, but couldn't detect a pulse. His skin was still warm.

I backed away carefully and surveyed the room. There was no evidence of a struggle, nothing disturbed or out of place, except for Joe Bellman. Nothing to indicate robbery. I looked for the gun but couldn't find it. The powder burns on his face suggested that he had been shot at close range.

I circled around and bent over to read the papers that were on his desk, but they related to a routine automobile policy. The pen lying on the documents was capped, which could be taken as a sign that Bellman had not rushed to deal with a sudden intrusion. His desk diary was open, showing a number of appointments earlier that day but none from midafternoon on, not even mine. I took a pencil from a mug and used the eraser to flip through the pages. There were scores of names and notes, but I saw nothing that rang any bells.

Still using the pencil, I pulled the filing cabinet drawers. They were all full, the tabbed files neat and apparently undisturbed. Of course, the killer could have taken individual papers; there was no way of knowing. But whatever Bellman's scheme was, I thought he probably had kept it all in his head and not put any of it down on paper. Maybe somebody killed him because of a grudge about something unrelated to my cases. Or maybe Joe died because somebody wanted to be absolutely sure that he would never be tempted or forced to talk.

I poked through his desk drawers, but found nothing of interest. My eyes avoided the snapshot of Bellman's wife and kids. I took a quick look around the rest of the suite, the small storeroom, the toilet, and the outer office, but there was nothing unusual or obviously out of place.

It hit me that I had to speak to Chris right away. I went to her desk in the other room, found a directory, looked up her number.

"Hello?" a sleepy voice answered.

"Chris?"

"No."

"Is Chris there?"

"Just a minute." The roommate, the nurse who worked the graveyard shift at the hospital. She came back on the line. "No, Chris isn't here now."

"What time does she get home from work?"

"Who's this calling?"

I hesitated for a second. Well, no need to hide it—the police were probably going to fret about this call anyway.

"Jack Carlson. Just tell her I called."

"Jack Carlson. Okay."

"Thank you."

Then I called the police.

Chapter Eight

Det. Miller was unhappy; it showed. Dr. Gow was very unhappy, and he didn't mind letting us know that he had been just about to sit down to a late dinner when he got the call.

"Rib eye, too," he muttered, while jotting a few notes on an official form. He signed it and detached a carbon copy, which he handed to Miller. "You can get him out of here now. I'll do an autopsy in the morning, unless you can think of some reason why it should be done right away."

"No, tomorrow's fine," the policeman answered. "Bound to be the gunshot, isn't it? I mean, you don't see anything else?"

Gow shook his head. "I don't expect any surprises. I'll be there at eight A.M. You can come and watch if you want, and that includes you, Mr. Carlson," he said with a sharp look that openly dared me to challenge him on this death.

"Thanks, probably not," I replied.

"Give me a call, Doc, if anything odd turns up," Miller said.

Gow departed. A police photographer continued to take shots of the body and the office, while a young forensic man dusted some likely surfaces for fingerprints. To me it looked like a simple, efficient killing, and I doubted very much that any incriminating evidence had been left behind. But perhaps Miller had warned his people to be thorough because I was there. Besides, this one was clearly murder. Shot in the face, no gun left at the scene.

"Small caliber weapon, probably a twenty-two," he said to me.

I nodded. "Not much noise, but a lot of internal damage."

I had already briefly told him why I was there and how I had found the scene. Miller led me into a corner of the outer office and I knew he was ready to give me a thorough questioning. He had his notebook and pen ready.

"Okay, tell me again. In detail."

"The door wasn't locked," I said. "I had an appointment with him for seven this evening. I walked in, saw him, called you, and tried to get his secretary on the phone, but she wasn't home. You guys arrived, and that's about it."

"Uh-huh. You're an investigator, Carlson. What do you think?"

"It looks as if somebody walked in and fired a single shot. Stuck the gun right in his face and shot so quickly that Bellman didn't even have time to flinch or duck his head. They probably checked to make sure he was dead and then left. You found his wallet in his hip pocket and there's no obvious sign the office was searched, so I'd say it wasn't robbery. Just a fast, clean hit."

"Why?"

"To shut him up? I'm just guessing."

"Because of this business of yours?"

"I'd say so, yes," I replied. "It happening the day after I saw him, and just before he wanted to talk to me again. Of course, it's possible that somebody else had a grudge against him for reasons that have nothing at all to do with me. But I like the first idea better."

"There something you haven't told me?" he demanded, putting a little edge in his voice.

"No. The only thing that's new since I saw you earlier this afternoon is that Bellman's dead now."

"You sound like you expected it."

"No. If anything, I thought *I* might be at risk, that he was trying to set me up for something by arranging to meet me here at a time when the building would be empty. But I can't say I'm all that surprised. If he was involved with some others in fraud and possibly even murder, then he'd be the first to go."

"Uh-huh." But the detective didn't look as if he put much stock in what I was saying. He was giving me the hard stare that all cops practice in the mirror every morning when they shave.

"Now, tell me about that girl again," he said. "I was kind of interested to hear about her. You didn't mention her this afternoon."

"I didn't think of it because she didn't really have anything important to say. Just about what a nice guy her boss was, he had nice family, that kind of thing. We had a couple of beers, and that's all there is to it."

"Oh really? You see her last night, you come here, you find her boss dead, and right away you called her. Doesn't seem quite right."

"I called Chris to let her know what had happened, and because it occurred to me that she might be in danger too."

"You think she was in on it with Bellman?"

"No, I doubt that. She didn't strike me as the type. But it's possible that the person who shot Bellman could think she knows something."

Miller now looked very unhappy. "Chris Innes might be the last person who saw Bellman alive. She may be a witness in a murder case. She might even be a suspect in it. I've tried to cooperate with you as far as your business is concerned, but you're an agent for a few insurance companies, that's all, and I don't appreciate your calling her like that, when you've found him dead and the police are on the way. You ought to know that some people could view that as interfering."

For him, that was a monumental speech.

"Hey, come on. I wasn't trying to interfere, and you know it."

"You heard me."

I could have argued the point with him, but I bit it off. It can be tricky getting along with local police. It doesn't matter if you're right about something; if they want to make life difficult for you, they can and will. Miller and his local prosecutor could dummy up some bogus charge. They would surely drop it later, but in the meantime I'd be an embarrassment to the insurance companies and out of the action. In my business, you have to stay cool and prepare for tomorrow.

"There is one other thing you might want to know," I said. Better now than later. "I didn't think much of it at the time, it just sounded unlikely."

"What is it?" Miller asked coolly.

"Well, Chris told me she thought her phone was being tapped. The phone company told her the line was clear, but she still kept hearing clicks."

Miller stared at me while he thought about it for a long moment. He ran the flat of his thumbnail along his upper lip.

"Carlson, I was going to have you come in first thing tomorrow morning and write up a statement for us."

"Sure, I'll be glad to."

"But now," he went on, "I think you'd better come back to the station and do that right away. I want your signature on something tonight. Then we'll see where we are with you."

I shrugged. "Okay."

Miller drove me there himself, left me with a desk cop, then disappeared. I've written a lot of reports over the years, so one more was no problem. I tried to keep it short and simple, repeating everything I had already told Miller about my contacts with Chris Innes and Joseph Bellman. I tried to keep the details to the bare minimum, but at the same time to include all the relevant facts. Still, nearly two hours passed before I was finally able to get out of the police station. The northern sky was lit up again as I hurried to my car. My head was a jumble of flashing thoughts and images—Bellman's ruined face, Chris, the garnet mine.

I went to Doran's bar first. I didn't really expect to find her sitting there quietly getting sloshed, and she wasn't there, but it was worth a look. The bartender said he knew Chris, but she had not stopped in that evening.

I drove to her street and cruised past her duplex. Miller's car was parked in front and there was also a black-and-white with a cop in it. I wondered if Chris had returned home and was being interrogated now, and if so, what she might be saying. I felt an unnerving sense of lost opportunity, because I had spent a few hours with her the night before and I'd come away with nothing much, and now everything was scrambled. I should have done better.

I drove around aimlessly for a few minutes, thinking about her. I had her pegged as a lonely young woman, but that was too easy. At the bar, she'd been almost prim in her demeanor and in the way she talked about her boss, how he treated her with respect, was a good, religious man, a family man. About men, she'd said maybe she was too fussy. But she wasn't fussy about me, and I was not an obvious target—I was at least ten years older than her, probably more. At her apartment, she turned into a seductress, taking control, leading the way. There were good things about her, and puzzling things, and maybe a small hint that vodka could be a problem in the works.

I found a gas station that had a pay phone outside. I pulled in and made a call to Steve to tell him what had happened to Joe Bellman.

"In the face? Holy shit."

"May have hit the cheekbone first, then went through the eye."

"Jesus. I didn't see that coming."

"Me either," I said. "I didn't even size him up as a suicide risk."

"You know, in spite of what I said to you back here, I was never really sure myself that all those claims were bad. But now, this leaves no doubt in my mind that at least some of them are."

"Sure."

"You agree?"

"It sure looks like he was silenced, and that's a real problem for us. It will be harder now to shake anything loose."

"What are you going to do next?"

"The only thing I can do is start tackling the beneficiaries and the witnesses. And I want to see Chris Innes again, when the police are through with her. There's an outside chance they will squeeze something out of her. If they don't, I will certainly try, but I have a hard time seeing her as a suspect."

"But she may know something."

"Right."

"Turn on the charm, Jack."

I had to laugh at that.

"Hey, are you all right?"

"Yeah, why?"

"I don't know," Steve said. "You went silent for a minute, kind of like you were distracted there."

I was distracted. I was looking at the sky.

"No, I'm okay," I said. "Look, I've got to go, Steve. I want to try to catch up with Chris Innes tonight."

"Okay. You take extra care now."

"I will."

"And get back to me."

"Right, tomorrow or the next day. Bye."

I hung up the phone. I'd been drifting, no question. The reds and purples were flashing and rippling across the blackness overhead, and I was sure I could hear a faint chant or singsong somewhere in the distance. This fucking town. The aurora, the elusive voices, the chill breeze in the night, the lonely street in the quiet town out in a remote area—all of it somehow seemed to envelop me then, and my mind felt a brief shiver of panic. For no real reason that I could imagine. I looked through the glass into the gas station, but the clerk must have stepped into the back room. No one around the place, no cars on the road. I didn't like being there, and I remembered the brief mental spasm—hallucination?—that I had experienced at Winthrop's garnet mine that morning. And then the white shapes racing through the graveyard last night. *It's this town. Or it's me, slowly losing it.*

I drove back to see if Chris was home. The cops were gone, but the lights were out, the place completely dark. I knocked on the front door and rang the bell just to make sure, but nobody answered. I wondered if she was at the police station. I drove back to the inn, hoping she would call or drop by.

I couldn't get to sleep until I'd put away three beers, the local lager. I was pushing forty, but I was in good health and I had a reasonable attitude toward life. Nothing in my history. So what was going on with me? I felt embarrassed by myself. I was a professional and proud of it, but for the first time in years I felt as if I'd made some blunder that I didn't even understand. That was the worst part. The uncertainty, the aftertaste of panic and fear that seemed to indicate deeper troubles, as if my brain were betraying me

* * *

I thought I was dreaming that I'd forgotten to lock my door, and that someone with a gun burst into the room. *Now you die, idiot.* I saw gray light in the window. The noise came from the door, someone rapping sharply on it. *What the hell?* I slid out of bed, got to the door, and opened it. Uniformed cop—no, two of them.

"Come on. Miller wants you. *Now.*"

Chapter Nine

Chris was slumped behind the steering wheel in her car. She had a bullet hole in her right temple and the gun was on the seat beside her. The air was cold and raw, and there was a heavy mist that couldn't quite work itself into a drizzle. It was twenty minutes to seven. The same team of cops worked quietly, doing the same sort of things they'd done the night before. Dr. Gow hadn't put in an appearance yet, but he would no doubt show up before long.

I stood under a tree just outside the yellow tape, trying to stay dry. I felt bad, really bad for Chris. Some measure of responsibility for her death belonged to me, and I didn't even bother trying to rationalize it away. I smoked a cigarette, but that didn't help. A lightly wooded area off a gravel road in the countryside, a few miles from town—on another day, it was probably a pretty place.

Miller had already told me how an elderly man had come upon the scene. He lived somewhere in the vicinity and was on his way to a local pond to do a little sunrise fishing. He noticed a car where a car didn't belong, went to take a closer look, and nearly killed himself rushing home to call for help. The old fellow was still pale and shaken as he sat in one of the squad cars.

I didn't know why Miller had his men haul me out there right away. By now he might even have suspected me, so maybe he wanted to see how I reacted at the scene. He did watch me carefully when I arrived. I don't know how I reacted; I was still groggy and I felt numbed by what I was seeing. Miller didn't say much, he merely pointed out the gun, the fatal wound, and the fact that the car did indeed belong to Chris. I couldn't think of anything worth saying, so I looked and nodded. Then I moved back under the tree and tried to collect my thoughts.

Gow appeared in an immaculate ten-year-old town car, driving very slowly so he didn't kick up any pebbles and scratch it. He went straight to work. Miller exchanged a few words with him and then came over to talk with me. That was his style, I recognized: speak to someone, drift away, then come back at them again, and so on.

"When was the last time you saw her?" he asked.

"Monday night. We met at Doran's bar."

"You see her or speak to her at all yesterday?"

"No."

"Last night, early hours this morning?"

"No. After I left the station last night, after I wrote up that statement for you, I went to her place, but the lights were off and nobody answered the bell."

"Why'd you go there?"

"To see her and talk, make sure she was okay."

"Then what'd you do?"

"Drove back to the inn, had two beers at the bar in the restaurant, and I took a third one upstairs to bed with me."

"You must be disappointed," he said.

I wouldn't have chosen that word for how I felt. "Why?"

Miller shrugged. "This kind of knocks down your theory that Joe Bellman was murdered to shut him up about that insurance stuff."

"How so?"

"Aw, come on now, Carlson. Even you can see that this girl must have had something going with Bellman. They wouldn't be the first boss and secretary to get it on and they sure as hell won't be the last."

"She was pretty emphatic telling me that wasn't the case."

Miller looked at me as if I were simple. "You want to put a little money on it? You think that gun in the car isn't the same one that killed Bellman?"

"No, I'm sure it is."

"Well?" As if that proved it.

"Why would she shoot him and then herself?"

"The usual. He probably strung her along. He told her he intended to divorce his wife and marry her. Probably swore that he loved her every time he slipped between her legs. Maybe he finally told her it wasn't happening, tried to break it off, or maybe she just got tired of waiting, tired of his dodging and procrastinating, and she confronted him about it, they have a scene. She loses it, bang, Joe's dead. She doesn't go home, she drives around, whatever. She's got nowhere to run to, she knows she can't escape. She killed her lover, her life is in ruins. Despondent, she ends up out here. Same gun, same end."

"*Crime passionel,*" I contributed.

"What?"

"Crime of passion."

"Crime of passion, exactly."

He had it all worked out. I wasn't sure what to say, because this could take me down a road I didn't care to travel.

"I don't believe it," I said.

"What part don't you believe?"

"That there was an affair. That she shot him. Or herself."

"Why not?"

I was weighing it. I couldn't tell him that Chris and I had fucked our brains out together. She was dead now, but it still felt like some kind of huge betrayal of her. I saw it as confirmation of her insisting that she wasn't romantically involved with Bellman, but what would Miller make of it? The way he was talking, he might just laugh and say it proved that she was a no-good slut who was fed up with Bellman for not coming through on his promises. And it would get out, and for a lot of people it would be the last detail that people heard or thought in connection with Chris Innes. It wouldn't make me look good either, but I could handle that.

"I'm just not convinced yet," I said. "If she and Bellman had a thing going, somebody else *had* to know about it. Did you talk to her roommate, the nurse? What did she say?"

"Jenny Randall—she didn't know who Chris was involved with, but she had the impression that there might be somebody. As for other folks, now that this has happened I expect we'll hear something before long."

"I can't believe that two single women shared an apartment and they didn't discuss their love lives."

"Night shift, day shift," Miller said. "They didn't spend a whole lot of time together. They weren't old friends, it was economics, sharing rent."

Dr. Gow approached us then. He had put on a rumpled tweed hat and looked as if he wanted nothing more than to go back home to bed for another hour. But I knew he wasn't.

"All yours," he said to Miller.

"Anything special?" the detective asked.

"No, just what it looks like."

Miller nodded. "Thanks, Doc."

Gow turned to leave.

"You through with me?" I asked Miller.

"Yeah, for now."

I hurried to catch up with Gow. "Doctor, are you going in to do that autopsy now?"

"Yes, I am."

"Mind if I hitch a ride with you?"

"Not at all," he said with no enthusiasm.

"Thanks."

He was a slow and laborious driver, but I didn't mind. The car was warm and comfortable, and Gow put on some soothing music. We said nothing for a few minutes as he proceeded cautiously back to the main road. He seemed to relax when we were on asphalt and he glanced briefly in my direction.

"Did you just want a ride into town, or are you coming along to watch me at work?"

"I'm curious about the wound."

"The one on Joe Bellman?"

"Yes."

"What about it?"

"The gun was close to him when it was actually fired."

"Why do you say that?"

"And he was hit on the right side of his face."

"Yes."

"The upper cheek area, lower part of the eye socket?"

"We'll see. It did look that way."

"Well, that could suggest a left-handed shooter."

Gow cleared his throat. "Why?"

"Line of fire," I said. "A right-handed shooter would have a tricky time making that kind of wound. I'm not saying it couldn't be done, but it does seem a little unlikely."

"If they were facing each other square-up, you mean."

"Yes."

"But there'd be nothing to it if the shooter happened to be standing a couple of steps to his left," Gow pointed out, wagging one finger as he clutched the wheel. "Coming at the victim from the victim's right side. Then, a right-handed shooter would have the gun in about the same place where you had it for your left-hander. Am I right, or am I missing something?"

"No," I admitted. "That's true."

"Well, there you are."

"But why would somebody do that?"

"Do what?"

"Walk in and then step to the left?"

"Perhaps they were both jockeying around, arguing."

"I know, I'm just curious."

"*Pfft.*" Gow shook his head. "You have to find a mystery in everything, Mr. Carlson?"

"No, but I've got one or two here."

"You've made a career out of this sort of thing, have you?"

"A career of sorts," I amended.

"How did that happen?"

"Miller's job wore me down."

"I see."

"What about you? Have you been practicing medicine here for most of your working life?"

"Just about."

"Were you born in Winship?"

"Yes, I was. Delivered by my father, as a matter of fact."

"He was a doctor too?"

"And his father before him."

"It must be nice to get the money thing out of the way early on," I said, and to my instant relief he chuckled at that. "The country's pretty out here and the town seems pleasant. What's it like?"

"Oh . . ." He took so long I thought that was all, but at last he finished vaguely, "About average, I guess."

The sky was a little brighter, but the air was still full of cold mist when we parked in a reserved place behind the hospital. Dr. Gow led me to a long, low one-story brick wing. He looked at his watch and scowled. I felt the same way.

"Is this the only hospital in town?" I asked.

"No, there's St. Mark's, on the other side of the river."

"Do you know Jenny Randall?"

"Of course."

"What's she like?"

"She's a very good nurse, I believe. I don't see her much—she works here at night. Why do you ask?"

"Until last night she shared an apartment with Chris Innes."

"I didn't know that." He seemed genuinely surprised. "Too bad. She'll be very distressed, I'm sure."

"Doctor, are you going to do an autopsy on Chris too?"

"Yes, it's required."

"You didn't autopsy George Winthrop."

Gow stopped and gave me a very rich smile. "He autopsied himself when he did that. Not a very good job, I'll grant you."

I had to smile too. "Will you run tests to see if Chris was given any kind of drug or anesthetic?"

He sighed. "The standard drug and alcohol tests, yes."

"Would that include something like chloroform?"

"You think someone rendered her unconscious, took her to that place and shot her, making it look like suicide?"

"Why not?"

"Believe me, the smell of something like chloroform or ether would have been very obvious in the confined space of that car."

"But you will check? Nasal swabs, whatever?"

"Mr. Carlson, I will find what I find."

"Okay." I'd pushed him enough for the moment. "Thank you."

"You're welcome."

The autopsy on Joe Bellman confirmed only

the obvious fact that he had died as a result of the single gunshot wound to the head. I left as soon as it was clear that Dr. Gow was not going to make any startling discoveries about whether the shooter might have been left-handed or right-handed.

"Do you want to be here when I do the girl?" Dr. Gow asked when I reached the door.

"No," I replied after considering it for a moment. "But I'd appreciate it if you would give me a call when you get the report on the blood and tissue samples. I'd like to hear the results."

"For both of them, I assume."

"Yes."

"It could be a few weeks. It depends on how busy the lab is. Unfortunately, we have only one lab for the entire upstate region."

"I'll give you my number before I leave town."

"And when is that?"

"I have no idea. Maybe I'll still be here."

He chuckled at that. I didn't.

I walked the few blocks to the Birch Inn, picking up a copy of the *Winship Journal-News* on the way. I read it over three cups of coffee on the front veranda. It was still cool and damp out, but I thought that if I went up to my room I'd get back in bed and fall asleep. The paper carried a short front-page report on the shooting of Joe Bellman. It offered no new information and it suggested that Joe had simply been the unfortunate victim of an office burglary. Sure. I put the paper aside and lit a cigarette.

I couldn't avoid thinking about Chris any longer. It was no good telling myself that her death wasn't my fault. Of course it wasn't, and yet . . . I'd spent time with her, we'd made love, fucked, and that always makes it different, to me anyway. And I had failed, somehow. She should not be dead. I had dismissed her fears of her phone being tapped. I hadn't warned her that if she knew anything she might be at risk. I had handled the situation with her all wrong.

Maybe I was even wrong about her and Bellman. Could it have been nothing more than a banal affair that suddenly went haywire, as Miller thought? I doubted it, but I doubted myself too. Maybe I was fooling myself, reading too much into the fact that a woman took me to bed. This case felt like an impossible mess.

I stared at the town green across the street, but what I saw was the image of a young woman's face frozen in death. Her eyes were shut, her expression blank, no sign of fear or sudden terror. It told me nothing, but I couldn't get it out of my head. The last thing *I* had seen in those eyes was joy.

The rest of the morning was a loss.

Chapter Ten

That afternoon and the next few days were hardly any better. My best two potential sources of information were dead. I talked to some of the witnesses named in the police reports, but none of them had anything helpful to say. They were cool and curt to me, and I was reminded yet again that not many people feel sympathetic toward insurance companies.

I slipped into the church and sat at the back for Bellman's funeral service, but that was another waste of time. His wife appeared to be on the verge of a complete breakdown, though she managed to get through the ceremony. His kids were dazed, lost behind blank expressions and vacant eyes, and they moved like robots. The few people who noticed me seemed to know instinctively who I was, and their faces curdled. I left quickly just before the funeral was over.

It was more of the same the next day, in the same church, at the funeral for Chris Innes. Like

Bellman, she drew a big crowd. Her family looked more stoical and reserved. I didn't see Bellman's widow in attendance.

The person most visibly distraught at Chris's funeral was an attractive dark-haired young woman. I thought she might be Jenny Randall. I hadn't been able to get her on the phone, and she was not at the apartment the three or four times I went there. Perhaps she had moved back in with her family for a few days, or she might simply have decided not to answer.

I finally caught up with her late on Sunday morning, the day after Chris was buried. I'd decided by then that my best chance would be in person, and I was relieved when she actually responded to my knock. She was indeed the woman I had noticed at the funeral service.

"Are you Jenny Randall?"

"Yes."

"My name is Jack Carlson. I—"

"Prove it."

She looked tired and drawn, but wary. I took out my wallet, extracted my driver's license and held it up. She leaned forward and peered at it through the locked screen door.

"I don't blame you for being cautious," I said, pleased that she hadn't told me to get lost.

"What do you want?"

"I had a drink with Chris last Monday night."

"I know."

"I'd like to talk to you about her."

"Let's get it over with," she said with a resigned tone. She slid the lock and turned away. "Come on in."

"Thank you."

I followed her up the stairs, down the short hallway, and into the living room. The air was stale and there was a week's dust on the furniture, obvious signs that the normal routine had recently been interrupted.

Jenny sat in one armchair and I took the other. She wore an oversized gray sweatshirt with the sleeves pushed up and baggy green shorts; she was barefoot and her hair hung in tangles. She looked as if she had awakened not long before.

"Chris mentioned me to you?"

Jenny nodded. "I dropped her off at Doran's."

"Oh, right."

"And the police told me about you."

"Oh? What did they say?"

"That you were here supposedly to investigate Chris's boss, and that you would probably try to contact me."

"That's right."

"And they said that if you annoyed me, to let them know, and they'd take care of it."

"Did they?" I smiled.

"Yes." She didn't.

"Tell me first, if I'm annoying you, and I'll stop."

"What do you want to ask me?" But before I could speak, she continued. "The cops questioned me for hours. I told them all I know, which is nothing. Chris didn't talk to me at all

108

about the insurance business, and I probably wouldn't even have listened to her if she did. I don't know anything."

"She must have talked about Joe Bellman," I said.

"Not much."

"How did she feel about him?"

"She liked him."

"But that's all?"

"Chris wasn't the type to fool around with a married man."

"You told the police that?"

"Many times."

"But they didn't believe you?"

"No." Resentful, a bitter look in her eyes. "You must have seen the story they put out in the newspaper."

"Yeah, I did."

"It's bullshit."

"Do you think Chris would take her own life?"

"Not for him. The only thing is, Chris was kind of unhappy about her life, in general. But not to the point of suicide, not even close. I told the cops that, but they kind of slanted it their way."

"Why was she unhappy?"

"Her boyfriend, Greg, split a few months ago."

"That's all? I mean, was there more to it?"

"It's the whole thing," Jenny said. "She didn't have anyone to take his place. She wouldn't say so, but you could tell. Chris wanted to be married, to set up house and start a family, that stuff. She wasn't into being young and single anymore. But it was more a matter of her being impatient, not desperate. Chris was not suicidal," Jenny declared firmly. "And she didn't own a gun."

"Would she know where to get one?"

"If she wanted one she would have gone through the procedure and bought it legally. But she never did—that I knew."

It was an interesting point. The only new thing I'd learned from Miller in several days was that they had traced the gun that killed Bellman and Chris to its original owner, a casino employee in Atlantic City who had reported it stolen more than three years ago. The man had since died in a car accident, and the gun might have passed through any number of hands. It was even possible it could end up in the possession of a young female secretary in a small rural town hundreds of miles away. That part was rather unlikely, but of course the cops didn't see it as a problem.

"So, you don't think Chris was having an affair with Bellman and you don't think she shot him and then herself?"

"Of course not."

"And the official story—"

"Is bullshit."

"Have you told anyone else that?"

"Like who?"

"The newspaper?"

Jenny smiled mirthlessly. "They didn't ask me anything, and I'm not about to call them up."

"Why?"

"They'd treat me like a crank or an emotional hysteric. And it's just my opinion. Besides, I have to live here." She added, "Though maybe not for much longer."

"Why?"

"I hate this town."

"Why?"

She gave me a look like I had no idea. "Do you want coffee? I'm going to make some, I need it."

"Sure, I'll have a cup," I said, and I followed her down the hall to the eat-in kitchen. "What about her family? Did they ask you anything?"

"They don't want to know," Jenny said as she set up the coffeemaker. "Chris wasn't real close to them."

"They wouldn't talk to me," I told her.

"Well, they're pretty much a waste of time anyway. Her old man is a tight-ass wimp and her mother drinks. Her brother is as thick as a couple of two-by-fours and her sisters are all wrapped up in their own married lives and their wonderful kids, that kind of thing. All of which may explain part of Chris's unhappiness. She was in her hometown, she had her family nearby, and she very much wanted to be a part of it. But she wasn't."

"You two talk much? You work nights, she worked days."

Jenny gave me a look. "Two women share a place together, and you're asking that? Of course we talked."

"Did she ever work late at the office?"

"Hardly ever."

"How did she seem the last few weeks?"

"About the same as usual."

"She wasn't nervous or anxious or worried about anything?"

"No."

"Nothing unusual about her daily habits? When she came and went, what she did?"

"No, not at all."

The coffee sputtered and dripped. Jenny and I sat down at the table by the back window. Outside, the lawn was strewn with dead leaves from a dwarf apple tree choked with suckers. Jenny took a cigarette from a crumpled pack on the table and lit it.

"You ration them," I said.

"Yes." Now she faintly smiled.

"Same here." I fished out one of my own. "Jenny, Chris was telling me something about your phone being tapped."

"She thought so."

"What about you?"

"I don't know," she said with a shrug. "I heard the clicks, same as she did, but I don't know if that meant that somebody was listening in, or if it was just noise on the line. I don't know the okay clicks from the bad."

"But she was convinced—at least it seemed that way to me. Did she worry about it a lot?"

"Yeah, it bothered her. She even went down to the telephone company office to talk to them about it. They checked it out and said everything was okay."

"But she didn't believe them."

"We both heard the sounds again."

"Who did she think it was?"

"She had no idea."

"What about you?"

"Me either. I mean, I knew it couldn't be anyone interested in me, because my life is even duller than hers was." The coffee was ready, and Jenny got up to serve it. "So I just decided that there was no point in worrying."

"Did Chris change her behavior because of the phone?"

"Maybe she didn't use it as much. I don't know."

"Did the two of you do much together on weekends?"

"More the last few months, after Greg broke up with her. She was moping so much that I made an effort to cheer her up and get her to go out and do things, so she'd get over it sooner."

"Even though you both had different schedules all week long, you and Chris were pretty close friends?"

Jenny nodded. "Yes." Tears began to fill her eyes, and she looked down to blink them away. I stubbed out my cigarette and went to the counter to get the carafe of coffee. I refilled her cup and mine.

"One of the things that bothers me," I said gently, "is this business about the phone. Chris met me because she wanted me to know that Joe Bellman was a good, honest man, who would never get into any kind of criminal activity. But at the same time, Chris is sure her phone is tapped. And if it was, from what I've heard the only reason can be because she worked for Bellman."

"I know."

"Somebody thought she knew something."

"What do you think he was doing?" Jenny asked.

"Fraud, for a lot of money. But don't ask me exactly how it worked, because I don't have that part figured out yet."

"Well, as far as I'm concerned, you could be right. Chris was just an innocent victim who got caught in the middle of something that she had no part in, and I think it's so evil that she was killed. They not only took her life, but they took her good name as well. I hate them. I hate this whole town."

I had found one person who agreed with me about the case. I was impressed by Jenny's loyalty, and the raw anger she displayed. But I didn't see how any of this could help me toward a breakthrough.

"You're sure that Chris didn't know anything? She liked her boss—are you sure that she wouldn't look the other way or help him on something that wasn't quite right, if he asked?"

"Obviously I have no way of knowing for certain, but I don't think she would cross that line. She wasn't in love with him, and she certainly wasn't in love with her job. The kind of work Chris did, she could just quit and get another job." Jenny took a fresh cigarette, but she didn't light it. "Besides, I don't think he would bring her into it and put himself at risk. How could he be sure that she would go along with him? And if she said no, then he'd have a problem, because she'd know that he was doing something crooked."

"Yeah, you're right," I told her. "I didn't really believe that she was involved, but I had to ask."

"You know what I think?"

"What?"

"I think you're going at this backwards."

"Backwards?" I was surprised. "Why?"

"Because everything you're asking me is about Chris, and her boss, and her job."

"Yes, of course it is," I said, puzzled.

"Maybe you're missing the rest of it."

"The rest of what?"

"Winship."

"What about it?"

"You're the investigator. What do you think?"

I wished people would stop saying that to me. "I imagine the winters are kind of rough up here."

Jenny laughed and shook her head. "Yeah, you see?"

"So tell me."

"Winship is rotten."

"What do you mean?"

"It's corrupt," she said. "There are all kinds of

shady and crooked deals, sleazy business, private clubs and societies going on. The whole county is like a little kingdom run by Winship and Schramburg, and they are far enough from anywhere so that nobody bothers them. *Nobody*."

Jenny lit up, excuse enough for me to have another one as well.

"Sure, but it's like that in most towns and cities. Local government always draws some people who see it as a franchise for their own enrichment. Maybe out here it's worse than usual, but I'm not a federal agent. I'm here to investigate some insurance matters. I can't start trying to unravel the whole town."

"You should," Jenny insisted. "You know that there are some other people involved, and if it was big money fraud?"

"Yes, I think it was."

"Well, then, it was probably some very important people here who were behind it from the beginning. The people who really run things, not just some two-bit con artists."

"Jenny, I—"

"What did you think of Penny Lane?" she asked suddenly.

"Penny Lane?"

"Not the Beatles song," she said with a laugh. "I guess you haven't found it yet. Penny Lane is the local nightlife, down in the south end. Take a look. You might be surprised."

"Okay, I will," I told her impatiently. "But,

116

Jenny, who am I supposed to focus on—town hall, the police, the Jaycees?"

"Yes," she answered immediately. "All of them. Start where you want, but they're the ones. They control things, and they're like the Nazis, man. Believe me. Even the churches. *Especially* the churches."

"Right, okay."

I liked Jenny, but she seemed to have said everything useful that she could, and we were off the edge of the diving board now.

"You've seen the churches?" she asked.

"The ones around the green. I'm staying at the Birch Inn."

"Right, they're five of them there," Jenny said. "Did you notice anything odd or strange about them?"

"I wasn't looking. The odd and strange finds me all by itself."

"I'll tell you something else. Some people have disappeared here. In Lauck County. Schramburg. *Winship.*"

"What do you mean, disappeared?"

"Disappeared," she stated flatly. "No searches, no official investigations, no news reports. They just disappeared."

"What people?"

"Summer visitors, people passing through, people who lived here all their lives. Your hear something, then the story just dries up."

"Let's go back to the churches. I've heard

what sounds like a choir singing late in the evening, a children's choir. And whatever they were singing, I'd never heard it before. I couldn't even tell you the language—in fact, sometimes it isn't even words."

"Yes," Jenny said, smiling. "Yes."

"Well, what is it?"

"I've heard it," she told me. "But I don't know. People will tell you it's the way the wind blows through the rock formation on Pioneer Cliff, or the way the cemetery is aligned and the gravestones face. You can explain anything."

I wanted to get things back on track, wherever that was.

"Did the cops tell you that you might be in danger?"

"No."

"They didn't offer you any protection?"

"No. Why would they?"

"Because you were Chris's roommate. If someone thought that she knew something and killed her to silence her, they might wonder if she had told you."

"She could have told any number of people," Jenny said. "Besides, the cops believe that she shot Joe and then killed herself. End of story."

"Yeah, we're back to that."

I reached for another cigarette.

Chapter Eleven

It was the middle of the afternoon by the time I got back to my hotel room. On the way, I walked around the green and checked out the five churches. I saw immediately what Jenny had referred to—near the front doors of each one was a plaque that showed a cross on a shield, the same as the one at the old cemetery and on the local beer labels. Otherwise, they were ordinary churches as far as I could tell. One was Catholic, the rest an assortment of Protestant denominations.

It was a bit unusual to see churches showing a coat of arms, if in fact that's what it was—and I couldn't imagine any explanation. The shield and cross did kind of remind me of the Crusades, the Knights Templar and the whole stew of medieval Christianity, but that meant nothing. No matter what Jenny thought, it was probably just a typical community association involving some clergy, businessmen and town hall types, an excuse for ziti dinners, tag sales, good works and a lot of socializing. Perhaps some of the people in it were also engaged in far less honorable activities, but that hardly made it an evil, criminal organization.

I hadn't spoken to Steve since late Wednesday, when I had called to tell him about Chris and the way the police were treating the case. The twin deaths made it seem less likely that anyone would bother listening in, but even so, we talked carefully, offering no conclusions or opinions. Steve was very subdued. I could tell that he was thinking of pulling me off the case.

I was supposed to call him again on Friday, but I avoided it because I was still hadn't come up with anything concrete. Now I reached him at his home, where he was watching a football game on television. He barely gave me a chance to speak. He had given a lot of thought to the matter, he told me, and his enthusiasm was cooling. Bellman was my best chance, and he was dead. Now even his secretary was dead. I wasn't making much headway. It might be wiser to let the insurance companies decide which claims they could stomach paying and which ones they were prepared to resist in court (with a view to haggling).

It wasn't completely unexpected. I knew that the insurance companies would want prompt results—they always do. They do not want to pay hotel bills, meals, and other expenses indefinitely. I had been in Five Towns for more than a week and I had little to show for it.

Steve didn't even try to disguise his thoughts as he spoke, which meant he no longer cared, or believed, that anyone might be eavesdropping on us. So I didn't either. If I was about to be pulled off the job, it didn't matter. I argued.

"This is what they want," I told him. "This is why they hit Bellman and Chris. To block us."

"Maybe, but—"

"I still have some people to run down, and some leads that I want to follow."

"How long will that take?"

"This week."

"A whole week?" he protested.

"At most." I'd never spent two weeks on a case in my life. "Probably less."

We went back and forth for a while, but in the end the best I could get was a couple of days. I had to call him again at his office by five o'clock Tuesday afternoon. He didn't say it, but I knew that if I didn't have something solid for him by then I'd be on my way back home on Wednesday morning.

It really bothered me. In my line of work a good, thorough examination of the physical evidence is often enough to disprove the claim, and a stern, aggressive interrogation will frequently demolish a claimant's resolve. Such people aren't career criminals, merely desperate or greedy fools.

In this case, however, the usual methods

hadn't worked. It was different. It was bigger and deadlier, and I wanted it. But I was still scratching around on the outside, trying to find some crack I could force open.

I made some more phone calls, trying to line up appointments for the next two days. Witnesses, although they claimed they had not really seen anything. Names from the police reports. It was hard going. Nobody wanted to see me. I got the message. They were busy. Call again next week, and so on.

I gave up when my ear started to hurt. I rolled over on the bed and dozed off for a couple hours. After a steak sandwich in the hotel bar, I went out for a drive around town. By then it was after ten, and since it was Sunday I expected most places to be closed or doing very little business. And the central part of town was indeed very quiet.

Penny Lane wasn't listed on the map, at least not under that name, but I didn't think I'd have much trouble finding it since Winship is not big enough to hide a gaudy street. So I headed south, cruising slowly, taking in every building I passed, trying to see or feel something in them—I don't know what.

I'd gone about two miles when I came to a small iron bridge that crossed a low stream flowing toward the main river. I drove on, and suddenly it was like entering another country, or another town at least. The homes were triple-deckers in decay, tenements that stood so close they seemed to sag against each other.

There were more people out, though most of them were hanging around on the sidewalks, steps, and porches. So even Winship had its slum neighborhood. To be fair, it wasn't much of a slum compared to others I've seen, but it was obviously a few rungs down on the economic ladder.

I smelled the hops in the air before I spotted the familiar emblem of the Five Towns Brewery. It was located in an old brick building, one of many scattered throughout the neighborhood, and one of the few that was still used for its original purpose. I passed a number of bars and eateries, but saw nothing that made me think I'd found Penny Lane. When the buildings thinned out and the road ahead was dark with trees, I knew I had come to the edge of town. I turned back and zigzagged the side streets, heading generally west.

It was an alley, directly off the main river road. I almost drove past it, but the brief, sudden flash of bright light caught me. I had to park a couple of blocks away from it because of the numbers of cars already there. The alley itself was open only to pedestrians, and there were plenty of those.

I was impressed. I'd seen Boston's Combat Zone in its heyday, and it was smaller than this place. Here in a distant small city in an empty northwest county, Penny Lane was busy, even on a Sunday night. Vice was positively thriving in the wilderness, like a remnant of frontier boomtown days.

It was about a hundred yards long and the old mill buildings on either side had been converted into topless bars, strip clubs, peep show arcades and massage parlors, with a number of fast food joints wedged in between. There were two cops posted at the entrance of the alley, and I saw a couple more walking the beat inside, ready to deal with anybody who got out of line. That was an advantage, since people like to feel safe when pursuing their pleasures.

At first glance it all seemed fairly routine, much the same as any sin street in America—though most of them are situated in high-traffic areas, and this one was rather off the beaten path. I saw a small bar called the Golden Triangle that looked a bit less garish than the others. I went inside.

I was wrong—it wasn't a bar, it was a brothel. There was a large single room with a stone floor and some industrial steel columns. The pinup posters on the walls represented the only effort at ambience. Rock music came from an invisible sound system. It was loud enough to fill the emptiness, but it didn't hinder negotiations. Girls, and there were many of them, wandered around in high heels, dressed in bikinis or skimpy lingerie. There were also plenty of men, potential customers and mere gawkers who drifted through the place with keen eyes. Every now and then one of them would follow a girl upstairs. The place was as stark and functional as an Eros Center in Hamburg.

The girls were all young and fairly attractive; there were no tired old veterans in the crowd. I discovered some "health statements" posted around the room, claiming that the "employees" were tested and examined every week, so that customers could enjoy themselves with complete security and peace of mind. Uh-huh. It might be the age of AIDS, but you can still have some fun tonight.

Prostitution is illegal. You can zone an area for adult entertainment as they did in Boston, but you can't zone your way around a law. And yet here was a brothel operating in full view of the local police. Maybe Jenny was right, and the whole governing structure of Five Towns was in on it, accepting a share of the proceeds in return for protection. I wasn't shocked, but I was somewhat surprised that they were able to do it without attracting unpleasant attention. You couldn't keep this a secret for very long. The state would—*should,* that is—come in and crack down, gathering a lot of cheap publicity in the process. Obviously that wasn't happening.

It got more interesting. I checked out several places along the alley (what else was there to do on a Sunday night?). In the peep show booths the windows were open. For a few bucks you could fondle the girl of your choice, and for several more she'd fondle you. In the video arcades, pretty girls would offer to come into the cubicle with you and help you enjoy the films. There were live shows, and after each act the female "star" mingled with the audience, letting anyone cop a feel, often going beyond that to heavier action in the darker areas of the place. In the bars, there were plenty of dark booths. The girl who brought your drink stayed—to cuddle on your lap, practically in your clothes, if you so desired. Or you could sit by yourself and watch the hardcore flicks showing on the many TV monitors or simply enjoy the nudes dancing on runways. I had a couple of beers here and there, but I managed to resist the clinches.

Penny Lane was bigger, busier, and raunchier than I had expected, and it made no effort to hide anything. It's difficult for me to get worked up about violations of the vice code since I regard most of it as a moralistic waste of time, a trivial pursuit compared to the big crime problems that exist. The Europeans are more sensible about this kind of thing than we are.

I found a narrow bar at the end of the alley. There were a few working girls inside, but it looked fairly quiet. I went in, nursed a beer, smoked a cigarette, and tried to think. I was tired, and I no longer knew what I was supposed to be looking for. I didn't see how I could connect Penny Lane with Joseph Bellman or Chris Innes, or any of the insurance cases. Maybe Winship was as rotten as Jenny said, and maybe some of the people who ran the whole show also had a hand in Bellman's scheme, whatever it was. But even if that were true, knowing it didn't help me at all. What I needed was a name, a trail, a lead.

I couldn't start investigating everybody, the whole town.

My mind kept going back to Jenny and Chris. Two apparently fine young women, both pleasant and both attractive. But Chris was skittery as well, she had a kind of low-grade paranoia. And when Jenny relaxed with me and began to talk freely, she was the same way, only more so. It nagged me, it hung like a cloud in my brain. How did they reach that point?

I was leaving the bar, thinking of heading back to the inn, when a young woman grabbed my arm in hers, gave me a quick peck on the cheek and tugged me, almost forcing me to walk with her. I started to resist.

"Just walk with me for a couple of minutes, *please*. A really obnoxious guy has been following me around, hitting on me, and he won't leave me alone." The words tumbled out of her in a rush. "If he thinks you're my boyfriend, maybe he'll give up and go find somebody else to bother."

"Okay," I said. I glanced back over my shoulder, but I didn't notice anyone who appeared to be following us. "No problem."

"Thanks a lot."

She was wearing a light raincoat, and when the front flap opened a little in the breeze, I caught a glimpse of a flimsy outfit underneath. Her heels drilled a clatter on the pavement as we walked briskly almost half the length of the lane.

"Where do you want to go?" I asked.

"Let me buy you a drink," she replied. "Least I can do to thank you."

"You don't have to do that. It's no trouble."

"Oh, come on," she insisted. "There's a little bar up here, the folks who hang out there mostly work here in the lane and take their breaks there. It's nice and quiet, no loud music, none of the usual business on this street. Besides, I need a drink. This place is getting to me."

"Okay."

The bar was as advertised, and we sat in a booth near the front door. She had a spritzer and I had another lager. She took the seat facing the door and window, so she could see that guy if he turned up outside.

"I was about ready to put the cops on him," she said. "But nobody around here likes it when the cops have to step in. My name's Kelly, by the way."

"And I'm Jack."

"Nice to meet you, Jack. And thanks again for being a gentleman and helping out a lady in distress."

I smiled at that. "You're welcome."

Like most of the women I'd seen in Penny Lane, she was pretty, with a look of frosted glamour, but not really beautiful. She was originally from Covington, Kentucky—"Kind of a loose town itself," she added with a laugh—but she had been all over the country since then. She was a dancer—"*Just* a dancer," she emphasized. Kelly was traveling with half a dozen other dancers. They'd been in Winship for two weeks and had another two to go before they would move on to some other city. They had people who lined up the jobs for them, put them up in local motels and arranged their transport from one city to another. The girls worked cities in loops—New England, New York-Pennsylvania-Ohio, the Upper Midwest, and so on. For the first time since I'd arrived in Winship, I was hearing someone's whole story without having to ask for it.

"At my age," she went on, "it's a good job. It pays well and I like to travel. There are some hassles and some creeps along the way, and it's not a business you last in for a long time. Even if you wanted to, you get old fast. So, I wire money to my bank account every week and as soon as I've got enough of a nest egg, I'll walk away from this."

"And do what then?" I felt I had to ask.

"I'd like to find a nice medium-sized town, one with just enough of a customer base in the immediate area, and open up a boutique."

"What kind of boutique?"

"I don't know yet, but it'll be something kinda chic."

Then I had to answer her questions—I was in the insurance industry, I was in Winship for a few days on business, and I was unmarried.

"That's all pretty cool," Kelly said, pulling her raincoat off. She was wearing a dark red, low-cut top made out of some clingy material that accentuated her full breasts. She caught me noticing them and smiled. "Not saying you're old or anything, but I do like men who are a little older, smarter, more solid. I've had to deal with too many boys who can't hold their liquor or their tongues."

I smiled. "So, you like men who hold their tongues?"

"Oooh, watch out for the quiet ones," she said. Then her eyes fixed on mine and a different kind of smile formed on her face. "Not *that* way, no."

Maybe I just needed some company, or maybe it was just that Kelly was so easy to look at— whatever, I was kind of enjoying her company. I had thought she probably had a hook or a hustle in the works with me, and I wasn't going to bite on either, but it didn't feel like that. It felt like relaxed, mildly flirty chat, nothing more. A few minutes later, our drinks were about done.

"Thanks for the drink and your company," I said. "I enjoyed both."

"Oh, my pleasure. And thank you again for helping me out." She started to pull her raincoat on. "Are you going back down the lane to check out more of the nightlife? I can tell you where to avoid."

"No, I'm heading back to my hotel."

"Where are you staying?"

"The Birch Inn, downtown."

"Want to share a taxi?" Kelly asked. "I'm finished working tonight and I'm going back to the motel. It's in the same direction as downtown."

"I'll drop you off. I've got a car."

"Oh, even better."

As soon as we were on the road, Kelly turned toward me and started talking nonstop again. I tried not to keep glancing at her legs and very short skirt. She went on about the worst part of her job being the loneliness on the road and in strange cities, how all of the men she met were losers or creeps—"present company not included, obviously!"—and most of the other girls were either silly or bitchy or just plain dumb. Kelly said she missed being around normal people.

"That's why I'm enjoying your company so much."

"Thank you." I smiled. We were at a red light and I was watching for it to turn. "But I wouldn't say I'm that normal."

"Hey, Jack," she said. I turned to look at her—her legs opened a little and her hands lifted the front of her skirt just long enough to flash me a glimpse of the purple thong she was wearing. She started laughing. *"Oh yes you are!"* I was laughing along with her then. Kelly slid close to me. "Am I being too *fresh* with you? Is that the word? Too—"

"I love fresh. You be as fresh as you can be."

"Oooh, yeah, daddy." She rested her hand lightly between my legs. "Good thing we're almost there."

In Winship I was having more nightcaps with women I'd just met than I'd had on the last ten jobs combined. The motel Kelly was staying at didn't belong to one of the top chains, but it was good; I'd have used it myself. There were twin beds in her room, though it looked like she was the only occupant, a few of her things dropped here and there, mostly on one side of the room. She put the DO NOT DISTURB sign on the outside of the door and locked it. She hung our coats in the closet and then went straight to the dresser with a bottle sitting on it.

"Let's see, we've got bourbon or . . . bourbon."

"No thanks, I'll have bourbon."

"In that case, we're in luck!"

Kelly took a couple of plastic motel glasses and poured generously. We touched glasses and sipped. She just stood there looking at me. So I put my drink on the dresser, then did the same with hers, and I put my arms around her and kissed her. She sank right into it, into my embrace. I loved the way her breasts pressed against me, the feel of the small of her back in my hands. We kissed long, slowly, deeply, and when we did break, we both kind of gasped and caught our breath.

"Damn." Her voice was almost a whisper.

"What?"

"I haven't had a kiss like that in . . . some time."

"You know what? Neither have I."

We stood there for a few moments, looking at each other.

"You want to sit down, or . . . what?"

"I think I'll freshen up," I said, nodding toward the bathroom.

"Me too," she said. "I want to change. You go first."

Nothing unusual or wrong in the bathroom. The usual female stuff, the walls, ceiling, and fixtures all clear. When I came out a couple minutes later, Kelly went in carrying a small tote bag. I took my shoes and socks off and padded around the room, checking everywhere—the lights, the pictures on the walls, the furniture, under the beds, the mirrors—every inch. I wouldn't have even been there if I'd felt any vibe that it might be a setup, with a mic, a camera and tape rolling, but I had to check. Nothing. I hoped I hadn't overlooked anything, because that could turn into an embarrassment. But this case was not going anywhere anyway, Steve was just days away from pulling the plug on it, and sometimes the situation you're in at any particular moment really is exactly what it appears to be. I was in that room because I wanted to be there.

I picked up my drink and sat down in one of the armchairs a few seconds before Kelly came back into the room. She moved quickly, picking up her drink, her long dark hair floating in the air. She was wearing a man's white shirt, half unbuttoned, long sleeves flapping loose as she walked. The shirt reached down just over her ass.

"You alright, daddy? Anything I can get you or do for you?"

"Come here."

She stepped closer and stood right in front of me, her legs parted. I sat forward on the edge of the chair, slid one hand up her thighs, under the shirt. I pulled the shirt open so I could suck her nipples. I kissed her again, slow and long. My finger explored—no thong now—and she was wet.

"I love your hands, daddy," she murmured. "And your tongue."

I was kissing her again. "Suck my tongue."

She did, eagerly. At the same time, she unbuckled my belt and pushed my pants down. Then she knelt down, fondling and stroking me lightly. She looked up and smiled at me as she teased the tip of my cock with her tongue.

"You know what, daddy?"

"What?"

"Tomorrow is my day off. No work."

"So?"

"So . . ." Sucking. Licking. Her deep blue eyes looking up. "If we had a whole day together . . . how many times do you think I could make you come?"

After the second time, we were lying under the sheets, cuddling and smooching lazily. Something occurred to me and I nodded my head toward the other bed in the room.

"Do you have a roommate coming back here tonight?"

"I did have. Keisha," Kelly said. "But she disappeared last week."

"Disappeared?"

"Yeah. She didn't tell anybody she was quitting, but her stuff was gone and so was she. It happens, girls get fed up and split, just like that. When nobody is looking." Then she slid her body onto mine and started tonguing my lips. "Anyhow, it's cool. You can stay."

Chapter Twelve

Maybe I should have spent the day with her. It was very tempting, but I was in Winship on business and I told Kelly I had work to do.

"What kind of work?"

"Insurance."

"Oh yeah. Tell me about it."

"It's too boring to go into," I said.

"I don't care. I'd like to hear. It sounds so *normal*."

"Maybe later," I said, trying not to read anything into her curiosity about my work. "I'll be back at the Birch Inn around five this afternoon. If you're free, give me a call and maybe we can do something."

She pouted. "Okay." Little girl voice.

I left, and from that point on things went downhill for me that day. Maybe the next day, or both, I'm not sure. I had a sense of control, as much as any person ever can have, and I knew my world and I was used to it. It didn't work brilliantly, but it worked just well enough, and I was able to live with that. But I seemed to be losing that control; I felt eroded with doubt.

Item: A message from Dr. Gow at the inn. I call him back. He tells me that he cashed in a couple of favors to have the toxicology tests on Joe Bellman and Chris Innes speeded up. The results are negative for both. Chris had a blood-alcohol level of .05, which is below the legal definition of intoxication. But since she did not die until early in the morning, it is quite possible that she had been drunk much of the evening. No drugs, no medicines. The results mean nothing, though Gow sees them as conclusive. By way of consolation, perhaps, he invites me to dinner. I thought of Kelly, but Gow was part of my work, so I had to go.

Item: Det. Miller has no news for me, because there's nothing left to investigate. Has any witness come forward to say Joe and Chris were having an affair? Well, not yet. Where did Chris get the gun? It doesn't really matter. There was no bottle with her in the car, so where did she drink? Oh, somewhere. I wanted to press him on this, but he cut me off.

"You still don't get it, do you," he said. "None of this is about murder the way you're thinking. It was a case of love gone bad, that's all. Yeah, Chris shot him. She killed him and that's murder, but the girl went off the deep end over love. There just isn't any cover-up or conspiracy like you're trying to sell."

I asked him about Penny Lane. He told me that the street was zoned for adult entertainment, had been for several years. No trouble, no spread, no rise in crime. On the plus side: good business and increased tax revenues. What about the illegal stuff—the live sex, the prostitution? When it gets out of hand, they clamp down on it, and then life gets back to normal. Miller looked somewhat disappointed in me, as if he had once considered me a man of the world and now I was coming on like some fussy old prude.

That was all as expected.

Item: A sweet old woman cooks great meals for Dr. Gow. His house is too big for a single man, but it is full of antiques and books. It has a kind of scholarly glow and warmth, though it is in fact a bit on the chilly side. He tells me that the cross and shield I've seen all over the place is the symbol of the Order of St. Michael, a community-religious type fraternal organization devoted to good works.

"You mean like the Elks, the Lions?"

"Yes," Dr. Gow replied, "but with more of a religious element. Christian, cross-denominational. A private organization, unaffiliated."

"Why is it even on the bottles of local beer?"

"It's just an old symbol in this area. Some of the earliest settlers in this valley brought the Order with them from the old country, and I think it was a help in bridging ethnic differences. The five towns became one, thanks in no small measure to the common associations in that group. And it has continued through the years to this day."

"Interesting." The Raccoon lodge, I was thinking.

Gow and I swapped tales of mutilations. He especially liked my account of Hopeville, West Virginia. After dinner we sat in front of the fire for a while and sipped Benedictine in silence. I wondered why he invited me, I wondered why I accepted. I wondered why he never married and had a family. Maybe he did and something happened. He nodded off. I thought of Kelly. Later, Gow said good-bye to me as if he knew that I'd be leaving Winship soon.

Item: In a room at city hall I studied a group of maps of Winship. They showed all the property lines. Something called the St. Michael Development Corporation owned several large parcels, including a great deal of open and wooded ground that surrounded the town residential areas. St. Michael land bordered the Winthrop farm, as well as property owned by several of the other families who were involved in the insurance claims.

"Who, or what, is the St. Michael Development Corporation?" I asked the clerk at a nearby desk.

"A group of developers, I guess."

In the records, SMDC showed a local post office box for an address. There was no listing in the telephone directory. Then I thought to check Penny Lane on the map. Numerous properties were shown, all of them owned by different people or companies, but none of the names suggested anything to me.

Item: Det. Ray Brandt is back at work after a bout with the flu. Brandt handled some of the accidental death cases. The man was short, had a prickly fifties crewcut, and wore a perpetual half-smile that made him look like some new kind of rodent. Ray wanted to help. Sure he did. He gave me all the time I wanted. But nothing Ray told me was of any use.

Item: It was probably too soon, but I didn't have much time, so I worked up my nerve and drove to Bellman's house, hoping to persuade his widow to talk with me. The small car was in the drive, but the big sedan was not. I heard the doorbell loudly ringing inside, but there was no sound of movement. No one answered. The house even *felt* empty to me. As I turned to leave, an elderly man approached from across the road. He stopped a safe distance away from me.

"Can I help?"

"I'm looking for Mrs. Bellman."

"They're gone."

"Where?"

"Staying with relatives."

"Can you tell me where?"

"Nope. Out of town."

"Are they coming back?"

"Who're you and what's your business?"

"Thanks."

I leave. The old guy made a point of peering at

the plate on my car, as if he intended to call the police. Yeah, pops, you put out a BOLO on me.

Item: Maybe it was the next day, Tuesday. I called Kelly, and she answered. She thought I had dropped her. I apologized more than once—pressure of work, etc. Told her I wanted to see her and would, soon. She said okay, her pouty voice. This job reeked of failure, so of course I wanted her, a woman.

Night. I drove by Penny Lane. Plenty of cars were parked in the area, so it had to be busy again. But I didn't stop. Kelly would be dancing, and I didn't want to see her working, the crowd enjoying her, folding money in their hands to slip under whatever little thing she might have on.

I wasn't going anywhere in particular, just driving for the sake of it, and to let myself think. I stopped by the river and got out of the car. A quiet area, a small park with benches facing the water. There were many such spots scattered around Winship. This scenic valley. This pretty place. I lit a cigarette and walked.

I was north of the green, beyond the old cemetery, but still close to the center of town. Here along the river the shops and offices were closed now and the nearest houses were a couple of blocks away. The river was wide and calm, and the only sound it made was a soft splashing against the stone embankment.

The sky was full of dramatic flashing colors, more vivid than I've seen on any previous night, but by then I was sick of the show. The red, purple, and blue lights had a metallic, poisonous character.

I thought again of Dr. Gow. No wife, no family. Perhaps I was curious about that absence in his life because it was the same way with me. Would I end up like him, in some sepulchral house? But at least he had his community involvement, his practice, many people who revered and depended on him. That is a kind of family. More than I had. And Kelly thought I was normal. The fuck I am.

I spun around at the sound of a tiny voice. It was a little girl, surely not more than eight or nine years old, standing only a few yards away from me. I was startled to see that she had no clothes on, just a large bath towel, which she held wrapped tightly around her. Bare feet. She looked nervous and scared.

"Hey, who are you?"

She didn't answer. I took a step toward her and she backed away. I stopped, and so did she. I was thinking that she might be the victim of some abuse at home and that she may have run away to escape a bad scene. I had to find out who she was and get her some help. I smiled at her.

I took another step toward her, but she backed away again. But this time she kept going, moving toward the middle of the park.

"Hey, I'm not going to hurt you, but you can't be out here alone like this. Let's go get some help. I'll take you."

She stopped and looked back at me, but didn't

come any closer. She stood there and stared forlornly at me.

"Come on, honey. Do you want to talk? Are you hungry, do you want to go get some ice cream, or pizza, a burger?"

The little girl didn't answer me. She turned away and started running. I was annoyed because I felt I couldn't just let her go, alone outside at night. I start to follow. I'm annoyed, but I don't want to scare her and cause her to scream. I had to follow her. If she wouldn't let me help, I hoped to see her return to a house nearby, her home, and go safely inside. She didn't go very far, through some trees and shrubs, into a small grassy area. She sat down, as if she were waiting for me. Or just catching her breath, as I was.

"That's better," I said as I slowly approached her. "Now, how's about you tell me your name? Mine is Jack."

She stared at me, and even through the darkness I could see the tension in her face and the way her whole body was trembling. It infected me at once and I glanced anxiously around. We were in a clearing that was ringed by several tall elms with thick trunks. I tried to maintain a normal tone of voice.

"All I want to do is help you if I can. What's your name, honey?"

She stood up and hurried away again. I watched, but I didn't move. I expected her to go a certain distance and then stop again, waiting for me to catch up to her. I was losing my patience. She shouldn't have been out there alone, but I was tired of playing games. This time, though, she didn't stop, she kept going. I didn't move; I felt like I *couldn't* move. I saw car lights flash by in the distance, the same direction she was going, so I figured she would reach the street. I was glad. She would be someone else's problem.

A breeze ruffled the fallen leaves on the ground at my feet. I looked up and saw that the lights were still coruscating in the blackness of the sky. I didn't want to be there. I wanted to forget that town and get away.

Too far from anywhere.

I felt lost, dizzy, just like that night at the gas station when I called Steve and suddenly felt unhinged for a couple of minutes. I thought I could feel the ground vibrating, humming beneath my feet. *Help*—the word echoed in my mind. The little girl had spoken to me. Was that what she had said? *Help*.

The earth humming right through my shoes, up into my entire body. A steady drone, low and unpleasant, just strong enough to set my teeth on edge and to press the bones in my joints against each other. I wanted to move. Something entered my consciousness then . . . voices. They were somewhere around me, nearby, unseen. The choir, though that is not the right word for it, the same as I'd heard before. Chanting, pointless vacant sounds, barking and yelping like beasts. It was a crazed music that flickered and flashed like the lights in the sky above—here, there, nowhere.

Then I saw bits of whiteness flitting through the shadows beneath the ancient elms. At the edge of my vision—I couldn't follow it, just glimpse it every couple of seconds. My eyes moved toward the river, but fog was rolling up over the embankment. Then I saw light close to me, *in the ground itself,* a dull luminescence seemingly moving through the surface of the earth, not over it or on the surface, but within, just below. It didn't appear to change the grass or the leaves; it fixed them in a pale yellow-green glow. Like an insect slowly engulfed by amber, I stood there, not quite able to move. The light all around me, the ground humming, the sky rippling with color, the wild voices of those invisible children.

Then they were all over me, five or six wild boys dressed in white tunics and dark pants. I tried to say something but I couldn't hear myself in their wailing din. They hit me, pummeled me, and when I went down to the ground they thundered over me like cattle, kicking and stomping me. Crushed by kids in the park one night—it was a bad end. The ground glowed and I could feel the harsh light on my skin. It entered my pores like some kind of annihilating truth, and I was changed by it. I had a vision of some person looking down at a stain on the lawn later that morning and wondering what it was. That was me. But the light didn't burn, it didn't consume my flesh. The beating continued, pain filling me, pushing me far beyond thought and emotion, beyond all sensation, my body locking down.

My face was pressed into the soil. The soil filled my nose and it felt like it was falling into my ears—or I was falling into the earth.

Chapter Thirteen

I opened my eyes. I was lying in bed in what appeared to be a hospital room. I was by myself. The room was dark because the curtains were drawn, but a little daylight got through, creating a brownish gloom. I didn't feel restrained, but I couldn't move. I lacked the strength even to raise my hand. I felt so stupid that I had a hard time forming a thought. It never came. I noticed a telephone on the table beside my bed, as well as a button to ring the nurse. Now that was a thought. But I still couldn't move. Oh well. Maybe later.

I heard something, and I was awake again. A man younger than me stood in the open doorway. He was wearing a white jacket. He smiled and said, "Ah." Then he said, "Hello." I tried to answer him, but the words didn't come. And then he disappeared.

The room was darker the next time I surfaced. It took me a few seconds to notice that Det. Miller was sitting beside my bed. He smiled at me, the way people smile when you've just made a horse's ass of yourself.

"I'm glad to see you're still alive."

"I'm not sure I am," I said when I finally managed to get my mouth working. "What time is it?"

"Almost seven. In the evening."

"What day?"

"Wednesday."

"This the hospital?"

"You must be a detective," Miller said.

"What happened to me?"

"That's what I'd like to know."

"I don't remember." I did, some, in bits and flashes, but I didn't want to try explaining all of *that* to a policeman.

"You don't remember anything?" he asked sharply.

"I think I got beat up."

"By who?"

"I don't know. I didn't see them."

"There was more than one?"

"Yes. Seemed like five or six of them."

"Go on," he prompted. "Don't stop now."

"I was in a park. . . ."

"Ryder Park. What were you doing there."

"Just taking a walk. Having a smoke, thinking."

"And?"

"And they came out of nowhere. They hit me, kicked me, they knocked me down and stomped me."

"Then what?"

"That's the last thing I remember." I suddenly became aware of my body. The terrifying idea that I might be paralyzed came to mind. "Hey, am I okay? I can hardly move, I feel like a dead weight. What did they do to me?"

"Take it easy," Miller said. "You're okay. You'll have to see the doctor to get a complete rundown, but from what they told me you've got a bunch of cuts and bruises. Oh, and a concussion. Not as bad as it could've been, I guess," he finished, sounding a wee bit disappointed.

"How did I get here?"

"Ambulance. One of our cars checked out the park at about twelve-thirty last night. Routine downtown patrol. They spotted you lying on the ground."

"Did they see anybody else in the area?"

"No."

"They didn't notice anything unusual?"

"Matter of fact, they did."

"What was it?"

"Did you happen to have your clothes on?"

"Yes," I answered. "Of course I did. Why?"

"Because you were naked when they found you."

"Naked? I was naked?"

If somebody took my clothes off while I was unconscious . . . instinctively, my butt tightened, and it felt as usual, apparently no damage done.

Miller nodded. "Your clothes were scattered

around, not too far away. I think we found everything—let me know if anything's missing."

"What about my wallet?" I asked.

"Wallet, credit cards, keys. They were all in your pockets. How much cash were you carrying?"

"Fifty, sixty dollars."

"Fifty seven and change," Miller said. "You weren't robbed, Carlson. Maybe you just got up somebody's nose, and they decided to let you know about it."

"I wasn't followed. I watch out for that."

Miller smiled at that. "Somebody found you."

"Yeah, they sure did. So, are you guys actually investigating this?" I think I hid my smirk as I said that, but hopefully not very well.

"Give me a description. Give me a suspect."

"A gang of teenagers," I said. "And they were all kind of dressed the same, white tunics or overshirts, and dark pants or jeans."

"I'll make a note of that. Anything else?"

"Maybe more details will come back, but for now, no."

"You heading out of town soon, or what?

"I don't know."

I closed my eyes. It took a minute, but then he left. And not long after that, I really was asleep again.

A nurse propped me up and gave me a bowl of broth. It hurt. She told me that Dr. Jolley would be in to see me soon. He arrived a little while later. The official damage: concussion, a slight fracture of the left forearm, which explained why it was tightly taped, and numerous cuts, abrasions, and contusions. I had a few stitches. I would have headaches and be in pain for a while, but they could give me something for that.

"Can you tell me how bad the concussion was?"

He wiggled his fingers scientifically. "I'm guessing mild, based on the way you appear right now. If the headaches last more than a day or two, you're getting into the middle range, moderate. Either way, you should take it easy and limit your activities for the next several days, for full recovery."

"When can I leave?"

"Later today, if you feel well enough. I'll come back and we'll get you up on your feet and see how you do."

"Doctor, how did I get a private room?"

He laughed. "It's the off-season."

"I don't suppose I can get a drink."

"I'll have the bar send up a pitcher of martinis."

"Or a smoke."

"Not in a month with a vowel in it."

"Can I use the phone?"

"Please do. We need the money."

After he left, I was thinking of the real message that had been delivered to me the previous night. It was the same thing Jolley had just told me: *limit your activities.*

* * *

I thought about calling Steve. He would be worried, or more likely pissed off with me, because I hadn't phoned earlier, as we had originally planned. I was unconscious. Stampeded. A herd of yelping little guys in white. Oh yeah, and the earth was lit up in a cold fire. Nothing astounding, just the usual hazards of being in the insurance racket. Steve would have to wait. I thought that maybe I would be able to speak to him the next day and somehow tell him what was going on. Provided I could make some kind of sense of it myself in the meantime.

It began to hurt, as promised. All over. But I didn't want them to give me a painkiller—I don't know why, it was just one more irrational fear—so I grimly stuck it out until sleep gave me a break.

A warm hand on my forehead. The room was dark, but I was in a cone of light from the reading lamp over the bed. It was Jenny Randall, crisp and competent in her whites.

"How are you feeling?"

"Okay." It took me a few seconds to wake up. "Ouch. Maybe not quite okay."

"Do you want me to give you something for the pain?"

"No, I'll survive. It's good to see you."

"You're lucky to see anybody."

"I can't argue that one."

"I told you about them."

"You don't know the half of it."

"What were you doing in Ryder Park?"

"I wish I knew."

"You mean you didn't see them?" she asked.

"I did, sort of."

I gave Jenny the same bare-bones version of events that I'd given Det. Miller. But more of it came out—the little girl, the wild singing and the ground tremors, the wave of kids who hit and trampled me, the light moving in the earth, my shoes, and how the police found me. It did me good to utter these things out loud for the first time, and as I spoke I realized that Jenny was probably the only person who would listen sympathetically. She didn't act as if I were crazy, although she did look a whole lot more worried by the time I finished.

"It's like that girl led you right to where they wanted you."

"Right."

"I have heard about that light in the ground, but I've never seen it myself and I never gave it any thought."

"What did you hear about it?"

"That it's some kind of unusual geological phenomenon having to do with the earth's magnetic field and local conditions. It appears in places, then vanishes, like the northern lights. People come to Winship to see it and study it, but most of the time they go away disappointed. And I guess it happens in a few other parts of the world too."

"News to me, but at least it's a kind of explanation."

"You were actually lying in it, or on it?"

"Yes."

"But it didn't hurt you."

"I was getting beat up at the time, so I'm not sure, but I don't remember specifically noticing pain caused by the light."

"What did it feel like?" she asked.

"I don't know. It's hard to explain. I thought I was about to be . . . obliterated. But whether that was what the light did to me or just the tremendous fear I felt, I don't know. It was only a few seconds, and then I passed out."

"Why do you think they took your clothes off, but didn't rob you?"

"To make me look like a fool. Which they did. To let me know that they could do anything they wanted to with me. And that's why they didn't rob me, so I'd get exactly the right message."

"What are you going to do when you get out of here?"

"I have no idea," I admitted. "In fact, I might be off this case already. My boss was fading on me a couple of days ago, and this won't thrill him."

"You should leave," Jenny said. "I'm going to. I'm sending my résumé out. Nurses can always find work."

"Speaking of which, why are you in uniform now?"

"It's my usual shift," she said. "You slept all

day and into the evening. They didn't bother trying to wake you and get you up on your feet. You're here for the night, so don't even ask about leaving."

"Wow, what does that mean?"

"It's good. Your body needed the rest. It helps you heal."

"I do feel better than I did last time I was awake."

"Good. I'll look in on you later."

"In that case, I'll stay awake."

Now she smiled. "Oh, don't bother."

The pain woke me sometime later. My head drummed and I felt every bruise on my body, but at least it gave me the sense that I was coming back to life, that I was not going to remain in a numb and immobile state forever.

I became aware of the sounds outside my room. An occasional clank, the whirr of the elevator, footsteps, wordless voices, all quite unremarkable—and yet because you hear them in a hospital in the middle of the night, they're somehow different from sounds you hear anywhere else.

But for the first time in days, and for no reason, I did feel relatively safe where I was. I knew Jenny was somewhere nearby and she was on my side. Besides, I was still alive—and if they wanted me to be dead, I would be. They had me. They could have easily killed me on the spot or taken me off somewhere into the forest and made me disappear permanently. Instead, they let me live.

What did I see? What really happened to me in that park? The more I thought about it, the less I seemed to understand. It was so bizarre and unreal, I was at a loss. A warning, yes. An unusual geological phenomenon? Maybe. In my line of work I've had some strange and astonishing explanations thrown my way, and most of them made me smile at the ways of the human mind. But now I was the one with the funny story, and I wasn't smiling at it.

Jenny brought me a glass of orange juice, which tasted good, and some cold toast and blah cereal, which didn't.

"How does your head feel?" she asked.

"Down to a mild patter, at least for now."

"That's very good. When they do clear you for release, today or tomorrow, give me a call and I'll come and drive you to your hotel." She jotted down her number on a small piece of notepaper and put it on the side table.

"Thanks," I said. "I'll probably walk it."

She laughed at that. "You won't be doing much walking anywhere for the next few days."

I set the food tray aside. "I want to try to stand up."

"Wait until the doctor comes."

"Stand right here, Jenny, please," I said in my best begging voice. "I just want to see how it feels, woozy or whatever. I won't try to walk."

She gave me a look. "If you fall, I'll kill you."

"Fair enough." I sat up slowly, slid my legs around, and planted my hands on the edge of the bed. She held my arm firmly in both her hands as I pushed off; my feet hit the floor and I got fully upright. Not bad, no dizziness, no feeling of weakness in my legs. "Not bad at all."

"Good, now let's get you back in bed."

"Just a second."

I took one step sideways, so I could still feel the bed touching the back of my legs. No problem. Another step, again okay.

"Hey, you said you wouldn't try to walk."

"Okay, okay." But then I took one step forward, turned around, took the step back to the bed and looked around at her. "Voila."

"Do you feel okay?" she asked.

I smiled. "I'm going to blow this clambake today."

Chapter Fourteen

"I guess they meant it," I said as I looked up at the towing zone sign. My car was no longer where I had parked it two nights before.

"I'll take you to the town garage," Jenny said. "It'll cost you."

"I'm sure."

"As long as we're here, show me where it happened."

"Sure."

"It's not too far for you to walk?"

"Not at all, I feel good."

She found a free spot to park her car. We went into Ryder Park, Jenny striding, me limping along in her wake. I was still hurting a little, but I felt too good being outside to let it bother me. The park looked pleasant and harmless. The sun was high and bright, and autumn leaves swirled down lazily in the sweet air.

"I think I was about here," I said. "I heard the girl speak one word, *'Help,'* and I turned around. Yeah, she was right about where you are now."

"And you followed her . . . where?"

"Just ahead." I pointed the way. When we got to the center of the park, surrounded by the tallest elms, I stopped. A clearing, not even big enough to call a meadow. "This is it, right here."

"Okay," Jenny said.

We both looked at the ground and kicked leaves aside. I had hoped to find the turf all dug up like a football field after the big game, but in fact it showed only minor signs of disturbance, about what you would expect to see from normal wear and tear in a public park.

"It's pretty firm," I muttered.

"Yes. Are you sure they were kids?"

"Kids, yes. Thirteen, fourteen, fifteen years old," I told her. "Not that they did much talking, but I could hear it in their voices, their sound. A kid that age makes a different kind of grunt and shout than an adult male does."

"It's creepy to think of them using kids to do that."

"Yes, it is." We were wasting our time in the park and I didn't feel like hanging around there any longer. "Let's go bail my car out," I said.

On the way, I told Jenny about my dinner with Dr. Gow and his comments on the Order of St. Michael, and also what I'd found out at city hall about the St. Michael Development Corporation and their extensive property holdings in and around Winship.

"You think they're the ones behind it?"

"I don't even know who *they* are," I said. "Some individuals in the Order and the SMDC? Yes—maybe, possibly, perhaps."

"Remember when I told you about the churches?"

"Yes, and you were right," I said. "I've never seen a sign or a plaque of affiliation on a Catholic church. They just don't do that, not even with their own organizations, like the Knights of Columbus."

"But St. Mark's, the Catholic church here, it has one."

"I saw. Another one of those weird little somethings that seem to be so common in this town."

It cost fifty dollars to spring my car. I wondered if Steve would dispute that when I included it on my expense statement. Jenny followed in her car as I drove back to the inn—in case I passed out and crashed on the way, I guess—and I honked to her as I pulled into the hotel driveway and she drove away.

Reluctantly, I made my long overdue phone call to him. He was deliriously happy to hear from me. He'd been worried, not pissed off. He was tired of waiting for me to ring him, so he called the Birch Inn early that afternoon, only to be told that my room did not appear to have been slept in the last two nights. They graciously said they would hold it in my name for another night—it was the off-season. Next, Steve called the Winship police and was referred to the hospital, but by the time he got on the phone with them, I had been released. Since then he'd been sitting around the office in some anxiety, not sure what to do or think.

I kept it simple. I told him I'd been knocked around pretty good, but was okay. That made him angry, and for a minute I thought he was ready to fight back. No more flirting with defeatism. But when I told him about some of the things I had learned—the Order, the SMDC, the property holdings—I could all but hear his eyes glazing over.

"Jack, Jack, Jack, please," he said, quietly but firmly cutting me off. "Listen to me. What you're talking about is a completely different level of investigation. Private associations, corporate entities."

"I know," I said wearily.

"You can't do that. Even if I sent a couple of guys up to help you out for a few days, you wouldn't be able to do it. If there is an organized criminal enterprise going on there, it needs a whole DA task force."

"You're right."

"Besides," Steve continued, "it's not our case. You're there on *our* case, remember?

"Yeah, but it's probably related to our case."

"Maybe it is, but it's *not our case*." I hated it when he spoke in that calm, insistent voice. "Do you have anything new for me on any of the claims?"

"Just how this other stuff factors in." A pause, so I threw in a little plea for the extenuating circumstance. "I just got out of the hospital, Steve."

"I know. I'm sorry and angry about what happened to you. I have to factor that in too, you know. You're at risk there."

"I'll take better care of myself."

He wasn't buying any of that. "It's going on two weeks, Jack. Two people are dead, your two best potential sources of information. And you were attacked badly enough to be hospitalized. So here's what we're going to do. It's Thursday afternoon, almost five o'clock. Unless you can call me by this time tomorrow with something *definite* that we can work with, some real lead, the job ends. We'll cover you through tomorrow night and you can drive home Saturday."

"Okay, Steve."

I was exhausted. He was right all the way. I knew I wasn't getting anywhere in the usual sense, but I didn't want to let it go yet. Maybe I would feel differently by the end of the day Friday.

The beating I'd suffered caught up with me again. It was all I could do to ease myself out of my clothes and slip into bed. A bad time to be going to sleep, but I needed it. If I awoke in a few of hours, I would order something to eat and then go back to sleep. If I made it straight through to morning, I'd take a nice, long, hot shower, eat a monster breakfast and then get to work again. Please let me sleep all night, I thought, and hold the dreams.

I heard a knock. Several knocks. The cops, I thought dimly as I struggled out of bed. They are masters at ruining sleep. I fumbled blindly, hit the light switch, and got the door open. It took me a couple of moments to realize that the person standing there was my friend. The dancer. Kelly.

"Oops," she said, looking me up and down, and then trying to see past me into the room. "Are you alone, is this a bad time?"

"Yes, no," I said, my voice thick with sleep. Then I realized I was standing there in my boxer shorts, nothing else. "Kelly, come on in."

"Thank you!" She must have taken a closer look at me as I shut the door, because she looked shocked when I turned around. "What happened to your arm? Good Lord, you're all black and blue. Jack, what happened to you?" "

"Yeah, well, it's been one of those weeks." I struggled into a pair of jeans and pulled on a T-shirt. "Things kind of went downhill after I left you."

"I told you to stay, daddy."

I was almost fully awake, and I looked at my watch: eight-thirty, the P.M. version. That depressed the hell out of me. I sat down on the edge of my bed; Kelly took one of the armchairs. She wore black slacks, discreet boots, a silver-gray blouse, and a charcoal men's blazer, with a silver and onyx choker. You wouldn't peg her for a dancer in a skin bar. A thought: "You're not working tonight?"

"I swapped shifts for today with one of the girls who does the lunchtime and afternoon crowd. She was glad to—the tips are much better at night."

"Oh, that's nice. Get a night off."

"I'm glad I found you still here," she said. "I thought maybe you'd finished your business in town and left."

"Hey." Sudden thought. "Did I give you my room number?"

"Yes, you did. Look, if I shouldn't have come—"

"No, no, that's okay," I told her. "I just didn't remember. I'm sure I did, but I had a concussion the other night, and some things are still a little foggy."

"Jack, what happened?" she asked with evident concern. "Did you get in a fight in a bar or something?"

I gave a short laugh and smiled at her. "No, nothing like that. Don't worry about it. I'm okay now."

She was giving me a big dose of the cocked-head look. "Doesn't seem like something that would happen in the boring old insurance industry. What'd you do, trip over the paperwork and land on those spiky, lumpy old numbers?"

I laughed. "It's good to see you again."

"Thank you!"

"I'm sorry I didn't call you again."

"I thought you left town, or just dropped me. Which I would've understood, no problem, that's the way it is sometimes."

I shook my head. "Things happened, I had work things to do, I was in the hospital overnight—"

"The hospital?" Kelly was out of the chair and sitting beside me in a flash, her hands holding one of mine, rubbing it soothingly. "A concussion? Jack, what is going on with you? You can't just say stuff like that and not tell me more. I came here tonight because I care. I wanted to see you, at least one last time, or else find out either that you'd gone or you didn't want to see me."

Another one of those sudden thoughts: *Why not?*

"Kelly, I really am connected to the insurance business. I'm an investigator, and we're about to break open a big case. Multiple fraud and murder."

"Oh my God."

"Some of their goons beat the shit out of me the other night, trying to warn me to back off, but it's too late for that."

"Oh my God. Jack, you make me wet when you talk like this, but I'm scared for you. If there's been murder, they'll do it again."

"Some big names in Winship are going down."

"Who? The mayor? The chief of police?"

I gave a little finger wag. "Enough of my work

stuff. It's good to see you, Kelly. I'm glad you came by. I was thinking about you, I can say that."

"Then how come I've been here all this time and you still haven't given me a kiss. Do you mind if I ask you *that*?"

"Trust me, you don't want to kiss me now. I just woke up."

"You want to sweeten up, daddy?"

"I won't be long."

"You better not be, or I'll come get you."

I closed the bathroom door and turned on the water, letting it run good and cold. I still believed she was who she said she was and nothing more, but I didn't regret anything I'd said to her. God damn, that was me in the mirror, and I looked like shit. I scrubbed my face until the skin tingled, brushed my teeth and gargled. Kelly and I had the bathroom trip down pat.

"That's better," I said as I came out of the bathroom. She was standing in the middle of the room, her back to me. Kelly was still wearing the charcoal blazer. She moved her head slowly, looking back at me. Smiling. She turned around and faced me. All she was still wearing was the blazer and the choker.

"Jack."

"Hmm?"

"Can I tell you something?"

"Sure."

"It's kinda bad."

"That's okay," I said. "What is it?"

"It's going to sound really crazy."

"I've heard crazy a lot up here."

"The other day, Tuesday," she said. Kelly took a cigarette from my pack on the table and lit it. "Tuesday afternoon a bunch of us were all hanging around the motel, waking up, relaxing, watching the soaps like any other day. And we decided to go for a drive and see a little of the countryside, stop somewhere different for a meal. It was kind of crappy out—"

"A heavy mist," I said.

"Right, but you can go crazy sitting around in a motel room all day, so we decided to go, and Julio—he's our driver—said, fine. So we went, and we drove around for an hour or so. Nice countryside, nothing special."

"Mm-hmm."

"Then we saw this dirt road, winding down through a pretty meadow, and it looked like the entrance to a park, but there was no sign. So we said let's see where it goes, and Julio drove down the road, through the meadow, around a big clump of trees, along the bottom of a hill. We went maybe half a mile and we came to an open area where the road just ended."

"No buildings, cabins?"

"Nothing. But there was a path leading ahead into the trees, so we decided to see where it went. Maybe there was a lake on the other side. What we came to was a clearing, surrounded by trees. It looked like forest on the far side. Just this empty clearing about the size of a . . . a baseball field."

"Was it a baseball field?"

"Ha ha. So we poked around for a couple of minutes and thought it was a whole bunch of nothing, and we headed back to the van. And we just got to the path, and Julio says, 'Where's Amber?' She was gone. She was in the van with us, she walked down the path with us, and then she disappeared."

"In thin air, just like that?"

Kelly nodded. "Now, I knew Amber. She and I have shared rooms in other places. She was no headcase. If she decided to get out of the business, she wouldn't just run off in the middle of the woods and leave her things behind."

"How far away was she, last time you saw her?"

"I don't know, I wasn't paying attention to stuff like that."

"What did you all do about it?"

"We ran around all over that place calling out her name, looking in the brush and trees. We spent just about an hour doing that, thinking maybe she was mad about something and was off sulking by herself."

"No sign of her?"

"Nothing," Kelly said.

"I don't know. I don't know what to make of that."

"Jack, I'm scared. Two girls, two weeks."

I rolled over on top of her beneath the sheet

GET UP TO 4 FREE BOOKS!

You can have the best fiction delivered to your door for less than what you'd pay in a bookstore or online—only $4.25 a book! Sign up for our book clubs today, and we'll send you **FREE* BOOKS** just for trying it out...**with no obligation to buy, ever!**

LEISURE HORROR BOOK CLUB

With more award-winning horror authors than any other publisher, it's easy to see why CNN.com says "Leisure Books has been leading the way in paperback horror novels." Your shipments will include authors such as RICHARD LAYMON, DOUGLAS CLEGG, JACK KETCHUM, MARY ANN MITCHELL, and many more.

LEISURE THRILLER BOOK CLUB

If you love fast-paced page-turners, you won't want to miss any of the books in Leisure's thriller line. Filled with gripping tension and edge-of-your-seat excitement, these titles feature everything from psychological suspense to legal thrillers to police procedurals and more!

As a book club member you also receive the following special benefits:

- **30% OFF all orders through our website & telecenter!**
- **Exclusive access to special discounts!**
- **Convenient home delivery and 10 days to return any books you don't want to keep.**

There is no minimum number of books to buy, and you may cancel membership at any time. See back to sign up!

*Please include $2.00 for shipping and handling.

YES! ☐

Sign me up for the Leisure Horror Book Club and send my TWO FREE BOOKS! If I choose to stay in the club, I will pay only $8.50* each month, a savings of $5.48!

YES! ☐

Sign me up for the Leisure Thriller Book Club and send my TWO FREE BOOKS! If I choose to stay in the club, I will pay only $8.50* each month, a savings of $5.48!

NAME: _____

ADDRESS: _____

_____

TELEPHONE: _____

E-MAIL: _____

☐ **I WANT TO PAY BY CREDIT CARD.**

☐ VISA   ☐ MasterCard.   ☐ DISCOVER

ACCOUNT #: _____

EXPIRATION DATE: _____

SIGNATURE: _____

Send this card along with $2.00 shipping & handling for each club you wish to join, to:

Horror/Thriller Book Clubs
1 Mechanic Street
Norwalk, CT 06850-3431

Or fax (must include credit card information!) to: 610.995.9274.
You can also sign up online at www.dorchesterpub.com.

*Plus $2.00 for shipping. Offer open to residents of the U.S. and Canada only.
Canadian residents please call 1.800.481.9191 for pricing information.
If under 18, a parent or guardian must sign. Terms, prices and conditions subject to change. Subscription subject
to acceptance. Dorchester Publishing reserves the right to reject any order or cancel any subscription.

and propped myself up on my elbows. A couple of little peck kisses. I had the feeling I was going to say something pretty stupid, but what the hell.

"Why don't you get out now? Don't tell anyone. When I pull out of here, you come with me. No strings, no promises, but I'll do everything I can to get you closer to that boutique. Some other work, some business courses. What you're doing now, you can't get out of it soon enough."

"Wow." Then she gave me a big hug and a bunch of wet kisses "Thank you, daddy, thank you so much. You just gave me a whole lot to think about."

Chapter Fifteen

I wanted to see that place for myself, and Kelly was pretty sure that she would recognize the turnoff road if she saw it, so we set off after breakfast the next morning and drove around the countryside.

"Is it on this side of the river?"

"Uh, yes. Kind of that way," she said, pointing in a general northwest direction."

"Good. Anytime you see something you think you recognize, you let me know. Buildings, anything."

"Okay."

"Same with any street or road you think you might have been on the other day. We'll check them out."

"Are you a government agent?" she asked.

"No."

"Are you sure?"

I smiled. "The case I told you about? I'm

working it from the insurance side. I work for the insurance companies."

"What exactly do you do?"

"Investigate suspicious claims."

"What kind of claims?"

"Accidental death, for instance."

"Killing people for insurance money?"

"Right."

"Is that what happened to Amber?"

"I doubt it. Even if somebody took out a policy on her they couldn't collect without a proper death certificate, and you need a dead body and a good explanation to get that."

"Then why did she disappear like that?"

"I don't know."

"*How* could that just . . . happen?"

"I don't know, Kelly. I wish I did."

"Jack, if Amber has nothing to do with the case you're working on, why do you want to see the place where she disappeared?"

"Something is rotten in the state of Denmark, my dear. A lot of peculiar things happen here, and they seem to be connected in some way. Amber *might* be part of it, somehow. Anyway, I just want to see the place. You never know, I might notice something that you and the others didn't."

I also wanted to check the records at city hall to find out who owned the property where Amber supposedly disappeared, and to do that I would need to have the exact location.

"Hey." Kelly leaned forward and pointed.

"That fork coming up, bear right. I remember seeing that sign for blueberries."

"Good."

"They extended our stay another week," she said a minute later in a subdued voice. "So I'll be here two more weeks, not just one."

"You don't want to stay?"

"No, I want to get out of here. There's a bad vibe hanging over everybody now. Two girls gone in two weeks. It's getting scary, especially the way it happened with Amber."

"*Can* you leave?"

"I gave my word, and that's as good as a written contract in my business," she said. "Yeah, I guess I could leave, but I'd have to go into a new line of work because I'd be on their shit list."

"Would they come after you?"

"Why bother?"

"To punish you?" I asked.

"No, girls come and go all the time. That's the way it is. They've got a big organization, coast to coast, ties with the better venues. They don't worry about every single bar dancer. But I'd probably lose my last week's pay."

"I've heard some horror stories."

"So have I, but that's usually with some independent guy who runs his own little joint. I'd never put myself in a situation like that."

"As opposed to a situation like this."

"Yeah." A sardonic laugh. "Oh, take that left."

"Good," I said, making the turn. "Maybe it's not such a bad idea."

"What?"

"Quitting."

"Ja-ack," she whined. "I'm not ready to quit."

"How much money do you need to start that store?"

"I'm guessing a hundred thousand."

"And how much have you got banked now?"

"Almost ten."

It all seemed a little unreal to me, but I tried to encourage her. "If you put up ten, fifteen percent, and you have a good, sound business plan, you can probably get a loan for the rest."

"Really? Wow. Hey, hey."

"What?"

"I think we're getting close," Kelly said, and then pointed ahead. "That way, that way."

We turned off onto a road that began a long, snaky downhill descent. "Munnford Road," I said as we passed the sign.

"This is the right one," Kelly said. "I'm sure of it, because we thought we were getting lost and we were hoping this would lead back toward town."

"Why didn't you just turn around?"

Kelly laughed. "Julio does left, right, and forward."

"How close are we now?"

"When the road levels off at the bottom of this hill, then it's like, not even half a mile more."

"See if Munnford Road is on the city map."

Kelly unfolded it and ran her fingers over the map as if she were reading it in Braille. "Here it is," she said a minute later. "Way the hell up in the the upper left-hand corner."

"Any side roads or streets shown running off it?"

"No, not until it hits Stone Bridge Crossing," she replied. "That's the way we went back to town. I saw the stone bridge."

Kelly was still peering at the map a few minutes later, when I spotted a gravel road trailing off up ahead on the right.

"Is this it?"

She looked up. "That's it," she said, her voice quiet.

Her description of the place had been pretty accurate. The road curled around a large grove of trees and then ran a good distance along the base of the hill. It came to end in an open area surrounded on three sides by trees.

"Looks pleasant enough," I said. "On a sunny day like this."

"It feels creepy. I don't want to be here."

"Come on." I opened the door on my side. "Show me."

Kelly made a face, but she got out of the car and led me toward the band of trees on our left. We found the narrow path, which wound through the woods for about fifty yards, and then we came out into the clearing. It was smaller than I had expected, but it was a beautiful meadow, almost perfectly round, encircled by tall pines and thick brush.

I turned to Kelly, who was hanging back a few paces, apparently reluctant to move another step. She clutched her handbag tightly to her chest.

"You okay, baby?"

"Let's go."

"We'll go. In a minute," I said gently. "Show me where you were standing, as close as you can remember. Don't worry, you'll be okay. Nothing happened to you here. And I'll be right beside you."

Kelly took a deep breath and let it out. "Okay. I was a little farther ahead here, and more off to the right." She walked past me and I followed along, a step behind. We went a short distance, maybe twenty paces, and she stopped, looked around, as if to get her visual bearings with the tree lines, and nodded. "Yeah, I was right about here, I didn't go any farther."

"Where were the others?"

"We all kind of fanned out a little," Kelly replied. "Just taking a look around, you know? But it's just an open field, a meadow. There's nothing else to see here, as you can see yourself. So, after a few minutes, we all started circling back, slowly, just walking, talking to each other, saying what a waste of time this was and what we wanted to eat for supper, that kind of stuff."

"What's your best idea of where Amber was?"

"I have this image in my head of seeing her up ahead," Kelly answered, taking one hand off her bag long enough to point toward the middle of the field. "Out there. She walked farther out into the field than the rest of us did, and I had a glimpse of her trailing behind us as we turned back to go. When we got out on the other side of the trees, where the van was parked, we noticed she wasn't with us."

"Okay."

"Where are you going?"

"Out there, around where you think she was. You can stay there if you want," I told her. "I want to look around on the ground—maybe Amber dropped something. I'll be right back."

"I don't want to be alone here."

"Come with me, then."

I walked slowly toward the middle of the field, scouring the ground for anything out of the ordinary. All I saw was meadow grass and dark soil below it. I glanced back at Kelly every few steps, and I was glad to see that she was following me, though still keeping a certain distance. I got to where I thought I had arrived at about the center of the meadow. I turned to look at Kelly while I was still moving, and I saw that she had a large hunting knife in her hand.

I was startled by the long blade flashing in the sunlight, and my toe dug into a large tuft of grass and I fell forward *the ground turns into barren rock and loose scree and the sky goes black and appears to be too close and I have nothing to hold onto the meadow grass gone the trees gone me still falling everything above flies away from me I'm thinking of the garnet mine that this time I won't be able to snap out of it get out sliding scraping the slope goes down down down the sun a small gray circle on the black far above the rocky gray slope rubbing my clothes shredding them my skin sloughing off all open nerve ends wet flesh burning I have no voice no breath inside of me no air outside nothing no more . . .*

Chapter Sixteen

My eyes opened and I saw Kelly standing directly above me and I saw the knife in her hand, the sun behind her half-blinding me, and I was gasping for air as if I'd been underwater too long.

"Oh my God, thank God you're alive," Kelly shouted, kneeling beside me and kissing my face. "I thought you had a heart attack and died. It didn't look like you were breathing."

"Is this where I fell?" I asked as I struggled to sit up and look around. Then I saw drag marks in the grass.

"No, I grabbed your feet and pulled you way back here."

"Why?" Though I was glad she did.

"I don't know. I was terrified, Jack. I thought . . ." A shrug.

"That the ground might swallow me up?"

"Maybe."

"Thanks, I had that thought too."

"What happened?" she asked.

"I just tripped and fell."

"Did you hit a rock?" She ran her fingers through my hair, looking for a cut or a bruise. "I don't see anything."

"No rock, just the ground."

"Jack, you've been out for five minutes or more."

"Wow. Yeah, it kind of stunned me."

Five minutes—that was worrying. Maybe I really did have a mild heart attack. I checked my pulse—maybe a little quicker than usual, but not much. I didn't feel any pain in my chest.

"Do you feel all right?" Kelly asked.

"Yeah, just a little shaken. What's the knife for?"

"I bought it yesterday," she said sheepishly. "I wanted something, some kind of protection. After Keisha and Amber disappeared. I was scared."

"Why did you pull it out here?"

"I was scared. I just felt better holding it."

"Scared of what?"

"I don't know." A helpless shrug.

"Kind of shook me up when I looked back and saw it the first time, and then again now, when I came to."

"I'm sorry."

"That's okay. Put it away, though."

"Okay, but please, let's get out of here, Jack."

"Fine by me. I've seen enough."

I cautiously stood up. My body felt okay, no new pains or injuries. Kelly and I didn't speak much on the drive back into town. I couldn't even explain to myself what had happened to me—hallucination, vision, psychotic episode?—and I didn't want to try describing it to her.

"Thanks for coming and showing me that place," I said.

"Huh, yeah."

"No, I mean it, Kelly. I did want to see it. Listen, I have a lot of work to do today and you're working tonight. I'll drop you back at your motel now, and we'll try to get together tomorrow during the day. Okay?"

"*Try* to get together tomorrow?"

"We *will* get together," I amended.

She gave me a big smile, leaned closer to me and ran her hand up my leg. "That's more like it. Oooh, you like it when I do this to you while you're driving? I can tell you do. I think you'd better hurry up and find a place to pull off the road, daddy, while we're still out here in the sticks."

Three times now it had happened to me. Winthrop's garnet mine, Ryder Park, and now in the clearing. Was it all in my head? Maybe I was just beat up by some teenage punks in the park, and all that stuff with the light in the ground was the work of my own disordered brain. The other two times, just me tripping by myself. That was maybe even scarier than any other explanation, that something was wrong with me, some part of my mind slowly coming apart.

But I felt good too, as if the incident had somehow given me an extra boost of energy. I went to city hall and checked the map page that included Munnford Road. The gravel road we had taken was not shown, but right about where I thought it might be was a small printed legend: *Wendell's Grove.* Had to be the right spot, because that whole area was part of a very large surrounding parcel of land, and it was owned by SMDC. What a surprise.

A few minutes later I was in a phone booth at the post office.

"Tom Shortt."

"Hey, Tom. It's Jack Carlson."

"Jack, hi. How's it going?"

"Fine, thanks. I'm glad you're in."

"I'm always in. You know I hate legwork."

"I need some help, kinda quick."

Tom Shortt was an old acquaintance. He operated his own private detective agency and he earned his bread and butter handling divorce cases, personal checks, and the occasional runaway spouse for wealthy folks. Tom also had access to a mainframe and databases that could provide all kinds of useful information on people, corporations, and property. Same kind of setup Steve had—but I didn't want to try this on Steve; that would probably be all he needed to hear to make him move up the five o'clock deadline to immediately.

"Is it a real job or a favor?"

"I'll pay, no problem," I told him. "I think it'll be pretty simple, but the thing is, I need the information like *today*."

"What do you need?"

"Anything you can find on the St. Michael Development Corporation. It's based in Winship, Lauck County."

"That where you are now?"

"Yes."

"Owners, directors, officers, financial statements?"

"All of that. Assets, as much as you can get."

"Is that all, just this one entity?"

"That's all."

"Okay. Sounds doable. Got a number I can reach you at?

"I'll be in and out of the hotel," I said. "Better if I call you when I get a chance. How long do you think you'll need?"

"I'll call my computer guy right now," Tom said. "He'll need a couple of hours, at least. Try anytime after two this afternoon."

"Okay, great."

"Jack, if he's tied up today, you're out of luck until Monday."

"Understood. Many thanks, Tom."

The clothes I was in were a little dirty and rumpled from when Kelly had dragged me across the ground, so I went back to the inn and changed. While there, I called Dr. Gow. It was time to throw some more questions at him. He probably knew Winship and its secrets as well as anybody. He was with a patient when I called, but I left a message and he rang me back a few minutes later.

"Are you all right, Mr. Carlson?" was the first thing he said.

"Yes, thanks."

"I heard you had some kind of trouble."

"Some kind is right."

"I'm sorry I didn't stop by to see you while you were at the hospital, but by the time I heard about it, you had been released."

"That's okay. It was no big deal."

"Good."

"I have some questions for you and a few more points to discuss. Is there any chance we could get together today or tomorrow."

"This afternoon is impossible, but you're welcome to come around to my house this evening."

"That would be fine."

"Eight o'clock? Earlier than that, I'll be with someone else."

"Thank you, Doctor, I'll see you at eight."

I hung up, and almost immediately the phone rang. It was Jenny Randall, sounding tired and cranky. She said she had some information she thought would be of interest to me. She was going to catch some sleep this afternoon, but she could meet me later, sometime early evening, before she went to work. I suggested we get together over dinner and she could choose the place. I owed her one. Six o'clock, the Golden Bowl, Chinese, downtown.

Then, for some reason, I thought I should call Kelly. It was in the back of my mind, bothering me, the thought of her walking around with that knife in her bag. Looked like a six-inch blade. When I first saw it, I did have the flash that I was wrong about her, that she was somehow tied in with the people I was investigating, and that she was there to kill me. But she easily could have, and didn't.

She had sounded so worried and fearful, and for all I knew she had good reason to be. But at the same time, the talk about opening a boutique didn't sound quite real to me, and she resisted the idea of getting out of the exotic dancer business at this time. Something she said came back to me—she was upset about having to stay on in Winship for an extra week. That was it; she didn't like it here, and everything would be fine as soon as they got to the next city on the loop.

I tried her number at the motel, but the line was engaged or off the hook. I tried several more times over the next hour, but the result was the same. If I let myself, I could feel kind of fucked-up about Kelly. There were things I liked about her, not just her looks and the great, uninhibited sex. She was down to earth, had a sense of humor and a great sense of fun—she was fun to be with.

I had even considered suggesting that she quit her job and leave Winship with me when I left. A place to stay at least for the time being, no strings or promises either way. Get another job, a "normal" job, take some courses and learn about accounting, how to plan, create, and run a successful business. It would be a way out of that whole seedy dancer's life, a way ahead for her.

Then I thought, You really *are* losing your mind.

"I'm afraid it isn't much," Tom Shortt told me when I phoned him a little after three. "St. Michael Development Corporation was closed two years ago."

"Closed?" I was at a loss for a second.

"June Fifth, nineteen seventy-six, to be exact."

"What does that mean? At the city hall the maps show SMDC as owning many large parcels of land here."

"The clerks just haven't corrected the entries on the maps yet, is what that part of it means," Tom said. "As for why it was closed, I would guess they probably just wanted to get out of the business of being a business, a corporation. Because that involves legal requirements, tax and benefit obligations, all kinds of things that can be burdensome. Besides, they did not do all that much in the way of active business over the last few years, prior to the change."

"Exactly what was their business, Tom?"

"Development, the buying and selling of commercial and private real estate. And they did that, they bought, presumably developed, and sold. But then, it looks like they were fairly inactive for a few years, and two years ago they decided to shut down the business. They created the St. Michael Conservancy, transferred their properties and other assets to it, and dissolved the corporation. The Conservancy holdings are mostly land and buildings, and it is a considerable amount in that area. The cash balance listed in the last statement was minimal, about what you'd expect for normal maintenance and improvements. Some investments, not large, nothing unusual."

"They could do that, just transfer everything?"

"Sure, as long as all the principals agree and they fulfill the legal requirements to dissolve a corporation."

"Please," I said. "Remind me what a conservancy is."

"A private trust, essentially. The purpose of any conservancy is to protect and enhance an estate, property, or body of wealth. To manage and maintain it and grow the assets."

"On whose behalf?"

"On behalf of the estate or property, the body of wealth itself."

"You're losing me here, Tom," I said. "I'm missing something."

"Remind you, huh? A conservancy is a not-for-profit entity. Ever drive down a country road and pass by a nature conservancy?"

This morning, you could say. "Okay, yeah."

"It's the same basic structure."

"Do you have any names, people involved?"

"No, that's about all that my friend was able to take down this afternoon. He can get back to it next week if you want more, and if it's there."

"Yeah, please. That's a help, Tom. Many thanks."

"No problem. Oh, and here. The listed address for the Conservancy is the law firm of Hall-Robertson, POB 15, Winship. You should be able to find their street address if you want to talk to them."

I scribbled it down. "Back to you early in the week, Tom."

Not-for-profit? Yeah, right.

I got Steve on the phone a few minutes before five. I had none of the kind of news he wanted to hear, so I didn't even try to run the St. Michael financial stuff by him. We agreed that the insurance claims, my investigation, didn't warrant staying in Winship any longer. No viable, immediate avenue of approach. Let the various companies do whatever they decided to do. Steve was cool about it, bucked me up. He and I had been through some losses like this before.

Tomorrow morning, I was on my own dime.

"You look beat," I told Jenny as we sat down at a table near the front window of the Golden Bowl.

"I am," she replied. "I got a couple of hours

sleep after I called you, but that's been it since yesterday."

"You're not going to work tonight."

"Yes, I am. I have to."

"Ouch. What're the hours on your shift?"

"Nine to six."

"The weekend's here," I said. "Get some extra sleep, take it easy."

"I hope to, but I'm on call."

"What kept you awake today?"

"I was at the library all morning. Looking up stuff for you."

"Jenny, you didn't have to do that."

"I wouldn't have, if you'd been in there doing your own research. Like I told you. Last week."

"I"m not sure what I should be looking up in the library, but it must be good, the way you're rubbing it in," I said. "What did you find?"

"It's a good little library. The Winship Historical Society has its own room there. Books, diaries, records—all local history."

"Okay."

"The Order of St. Michael seems to have started up in northern England or lowland Scotland three to four hundred years ago."

"Wait a sec," I cut in. "You went to the library and looked up the Order of St. Michael?"

"Somebody killed Chris, and you told me about the Order. I could sit around on my ass or I could go see if I could *learn* anything. Okay?"

"All right, go on."

"It was popular and had a lot of chapters, for

a while, in England, Scotland, Wales, and Ireland, but it was dying out there when immigrants brought it here to the United States. And it only took hold and lasted in a few small cities and towns here. Massachusetts, Connecticut, New York, Pennsylvania, Michigan, Minnesota, a couple of other places."

"Including Winship."

"Oh yeah." Jenny smiled and took another fork of her chili crab. "To boil it all down, St. Michael is Michael, the archangel."

"Right. I was brought up Catholic."

"An angel," she said. "And a saint."

"Yeah, so?"

"He is both human and of the angels, just as Lucifer was an angel but fell to the human, sinful level. Michael and Lucifer are twins, or—the same."

"This is interesting . . . a little wild," I said, "but how does it relate to the things we're dealing with here?"

"You can't reach God directly. Prayer—"

"I've noticed."

"Okay," she went on. "Michael and Lucifer are the intermediaries, the only two ways way we can reach God. *We* are the fallen angels. Christ is neither God nor the son of God. He is the brightest of the fallen angels. He is our prophet, our teacher, our guide back to union with God. But Lucifer is his twin, his brother. They are both the way to God."

"Jenny, when you say *our* . . . "

"Right, I mean *their*. This is what they believe."

"Good, just checking."

"And I'm just telling you what I found."

"Different ways to God," I said. "Same deal."

"Exactly."

"What else?" This theological crap was useless to me.

"Okay, I found a couple of local newspaper items about the Order. They hold three outdoor gatherings a year—spring, summer, and autumn. Festive celebrations, with lots of food, drink, games, and activities, restricted to members and their families, and they're held at a place called Wendell's Grove."

"I saw it on the map today at City Hall," I said. "It's part of their property holdings here. And I was at Wendell's Grove this morning."

"You were?"

"I just wanted to see it," I said. "It looks pretty nice, like a great place to hold a festive gathering outdoors. But I did have another moment with the ground."

"What happened?" Jenny asked with alarm in her voice.

"I tripped and fell, nothing serious. It kind of stunned me for a moment and I thought I had another weird dream-vision. It was over in a flash."

She gazed at me with uncertainty. "Are you all right, Jack?"

She said it like she meant "all right" as in all

right in the head. "I'm beginning to wonder too," I told her, and laughed to slide around it. "You did good, Jenny. This stuff is fascinating. I don't know how it all adds up, but it does make the Order look more cultish. Not simply a church social group."

"I know," she said. "If they truly believe that about being fallen angels, a part of God, then they may think they can do anything."

"Obviously, they do, if they're committing murder and other crimes. They don't think they're doing anything wrong. Just the opposite."

"But none of that explains the light in the ground, and the other things you say you saw or felt." She was back to my head. "Are you sure it was all real?"

"Yes," I said firmly. "No question."

"Are you sure they weren't just hallucinations?"

"They are sort of hallucinatory," I said, "but they come from outside of me. I'm not dropping acid."

"Did you ever?"

"Well, a couple of times, back ten years ago, when everybody was trying it. Just to see what it was like. This is different. And no," I added, "to answer your next question, I've never had a single flashback."

"But you did have a concussion a few days ago."

"The headaches went away in two days. By

Dr. Jolley's standard, that makes it a mild concussion."

"Okay. Let's see if we can start putting this together."

"You sound like you have a theory?"

"As a matter of fact, I do," Jenny said, sitting back in her chair. "Reading all that stuff about the Order today, I could see how a couple of things might connect. Some of the immigrants who came here and settled the Five Towns were members of this small Christian group, or sect, cult, whatever you want to call it. What do they find when they arrive here? A rare geological phenomenon, specific to this area. The ground glows and shimmers, and maybe the light really does move. But perhaps the people in the Order didn't think in terms of an unusual geological phenomenon. This was in the seventeen hundreds, remember. Maybe they saw it as a heavenly sign that this valley was a very special, sacred place."

"Pretty good so far," I said.

"They had the light in the earth, the unusual frequency of the aurora in this area, the lights in the sky. Even today, many people believe there are special places on the planet, like Sedona, Arizona, and Glastonbury in England, where the veil between this world and the next, or another universe, is very thin."

"I know, I know."

"Okay. The members of the Order in Winship probably brought their own rituals and customs with them, and may have developed more here. I'm thinking maybe the random chanting and the kids wearing those tunics might be something like that—the odd practices that most small, closed groups have, the kinds of things that serve to strengthen their sense of group identity. They have no meaning to anyone outside the group."

"Yeah, that was an odd practice they gave me."

"Or maybe what you saw and heard is what they always do whenever some of them know where the light is appearing," Jenny said. "Anyhow, the Order has held itself together here, and maintained its beliefs, down to this day. I'm sure a lot of them nowadays know that the lights are natural, either a geological anomaly or some kind of phosphorescence in the soil. But the lights are still a reinforcement for them, and this is still a remote, fairly isolated place."

"Far from anywhere," I said.

"It sure is." Jenny looked as if she had finished.

"Is there more to your theory?"

"I did some research for you," Jenny said, a bit sharply.

"Believe me, I appreciate it too. Everything you said makes sense to me, it's very plausible. But even knowing all that, I'm at a dead end."

"Why?"

"Bellman is dead, Chris is dead, and I'm not getting anywhere trying to kick information loose from anybody else. I don't even know if

Bellman was a member of the Order, but it wouldn't matter if he was."

"Why?" Jenny asked, puzzled.

"Because it wouldn't necessarily mean that the Order itself was involved," I told her. "Bellman could have cooked it up himself, along with at least one other person, who killed him to make sure he wouldn't end up talking."

"But the Order *could* be involved in it."

"Yes, but Jenny, I can't investigate them."

"Why not?" Her disappointment was showing now.

"The Order of St. Michael, the St. Michael Development Corporation, and the St. Michael Conservancy." I made an open-palm gesture. "That's way beyond what I could do. It would take a district attorney with subpoena power and a team of investigators to follow all the trails. It'd be like taking on a Mafia crew or any other organized criminal group."

I sounded like Steve, and hated it.

"They killed Chris."

"I liked her. One thing I'm curious about, though."

"What's that?"

"Did Chris have a drinking problem? Maybe just beginning?"

"No. Why would you ask that?"

"I got the impression she liked her vodka," I said. "I enjoyed meeting her and I was just hoping it hadn't been a potential problem for her."

"It wasn't," Jenny said. "Chris enjoyed a drink,

but there was no problem. Maybe it showed a little more when you saw her. But she was still getting over the breakup with her ex, and then you show up, asking questions of her boss, and I'm sure she picked up on the turmoil he was going through that day."

"Right."

"And they're going to get away with it."

"People talk. Sometimes it just takes time."

"They killed Chris and they're going to get away with it."

"They may. For a while."

Jenny had been staring down at the table, but then she looked up at me. "Did your boss yank the leash?"

"I'll be here through the weekend."

"Sure sound like you're quitting."

"I'm not done yet."

"Good. I'm sorry, it just makes me mad," Jenny said.

"I know, it's okay."

"What're you going to do next?"

I shrugged. "Keep gnawing at the edges."

Chapter Seventeen

Dr. Gow answered the door when I arrived at his house. He informed me at once that dinner had run a little late and the other guest was still there. It was Father Jimmy Royce, the pastor of St. Michael's Church in town. The two of them had just sat down to enjoy an after-dinner cognac.

"Would you care to join us for a drink?" Gow asked. "Or did you need to speak to me in private?"

"Thank you," I said. Lucky timing for me? I rather doubted it. "I'd be very happy to meet him."

"Ah, good."

Gow ushered me into the study and did the introductions. Father Jimmy was the picture of a country pastor, with curly white hair, a bulging waistline, ruddy cheeks, and fat little fingers. He wore thick round glasses that made it hard to see his eyes, even when he looked at you—they were like dancing blue marbles with no depth or features. Cigarette ash trailed down his jacket and tunic.

"You don't have to have cognac," Gow told me, gesturing toward a sidetable stocked with various bottles, "if you would prefer something else."

"I'll have some of that Dickel Number Twelve, if I may."

"Certainly." Gow poured a large measure in a crystal tumbler. "How is your work in town coming along?"

"It's leading me round and round."

"I'm surprised you're still here," the doctor said.

"So am I, half the time."

"Is there anything I can do to be of help?"

"I hope so, and perhaps Father Royce can too."

"Be glad to if I can," the priest said. "But it's Father Jimmy to you, same as it is to everybody I know."

I smiled and nodded my head in agreement. "Can either of you tell me anything about a group called the Order of St. Michael?"

Neither man showed any reaction.

"Aren't you looking into that matter with Joseph Bellman?" Gow asked, now looking puzzled. "The insurance claims?"

"That's right."

"What's the connection between that and the Order of St. Michael?"

"Maybe none," I said. "But Bellman was involved with some other person or persons in the crimes of murder and insurance fraud."

"Dear me," Father Jimmy said.

"You have proof of that?" Gow asked, peering intently at me.

"Not conclusive, not yet," I said with a smile. I was going to keep making it up for these two, talking as if I had more than I did, turning guesses into statements of fact, to see how they responded. Sometimes you have to lie just to shake things up a little. "But I've been here almost two weeks. I've had phone calls, tips, notes under my door. Bellman was a member of the Order of St. Michael and whoever he was working with may well be too."

"I can set you straight on one thing," Father Jimmy said. "Joseph Bellman was not a member. I've been actively involved in the OSM for years, decades, and he was not a member."

"I was just about to say the same thing," Gow said. "Whoever your source of information is about that, they're wrong."

"You're a member too?"

"Certainly," he said. "It's a fine community organization."

Father Jimmy spoke again. "As for anyone else who might be involved in the crimes you mention, even if they were members of the OSM, it wouldn't implicate the whole group. As a group."

"Not necessarily," I replied. "But it would

narrow down the field of likely suspects. How many members are there in the group?"

"I have no idea," Gow answered. "Jimmy?"

"A good few, a good few."

"Is it in the hundreds, would you say? Thousands?"

Gow chuckled. "Active or occasional?"

"I haven't bothered to look at the roll in ages," Father Jimmy put in. "But the number of families would be a few thousand. Count the wives and children in, and you're upward from there."

"Three hundred or so for the fish dinner every month," Gow said. "That's in season, of course."

The numbers were grim, but I didn't want to bog down now. I looked at Gow. "Doctor, you've had plenty of experience with the law, and I'm sure you can see where this will lead. It goes beyond insurance companies disputing individual claims. Everything goes to the district attorney, he'll have to start an investigation and it'll be much more intensive than I could do." Trying not to sound sarcastic, I added, "I'm sure the Order of St. Michael probably has nothing to do with any of this, as a group. But, a few bad apples. You know."

"Of course, we would all cooperate," Father Jimmy said.

"Of course," Gow echoed. "The Lauck Country District Attorney is Tim Matthews, his office is in Schramburg."

"Good man, Tim," the priest added.

That gave me a sinking feeling, but I hoped it didn't show. "What about the light, or phosphorescence, that appears in the soil around here? I heard about it and then I saw it for myself the other night."

"You're very lucky," the priest told me. "There's plenty of folks come here every summer hoping to see it, but most don't."

"It's a natural curiosity," Gow remarked. "Something to do with the mineral content of the soil in this area. Now and then it displays a certain luminescence. It's uncommon, but there is no mystery to it."

"It was written up in *Scientific American* some years back, I think," Father Jimmy said. "One of nature's odd little mysteries."

Time to change the subject again. "Father, I was surprised to see displayed on the front of your church the same emblem that's on the local beer label."

He chortled. "It does sound funny when you put it like that," he said. "But we're affiliated with the OSM, that's well known."

"I didn't think the Catholic Church permitted anything to be posted on their churches," I said. "I've never seen that done before."

Father Jimmy gave a shrug. "It was there when I became pastor to this parish all of twenty-two years ago, and I've never seen any reason to remove it. The diocese has never said anything to us about it."

"Twenty-two years?"

"That's right."

"Isn't that a long time to be pastor in one parish? I thought priests were moved to a new parish every five or ten years."

"That'd probably be the Diocesans you're thinking of," Father Jimmy answered. "Nice fellas. Good golfers."

"What order are you in?"

"The Archies, of course."

"The Archies? What is that?"

"The Order of the Archangel Saint Michael."

"That *is* Roman Catholic, I take it."

"If it isn't, I've made a terrible mistake."

Father Jimmy and Dr. Gow both chuckled at that.

"I'm not Catholic, as you can probably tell," I said.

"Nobody's perfect."

"Am I correct in thinking that members of the Order of St. Michael believe that men *are* the fallen angels, that St. Michael is the twin of Lucifer, or that Michael and Lucifer are two sides of the one, same angel—part angel, part human?"

That got their undivided attention.

"It sounds like you've been reading apocryphal literature," Gow said. "No wonder you're not making much progress on your insurance case. Isn't this rather far afield for you?"

I didn't get a chance to answer. "That's ancient history," Father Jimmy said patiently. "When the Order started up hundreds of years ago, they may have believed something along those lines. But the only people who pay attention to that sort of thing nowadays are scholars in universities, debating their different interpretations of passages in ancient texts."

"They don't believe that Christ himself was a fallen angel?" I asked. "Or that the Creation of the world was in fact the same event as the expulsion of Lucifer and his brothers?"

"Good Lord, no. Absolutely not."

"You didn't know you were in for a theological discussion as well as dinner tonight, Jimmy," Gow said with a dry laugh.

"No, I didn't. Not that I mind—far from it."

"Are both of you very active in the OSM?"

"It's more of an honorary thing in my case," the priest told me. "I go to the summer picnic, and a couple of the dinners they hold from time to time, but that's the extent of it. I have too many other duties to tend to."

"I'm too tired most of the time," Gow answered, "and too old all of the time. I go to one or two events a year."

"At Wendell's Grove?" I asked.

"My, my. You have been doing your homework." Gow shook his head, as if he found me an amazing specimen. "Yes, that is where they hold their clambakes and picnics, events like that. It's a lovely place."

"Yes, it is. Like a park," Father Jimmy chipped in.

"Are there any other branches or chapters of the Order here in the United States or overseas?"

Father Jimmy took it first. "I believe there are, but the OSM is a very small, locally organized group. I don't know anyone here in Winship who is in touch on a regular basis with chapters elsewhere. It's nothing like Opus Dei, for instance, which is centrally directed from it headquarters in Rome."

"The farthest thing from it," Gow said.

"That's right," Father Jimmy continued. "Here in Winship, it's simply a group of people, families, carrying on a benevolent spiritual and civic tradition that goes back a few hundred years. There's nothing more to it than that."

"How does any of this help you, Mr. Carlson?"

"Just trying to understand the background," I replied. "Sometimes that makes it easier to see what people did, and why."

We talked a few more minutes and then Father Jimmy announced that it was time for him to leave. He and I exchanged a few jolly words in parting, and I hung back as he and the doctor went to the door. Gow didn't look at all pleased when he returned to the study. He asked me to toss a log onto the fire while he refreshed our drinks.

"I can tell you have more to discuss," he said.

"A little more, yes."

He exhaled wearily. He trudged to the sofa and sat down in the middle of it. He smiled, though even when he smiled Gow had a way of looking very sad.

"So. What is it?"

"I had a good time tonight, Doctor," I said. "I appreciate your indulging me, giving me your time, and I liked meeting Father Jimmy."

"Yes, yes. You're welcome."

"But there is something very wrong with this town, and I can't just carry on skating around it, trying to rationalize it away."

"What is it?" he said again.

"That's what I want you to tell me, because you know what it is. Your family has been here for generations. You grew up here and you've spent most of your life in this town. If anyone knows this place and these people, it's you."

He waited so long to speak that he had to work up a rinse of saliva before his mouth would function.

"What are you talking about?"

I'd had too much of that posture. "Doctor, please. I'm talking about the light in the earth, which really does move, because I've seen it and felt its sting. I'm talking about those munchkins all done up in white who run around singing and yelping and chanting at night. I've heard them several times, I've seen them a couple of times, and they beat the shit out of me. You've got a picture-perfect town here, all neat and tidy, everything in its place. But you've also got a sin strip that would make large cities like Boston and Philly downright jealous. And you've also got this group, the Order of St. Michael, who have some very strange beliefs—no matter what you and Father Jimmy say about it. The OSM, which also happens to own significant parcels of land and commercial real estate in and around Winship."

"It doesn't add up to much, if you ask me," Gow said. "Take those curious ideas you attribute to the OSM—do you really think that a whole segment of the population here believes or even knows about such matters? Ordinary townspeople, teachers, lawyers, businessmen, hairdressers, farmers?" Before I could answer, he went on. "No one bothers with that, but even if they did, what possible difference would it make? Look at the denominations like the Mormons and the Seventh Day Adventists, you'll find beliefs that are equally if not more exotic. Religion is not a matter of legal or scientific truth, it's about faith."

"Doctor, I don't care about anybody's religion, except insofar as it influences their behavior in this world. In this town."

"If the light *is* a natural occurrence," Gow countered. "*If* the boys who you say assaulted you were just teenage bullies. *If* the Order of St. Michael *is* the benevolent Christian association everyone else knows them to be. You see my point? What do you have? Really, Mr. Carlson, what do you have?"

"Doctor, people disappear in this valley."

"Disappear?"

"Yes, disappear."

"I'm not sure I know what you mean," he said. "It seems to me that people pick up and leave—all over the country. Every town and city has its certain number of missing persons."

"No," I said. "I'm talking about people who really disappear, not just move somewhere else. As if they were swallowed up by the earth. Literally."

"Literally?" Some of the self-assurance was gone.

"Yes."

"This is getting silly." The hollow look in his eyes was impossible to decipher, but his heart didn't seem to be in his words. "It sounds like those stories you hear about people claiming they were abducted by aliens." He gave a slight laugh. "Perhaps the aliens live underground."

"How many more are going to disappear the same way?"

"Is this is all you have left to discuss . . . ?"

"I'll go in a minute," I said. "If I'm out of line with a personal question, just say so. No wife, no children? I don't get any vibe that you're gay. It's none of my business, but I'm curious why it worked out that way for you." I expected him to show anger and indignation, to lead me to the door, but he merely sat there, and his eyes were no longer focused on me. "I mean, a young doctor from a prominent local family, you would have had your choice of the local beauties."

"It is none of your business," Gow said. "But since you ask, I don't mind telling you. I was married, for more than two years. There were no children, and my wife died tragically before our third anniversary."

"I'm sorry."

A dismissive hand flutter. "Later, people told me I should remarry and have a family, but I never did. And at some point I even became comfortable with the knowledge that I would be the end of the family line."

"How did your wife die so young?"

"It was an accident," he replied, gazing evenly at me. "You and I are both in impossible positions, Mr. Carlson."

"Why do you say that?"

"You, because you don't believe anything. Me, because I do."

Somebody was at the window. We both heard it—the sound of scratching, tapping, hands slapping at the glass. We couldn't see anything because it was dark outside, but the noises continued—stomping feet racing around the house, hands slapping the walls, and those voices. The chanting and yelling had started, and now it rapidly increased in strength and intensity.

"There," I said. "What the hell is that?"

"What you're looking for," Gow replied. He appeared to be extremely upset, but he stood there helplessly, his eyes following the sounds outside. "This is what you wanted."

I went to his desk and picked up the telephone, but couldn't get a dial tone. I had no intention of letting them come at me again without giving them a good fight. I started to cross the room, intending to find the kitchen and grab a couple of knives, but Gow raised his hand to stop me.

"Don't bother," he said. "You'll be all right."

"Tell me what's going on," I demanded. "Or I swear I'll get a knife and go out there and draw some blood. It's the same ones who worked me over the other night, and I'm not going to let them do it again."

"I told you, you will be all right."

They pounded the outside of the house, and inside the study the walls were practically shaking.

"Why are they doing this?"

"I understand what they're saying," Gow told me. He reached into his jacket pocket and took out a small pill box. I wondered if he had a bad heart or some other condition that was being made worse by the insanity around us. Gow held a capsule in his hand. He looked at me. "I'm sixty-eight years old."

"*What are they saying, singing?* Tell me!"

He put the capsule in his mouth, bit down hard on it and swallowed, and that was when I knew it wasn't medicine. Gow's face went into a paralytic convulsion. I rushed to him and tried to force his mouth open, brushing bits of powder off his teeth. His eyes screwed up and seemed to vanish into his face. His cheeks were blossoming purple. I got a whiff of bitter almonds. I backed away. He thrashed some, his body bouncing rigidly like a carved log.

Outside, silence again.

Chapter Eighteen

"Are you on drugs?" Det. Miller angrily asked. I didn't bother to reply. I just stared at him. "That's your story? A bunch of schoolkids were running around outside, whooping and thumping and creating a ruckus, and because of that Dr. Gow decided to pull out a cyanide capsule and kill himself?"

"That's what happened."

"You're crazy."

"He said, 'I know what they're saying.' "

"And what's that supposed to mean?"

"That they, or whoever sent them, wanted Gow to end his life."

"Oh, I see. Now why didn't I think of that? I suppose they were singing instructions to him in some foreign language."

"I didn't understand any of it."

"And these were the same kids that beat you up."

"Yes," I said. "Of course."

"But you didn't actually see them."

"No. I was asking the doctor to tell me what was going on."

"You didn't look out the window?"

"By the time I did, they were gone."

We were in the kitchen at Gow's place, me at the table with a cigarette (my third since Gow's death), Miller circling around, agitated.

"Do you honestly expect me to believe any of this?"

"I don't care what you believe," I told him. "Why don't you just write it up any way you want? Isn't that the way things are done around here?"

"Fuck you, Carlson." He was glaring down into my face, but I didn't blink. I've met better performers. "You come to town and people start dying. The people you talk to."

"You're still here."

"I ought to lock you up as a material witness. Let you cool your heels in jail for a few nights and see how you like that."

"Maybe you ought to book me for murder. Maybe I pulled out the cyanide capsule and forced him to chew it."

"Don't think I wouldn't like to."

"You know you're going to write it up as an ordinary suicide case, so what's the fuss? Don't even mention the other stuff. I had a couple of George A. Dickels, I probably imagined the kids and all that. Don't make a big deal out of it."

Miller looked as if he couldn't tell whether I

was still being sarcastic or if I meant it seriously. I wasn't sure myself.

"Did you call anybody besides the police?" he asked.

"Not yet."

"You're a goddamn menace," he muttered.

"Yeah, but to who?"

"Everybody you come into contact with— Bellman, his secretary, and now Dr. Gow. He was a decent man. People liked him, me included."

"I'm sorry, but I didn't kill him. Can I go now?" I asked. "I have to get back to my snooping and nosing around, before somebody else disappears."

"What do you mean, disappears?"

"Like the others."

"What others? What're you talking about now?"

"People disappear in this area," I said. "They're swallowed up by the earth. Or maybe it's just that they get snatched and murdered for some reason. Like a club dancer working in Winship for a couple of weeks, and she disappears for no reason at all. There was another case this week, a dancer, I think. Gow told me about it tonight," I added.

"He told you what?" Miller demanded.

"About the people who disappear here. About the light. And about the Order of St. Michael— the OSM, the Conservancy, all that land and money."

What are a few more lies among friends? Gow had discussed those things with me, but he hadn't really told me anything. But I wanted to see how Miller reacted. He stood there, glaring down at me, but I could see that behind the glare he was perplexed. It was churning inside of him.

"You're a walking, talking crock," he said.

"If Gow wasn't old and weak and tired, and a risk to break down and start talking, why would they want him dead?"

"I don't have time for this bullshit."

"Just curious, Detective. Are you OSM too?"

"It wouldn't make any difference if I was," he insisted with another show of heat. "If a person commits a crime, I put him in jail. Doesn't matter if he's OSM or a Jaycee or my own brother. I'm a cop."

"That's what I thought."

He didn't miss the way I said it. He was right on the edge, and so was I. But he was also afraid of making a mistake. I was ashamed of myself for ever believing that Det. Miller was honest.

"Get out of my sight," he said, turning away.

I drove immediately to Penny Lane. Funny, I had mentioned a specific case, a dancer, but Miller never responded to it. He didn't ask me any questions, he didn't claim that I had to be mistaken, he didn't address it at all, and that is not the way he should have reacted.

I felt uncomfortable prowling around in the

fevered darkness of the club looking for Kelly. She was one of four girls dancing on a long runway. I slid onto a stool at the edge of her territory. A waitress brought me an overpriced beer. I watched. Kelly was busy, working a couple of customers nearby. She shoved her breasts and butt in the face of anyone who slipped some green beneath the waistband of her thong. Guys sat there, holding money up like buyers at a market. I wasn't Kelly's boyfriend, but I didn't like seeing her there. It was no help that she didn't notice me until I held up a five dollar bill.

At least she wasn't embarrassed. In fact, she was delighted to see me. I got the in-your-face tit-cuddle, and a tongue in my ear. We exchanged a few whispers and she lingered in front of me for more than one song. She could see I wasn't comfortable. Ten minutes later, she had a break, and she led me to a dark booth away from the crowd.

"I didn't think you'd come here," she told me, "but I'm glad you did. How are you feeling? Getting better?"

"Yeah, I'm okay. I tried calling you, but the line was busy. I was worried about you."

"You were?" She liked that. "The line's busy most of the time, unfortunately. Two girls and one phone per room, somebody is always looking for a phone that isn't being used. What have you been doing?"

"This and that," I said, trying not to laugh.

"Did you or any of the other girls tell the police about Amber?"

"No, of course not."

"I didn't think so. But they know."

"They do? How do you know that?"

"I just do," I said, "and I can tell you that they're not going to do anything about it. This whole town is dangerous, Kelly. Something's happening here. You're not safe. I think you should leave Winship as soon as possible."

She frowned. "*What* is happening?"

"My case is going to blow things up here soon," I said. "The people who are involved are getting desperate."

"I don't know, Jack. The money I make here is my future."

"Kelly, I'm talking about you *having* a future Just tell them that there's an illness in your family back home. Tell them you'll be back at the next city on the circuit. They'll let you go, and they'll hold your job for you."

"I don't know."

"If they don't, fuck it. Go anyway."

"Why would they worry about me?"

"People seem to die or disappear in this place for any number of reasons," I told her. "Isn't what happened to Amber enough for you?"

"I could have been wrong," Kelly said forlornly. "It could be that she walked away and we didn't notice. Maybe she just snuck off and left town."

"Did she take her things?" Kelly didn't speak. "She didn't leave, not of her own free will. The people who run this town are a part of it."

Then I told her about what happened earlier that night, the crazy scene at Gow's house, his suicide, and why I believed that the police really knew what it was all about.

"God," she said.

"Somebody's God, yeah."

"What're you going to do, Jack?"

"I'm getting out too, in a few days," I said. "I still have a few things to do, then I'll be ready to deliver everything I know to the companies—and to the district attorney and the FBI."

"Wow."

"If I go, can I go with you?"

"You shouldn't wait for me."

"But how can I leave?"

"Rent a car."

"If it's just for a couple more days, I might as well wait until you're ready to leave too," Kelly said firmly, her mind made up. "And who knows? Maybe I can help you out, one way or another—right, daddy?"

Chapter Nineteen

It was nearly three in the morning when I found Jenny doing her rounds of the ward at the hospital. She was surprised to see me, and she took me to a deserted lounge area where we drank some machine coffee and talked briefly.

"Gow's dead."

"I know," she said. "News went around the hospital about an hour ago. They said that someone was with him. Was that you?"

"Yes, I was there."

"And was it really suicide?"

"You could say that."

She gave me a quizzical look. "What do you mean?"

"Jenny, everything's bad, very bad. Tell me exactly what you heard about Dr. Gow's death?"

"Just that he had company and he suddenly killed himself," she said. "For no apparent reason."

"That would be the official word. But I suppose I should be grateful they're not blaming me for it."

"Not yet anyway."

"Thanks a lot."

I told her everything—what Gow and the priest had told me about the Order, my words with Gow as the house was surrounded by the same howling band that had beaten me up, the doctor's death, and my session with Miller. I told her the same things I told the detective.

She shook her head slowly, absorbing the information. "What I don't understand is why they haven't just killed you"

"Thanks again."

"You know what I mean," she said. "You're their problem."

"I know, but I'm not just another outsider they can make disappear. I was sent here by some big companies. They probably figure that if anything happens to me, it will only focus more attention on Winship and them. Easier to get rid of the people here who look like weak links or threats, even Gow. The other track, try to scare me off and also to convince me that I don't have a case against anyone here."

"But you do have a case?" she asked intently.

"Yes."

"Tell me again what Gow said to you, at the end."

" 'I know what they're saying.' "

"You're sure about that?"

"Absolutely," I replied.

"But how could they know what he was telling you? He could have been discussing the weather or anything."

"Right," I agreed. "That's why I'd say it was the priest, Father Jimmy Royce. He was there, he knew I'd spoken with Gow a number of times, he may have heard something Gow said, or that I said, and decided the doctor's time was up. But there is one other possibility."

"What?"

"The kids could have been sent to stiffen Gow's spine," I said. "To me, he looked tired of it all, tired and sad. If the message he got was to stay strong, maybe he just decided he couldn't do that anymore. He told me he was comfortable knowing he would be the end of his family's line, which is quite a comment, since he came from one of the oldest of the Five Towns families, OSM all the way."

Jenny was silent for a moment. "But there isn't much chance of finding out who killed Chris, right?"

"I think there is," I told her, although I was not as confident as I tried to sound. "Once this breaks, someone with lesser culpability will talk."

"What makes you think that you can break this case now?"

I put a finger to my lips. "Things, people, information. But the less you know, the safer you will be. You'll know soon. Everybody will."

"I'm scared for you, Jack.'

"I'll be all right. You watch yourself too."

We talked for a few more minutes; then I walked back to the inn. I needed some sleep, but I felt excited. Or deranged. I'd been busy lying to everybody, leading them on, bluffing, exaggerating, trying to convince someone, anyone, that I was onto the whole deal—all just to stir the pot. I didn't know what else I could do. Gnaw the edges, see what happens.

The doctor, the priest, the cop—trying to deceive or mislead them didn't bother me at all. It was a little different with Kelly. I enjoyed her company and she might well be who she appeared to be, a dancer who wanted to save enough money to open a boutique and live a "normal" life. I hoped she was. But it was remarkably convenient how she had entered my life. I knew she did dance, I showed up at the club and saw her there, so that part was true. But I couldn't be sure yet that she had not been recruited to look after me in Winship—keep his dick happy, find out as much as you can of what he knows, and lead him in these directions. It was Kelly who gave me the Amber story, but tonight tried to play it down. It was Kelly who was so fearful, but tonight didn't want to leave her job and get out of this town—at least not until I did. If then. It was Kelly who suddenly had a big knife.

There were a couple of nagging little things about Jenny, too. I had gotten the impression from Chris and Jenny both that they were not all that close as friends, that they didn't see much of each other because of the different work shifts they had. I'm sure they did talk and share some confidences. I was grateful to Jenny for the information she brought me about the OSM, but there's a part of my brain that always looks a gift horse in the mouth. I hadn't asked her to go out and look up anything for me, at least not directly. I hoped she really was just trying to be helpful because of her feelings about Chris, and not because she wanted to lead me in any certain direction to or away from something.

The other thing that still bothered me was the question of the night that Chris and I met at Doran's. There was no disagreement that Jenny had dropped Chris off at the bar. And Chris was there, well into a drink, when I arrived. But we met at ten, and Jenny's shift at the hospital began at nine. Probably a minor discrepancy. But Chris told me she had planned to walk back to her apartment, which was just a couple of streets away, and she asked me to give her a ride because of the rain. If she could walk home, why couldn't she walk to the bar in the first place instead of taking a ride from Jenny, who was supposed to be at work an hour earlier? I even wondered if Chris and Jenny both could have been acting in some way on behalf of the OSM.

There's a word for people like me: paranoid.

I wasn't sure what I was going to do until I stood on the veranda of the hotel and the church bells started ringing as if it were Sunday morning. But it wasn't, I reminded myself, it was Saturday morning. I walked across the green to see what was happening at the Catholic church.

There was a mass in progress, but Father Jimmy Royce wasn't the priest saying it. I found him a few minutes later, out back, doing his brisk duck walk from the vestry to the redbrick rectory. I trotted to catch up with him.

"Father," I called out. "Father Jimmy."

He turned, recognized me, and stopped abruptly. "Well, well, just the fella," he said. "Come along inside, Mr. Carlson. I'd like to speak with you."

Neither of us said another word until we were seated in his office, a light and airy room with golden oak bookcases, a large desk, and stiff chairs. A crucifix, holy pictures, pamphlets and tracts—all the expected religious trappings were in evidence. I tried to imagine Father Jimmy at his day-to-day work, arranging a baptism or a funeral, or discussing the sanctity of marriage with a pair of local sweethearts. Good old Father Jimmy. He pushed a few papers around on his desk, made a few illegible ink scratches on a notepad, and then looked up at me.

"What happened, son?"

"What happened?"

"Yes. You were there after I left."

"You want me to tell you," I said.

"Of course I do. I'd particularly like to know if he put up much of a fight at the end."

"What?" I couldn't believe it. "How do you mean, a fight?"

"It's important." I just gaped at him. "Perhaps I'd better explain, since you're not a religious man yourself. Suicide is a terrible thing, a sin against life itself, a sin against God. It used to be called the one unforgivable sin, though we try to be more understanding of the . . . stress . . . that people go through these days." He spoke the word "stress" as if he were choking on a dog turd. "If my friend the good doctor struggled against it at the end, that would be a sign he was sorry for what he had done."

"You mean, he had last-second repentance."

"Well put, the very thing. He was a dear man, a good friend to everyone who knew him, and he'll truly be missed. It would be a comfort to know that as he stood on the brink—"

"Spare me the Pat O'Brien act," I said.

"What?" He tried to look shocked, but with those blue eyes bouncing around behind the thick lenses he created a much nastier impression. Maybe that's just what I wanted to see in him.

"You know what happened last night," I told him. "And you know why, which means that you're still a little ahead of me. But I want you to know that I'm closing fast, and there's nothing you or any of the OSM can do about it."

He stared at me for a long time, probably weighing various approaches in his mind while trying to decide if I was serious or not.

"What exactly do you mean, Mr. Carlson?"

"I mean it's all going to come apart. Your quaint little sect, your gang of kids in white tunics, the Conservancy, the money. The crimes."

"That is what you propose to do, is it?"

"It's going to happen, with or without me." The reason I said that was to save my life, maybe. "It's too late. No one can stop it from happening."

"Really?"

"Yes." I gave him the eyeball right back.

Another long pause. I didn't much care for the approach the priest had settled on. His fat little fingers looked too calm, splayed restfully on the dark green blotter. His eyes had gone slo-mo.

"If you only knew," he said deliberately, "you wouldn't talk that way. But is there any point in our talking?"

"I'm listening," I said. "But no more bullshit."

"Are you a complete atheist, Mr. Carlson? I mean, were you raised that way from birth?"

"I served some time with the Lutherans. As soon as my folks stopped making me go to church, I stopped."

"May I ask why?"

"There was nothing in it for me," I told him. "Never felt a twinge."

"Other people do. Far and away most people do."

"They're luckier than I am. Faith is the gift I never received."

"Ah, well, at least you know the story of our Lord."

"Sure."

"Do you deny the existence of any spiritual or supernatural dimension to life in this world?"

"It exists. In people's minds."

"That's a start, I suppose. It would help if you believed in the existence of your own eternal soul."

"It would help if I had one," I replied.

"What would you say, Mr. Carlson, if I told you that on this planet there are a few, very few, special places where the ground itself is part of the spiritual dimension? Where the normal laws of science don't always pertain. Where the spiritual realm comes into real physical conjunction with our everyday world."

"You mean a crossing point to . . . what? Heaven and hell?"

Father Jimmy smiled. "Ah, you're almost on dry land now. Not heaven and hell, no. Nowadays we tend to play down any literal emphasis on heaven and hell because it makes people think merely in terms of rewards and punishments. And even I would have a hard time with the notion that they were located just the other side of some doorway up the road. What I am referring to is a purely spiritual or supernatural region that is every bit as real as the one we live in here."

"If it's not heaven or hell, what is it?"

"Another level of life. Another universe," Father Jimmy said.

"And who lives there?"

"The angels of light and the angels of darkness, and those who have passed on from here."

"Does that include atheists who pass on? If so, I'm in."

"You have an opportunity to understand," the priest said with a sorrowful look, "but you spurn it."

"Father, you will have an opportunity to hire a lawyer."

"Is that what you came here to tell me?"

"No, I guess I was hoping that you might tell me the truth about everything that's been going on here," I said. I smiled. "Silly me."

"Mr. Carlson," he started again after a slight pause, "some members of the OSM are having a special meeting tomorrow afternoon. Dr. Gow's wake is on Monday, his funeral Tuesday, but some of his closest friends want to get together before then to share our thoughts and memories of him."

"Very good of you, I'm sure," I said.

"I'm telling you this because I'd like to invite you to come along and join us," Father Jimmy said. "I think that if you meet some of our people, in that kind of informal setting, you would gain a lot. You might even find some answers for that unresolved insurance matter of yours."

"Really? Is somebody going to confess?"

"I thought you were here to talk to people and ask questions," Father Jimmy said, now looking sad. "Some of the people who will be there tomorrow were close to Joseph Bellman. They may be able to save you time and help you."

"At Wendell's Grove, I suppose?"

"Yes, at three o'clock," Father Jimmy said. "Will you come?"

"Thanks, but I don't think so."

"Why not?"

I stood up, ready to leave. "I may be gone by then."

"You're leaving Winship?"

"My work is pretty much done."

"You say, *pretty much?*"

Scratch a priest, find a lawyer.

"I have a couple of things left," I said. "If I finish them early enough, I'm out of here tomorrow. Otherwise, it'll be Monday morning. It's a long drive from here to . . . anywhere."

"I must say, you didn't sound nearly this . . . optimistic . . . about wrapping your business up when we spoke last night."

"Yeah," I said, turning to go. "What a difference a night makes."

Chapter Twenty

I had just about lied and bluffed my way offstage in Winship by then. There was nobody left to jive, including myself.

I sat on the hotel veranda and tried to focus on what I had, or thought I had. A group, a tightly wound sect that had taken an old line of apocryphal Christian faith and skewed it even more to fit their unusual situation: they had some lights in the sky and lights in the earth. Bizarre cultish behavior. The isolated location, freedom from scrutiny. Strange flowers grow together— the Norman Rockwell town oozing all the charm of home and church and school, the night shades of Penny Lane, and the almost tactile presence of ongoing unnatural death.

I was aware of the kids. I saw them everywhere. They were just kids, hanging around, playing, talking to each other. What did they do in this hothouse, what was their role? Were they merely trained to believe, and to go out and beat on people when ordered? Was there a secret language to this place, and were the kids so thoroughly indoctrinated that they knew it and could deliver an irresistible message to Dr. Gow? The ones I saw all looked normal, their gestures natural and spontaneous. They didn't look like zombies, they looked like kids, and they were around everywhere.

The hell with it. All of them.

I went back up to my room and called Kelly, and her good mood lifted me right away. I drove to her motel and we were soon fucking each other's brains out, and then lying tight together beneath the covers. I was drifting off a little.

"Jack?"

"Mmmn?"

"Anything else happen since I saw you last night?"

"Unh-uh."

"What're you going to do today?"

"Just hang around and take it easy," I said.

"Are you waiting for something?"

"Yeah, I should hear about a couple of things."

"Last night you told me you'd probably be leaving town, either tomorrow or Monday."

"That's right."

"You're definitely going?"

"My work is just about done here, Kelly."

"You got what you need to put those people away?"

"Most of it," I said. "The rest will begin to fall into place after I get home and meet with Steve and his people, write my report, and we put it all together."

"Wow. You are some guy."

I didn't think so. After a long pause, Kelly spoke again.

"What about me?"

"What *about* you?"

"I've been thinking about what you said."

"And?" I said when she didn't continue.

"I don't know."

"Do you want to come with me?" I asked.

"And do what?"

"Like we were discussing the other day," I said. "Get another job, take some business and accounting courses so you'll be able to put together a good plan and open that boutique."

If she was serious and decided to go that route, then things might become very interesting between the two of us. But if she was going to stay in the traveling exotic dancer business, I didn't see any place for me in her life.

"Maybe I could dance at clubs in the area around where you live."

"Do you really want to keep on dancing in men's clubs?"

I felt her body tighten slightly in my embrace.

"You mean, another job, like . . . minimum wage kind of stuff? Jack, I'm banking good money in this business."

"Then stick with it."

Her body pulled away from me a little then. "That sounds like good-bye."

"No, it's not," I told her. "If you leave with me, fine. If you stay on the loop, that's okay too. I'll give you my phone number, you can call and we can talk as often as you want. You have to do whatever you think is best for you."

"But I don't know what's best for me," Kelly replied.

"Maybe we both need to take a little more time to think about what we really want to do."

"Last night you said I was in danger."

"I had just seen a man take his own life," I told her. "That might have made me overstate things."

"So, you think it is safe for me here?"

"I don't know," I said. "Even if they've seen us together, there's no reason for them to consider you a threat. But who knows how they think?"

"Keisha and Amber weren't threats to them."

"Like you said, they probably left for their own reasons."

"Amber? Out there at that place?"

"I don't know, Kelly. Like you said, she could've snuck off when nobody was looking. Spur of the moment. Fed up, or fucked-up."

"And walk for miles?"

"First guy that came driving along and saw her?"

"That's true," Kelly said with a laugh. "Does that mean you don't believe that idea that she somehow disappeared in that meadow?"

"Probably not."

"Even after what happened to you in the exact same place?"

"There *is* something unusual in the earth around this town," I replied. "The luminescence, maybe the magnetic field sometimes has a temporary disorienting effect if you're in the right place. But beyond that, no. If Amber is actually dead, it's because someone killed her, not because she vanished through the veil into some other dimension or universe, or was swallowed up by the earth."

"I love it when you talk like that."

"What do you mean?"

"You're an intelligent man," Kelly said. "Believe me, I've met too many men who *aren't*. Sometimes, just listening to you talk makes me wet."

"Is that what you like about me?"

"Among other things," she replied in a teasing tone. "Hey, what'll you be doing tonight while I'm working at the club?"

"Not much. Probably sleeping."

"No! Come see me there, please? I want to see you."

"I'm not crazy about watching you with all those guys like that."

"Aw, it's just a show," Kelly said. "The only guy there who means anything to me is you. You didn't enjoy seeing those losers drooling over me and knowing you're the only one who could do anything you want to with me?"

"Maybe I did, a little," I said, smiling in spite of myself.

"I knew it, I knew you did!"

"And I do like it when you talk that way."

"Mmmm, you come see me dance tonight, daddy, and on my break I'll take you into a booth in that side room and I'll get down under the table and suck you until you scream."

"Kelly, baby," I said. Not knowing her.

"There's something else that I like about you," she said, her voice suddenly quieter, needy. "I feel safer when you're around me."

I stopped and bought a bottle of No. 12 on my way back to the inn. I sat in the armchair in my room, feet propped up on the coffee table, and sipped Tennessee whisky. And I thought. Even if everything Kelly said was true, even if her feelings were honest, and even if things went the best way possible for us now—still, I was thirty-nine and she was twenty-three, so I knew that the day would almost certainly come when she left me. If ever I had her. Did I want to go through that, older then, left alone once again, and feeling that I had crossed into some terminal zone?

Dumb question.

There was a message from Jenny for me when I got back to the inn, asking me to call her. Left a couple of hours earlier. I looked at the note again and picked up the phone. No one, just the machine. I left a short reply to her call.

I showered and dressed, and tried Jenny's number again—same deal. I went downstairs and had dinner—a steak, fries, and salad. It occurred to me that I might be overstaying. I was paying for everything myself now. It was not as if I actually did have anything out there that I was waiting to hear on. They could laugh me off and ignore me, wait me out. It might be just as well to leave the next morning instead of hanging around until Monday.

After my meal I took a walk around the city center, through Ryder Park. It was a cool autumn evening. Nothing, no chanting, no wind whistling through the graveyard, no lights in the sky or the earth.

I went to my car and drove around. I passed Jenny's duplex, but there were no lights on in her half of the building. I wondered if she had something to tell me, or if her call was merely to find out if I had any new information to share. Jenny had told me she was on call that weekend, so she could be working at the hospital. When I saw the medical complex as I was out driving, I parked and went inside to check. No, Jenny Randall was not on duty that night.

So she was out somewhere, and why not? It was Saturday night.

I went back to my room, watched some television, and slowly sipped another whisky. Part of me wanted to be lazy and feel tired, and just glide toward sleep. But I didn't feel tired, and I kept thinking about Kelly and Jenny—though not at all in the same ways. You see people as you want to see them, but also as they want you to see them, and the difference is all the difference.

I looked at my watch. She would be working now, a break every twenty minutes. I put on my jacket and drove to Penny Lane. Kelly wasn't dancing on the runway or the back bar stage. I went through both public rooms at the club, but I didn't see her anywhere. I bought a beer and waited for a while. Still no sign of her. I asked one of the bartenders about her.

"She didn't come in tonight," he said with a shrug.

"Is Julio here?"

"Julio?"

"The van driver," I said. "He drives the dancers."

"I don't know him. I just tend bar, man."

He sloped off to pour a drink for somebody. I hung around, but Kelly didn't show. When the other dancers took a break, I managed to intercept one of them, a gorgeous Asian chick. She was on her way to have a drink with a group of young business types, but I got her for a second.

"Where's Kelly?"

"Kelly? I don't know, man," she replied. "She wasn't with us when we drove in tonight. She must not be feeling well."

Sunday, late morning. My head felt empty, slow to put two thoughts together in a row. I tried without success to get Jenny on the phone. I rang the hospital, and after a long wait someone came back on the line and told me that no, Jenny was not on duty today. I called Kelly too, but again had no luck.

Was I supposed to think that both women had disappeared? Been snatched, and now were either dead or being held somewhere—like Wendell's Grove? It seemed too obvious—or was that what I was meant to think?

I drove to Kelly's motel and went to her room. The door was slightly ajar. I knocked on it anyway, pushed it open and stepped inside. The bed was made, the room tidy, and all of her personal things were gone.

"Can I help you?"

I turned around. A young man stood in the open doorway. T-shirt, jeans, bare feet. His dark hair was a little mussed, as if he'd gotten out of bed only a few minutes before. This crowd worked late, slept late.

"Are you Julio?" I asked. He nodded. "Where's Kelly?"

He shrugged. "She took off."

"When did she leave?"

"Who're you, man?"

"Jack Carlson. A friend of hers."

"Yeah, well, she didn't work last night," he said. "I think she told somebody she felt sick. When we got back here, I saw the door was open. She was gone, took her things and left."

"Did she check out at the desk?"

"No, she wouldn't need to. We handle that stuff for them."

"Why would she just leave like that?"

"Who the fuck knows, man? These girls do that."

"Like Amber? And Keisha?"

"Kelly told you, huh? Yeah, like them." Julio stepped inside the room and pulled the door shut behind him. "These girls, they all got problems, you know? One thing or another. They get fed up with the work, or mad about something, or just strung out, and they take off."

"Do they ever come back?"

He looked at me for a moment. "Sometimes, yeah. They make good money dancing. If they get their shit together, they can come back."

"Why would Kelly leave on a Saturday night, way the hell out here in this nowhere town?"

"Probably ran off with some guy," he said, a big smile forming on his face, the kind of smile that told me he had me sized up as a chump. "Some older guy with money, says he's gonna take her away and make her his queen. That how you met her, at the club? And you thought *you* were that guy?" He started laughing. "I think it was some other guy, man!"

The Sunday morning newspaper, still rolled up inside a yellow plastic bag, sat on the front porch of Jenny's duplex. I rang the bell, knocked on the inside door and waited. No sounds from within; no one answered.

* * *

I checked out of the Birch Inn, threw my bags in the car and started driving, but I wasn't sure where to go. Part of me wanted to leave Winship and the whole ungodly mess behind. File my report and expenses, and forget it all. I didn't see what I could do about Jenny and Kelly. Talking to the police would be pointless and it might well bog me down there even more. I had no leverage, no weapons, and no idea how to help either of the women—if, in fact, they needed help at all.

At the same time, it felt wrong simply to drive away. I told myself I wouldn't be walking out on them, but I knew I'd feel as if that was exactly what I was doing. Then it occurred to me that there was one thing I could do.

It was a little after three when I got to Wendell's Grove. Two men stood by a pickup that was parked beside the entrance to the gravel road. One of them waved me over and I slowed to a stop.

"This is private property," he told me.

"Father Jimmy invited me."

"Okay. Follow the road."

Brilliant idea. I drove on and parked at the end of the road, next to eight or ten other cars and trucks that were already there. Another couple of guys.

"Who're you looking for?"

"Father Jimmy," I answered.

"You know where the clubhouse is?"

"No."

"See that big rock by the edge of the trees?" he said, pointing to the tree line straight ahead. "There's a path that cuts behind the rock."

"Thanks."

I found the path, which wound through the trees for about a quarter of a mile before it came out in another large clearing. The clubhouse, a large log cabin with a wide veranda, was off to one side, near the bottom of the wooded hill. I saw a ball field, a little shimmer of water in the distance that might be a lake. A few men sat around at picnic tables, talking among themselves and drinking cans of beer from a cooler. A man sitting on the top step of the cabin asked me who I was and what I wanted there.

"Jack Carlson," I said. "Father Jimmy invited me."

"Hang on." He went inside, returned a minute later and held the door open for me. "Come on in, Mr. Carlson."

They were seated around a large table in the main room. The priest, the cop, and two other men I'd never seen before. Miller stared coolly at me, but Father Jimmy flashed his jolly pastor smile.

"Thank you for coming, Mr. Carlson," he said. "Do sit down and join us. Would you care for a drink? There's some beer, soda—"

"No, thank you."

I took a seat across the table from them. We were all silent for a moment and then I pushed ahead, anxious to get it over with as quickly as possible. Eat shit and try to act as if I liked it.

"I just came by to tell you that I'm leaving Winship," I said. "I've finished my work here. There's nothing more for me to do."

"Ah, and was it successful for you?" Father Jimmy asked.

"I don't see any reason for the insurance companies to dispute any of the claims," I replied. "I'm sure the checks will be sent out shortly."

"And the rest of your investigation?" The priest again.

"There is no rest of my investigation. The claims were it."

"Oh." Father Jimmy hesitated. "I thought you were concerned with the activities of the OSM and the Conservancy?"

"The claims appeared to lead me that way," I continued. "But it turned out to be irrelevant to my business."

"I see."

"I don't see any connection, and there are no people I now regard as suspect or complicit with Joseph Bellman and the insurance claims."

"Well, well," the priest said. "It sounds as if you have wrapped things up quite thoroughly. I'm glad your work has been successful for you."

I stood up to go, then looked at Detective Miller.

"You know Jenny Randall, the nurse? Shared

an apartment with Chris Innes?" Miller gazed at me and nodded his head once. "I've been trying to get in touch with her the last couple of days, just to say good-bye, but I haven't been able to find her."

"Maybe she went away for the weekend," Miller said.

"No, she was on call at the hospital this weekend."

"I'll look her up," the cop said. "Make sure she's okay."

"Thanks."

I was going to mention Kelly too, but at that moment I couldn't see any point to it. Regardless of whether or not these people knew anything about disappearing dancers, it would accomplish nothing useful and it might even be foolhardy for me to express my concerns again now. In some obscure way, my silence felt like a small betrayal of Kelly. But was it?

I nodded briefly at the group of men on the other side of the table and turned to leave, feeling self-conscious as I crossed the room and went out the cabin door. Did they believe me? Did they even care what I said or thought? I had to hope that Kelly and Jenny were alive and safe—somewhere, for reasons of their own—and not in any danger because of me.

The men outside were still sitting around, talking and drinking beer, and they barely took notice of me as I left. But I had only taken a few paces toward the path through the woods when a blast of pain tore through the back of my head, my vision blinking wildly, blotting up with darkness.

I opened my eyes and saw the aurora borealis flashing, shimmering above in the night sky. I was on my back, arms and legs outstretched, tied to tent pegs staked in the ground. I tried to move, but couldn't budge at all. Duct tape over my mouth, wrapped completely around my head. The only movement I could make was to turn my head, which created new waves of pain from the raw wound on my skull. I saw Kelly, taped and staked out the same way, a few feet from me. Her eyes were frantic with fear, staring hopelessly at me. I raised my head, craning my neck to look around and see more. I could make out the darker shadow of the tree line in the distance, a distance that felt familiar. I could see how it circled around—we were in that clearing, the meadow where Amber had supposedly vanished and where I'd had that fall and hallucinatory incident.

Kelly and I appeared to be alone there; I couldn't see anyone else. I tried to get free, yanking my arms and legs, but I couldn't create any give with the pegs in the ground or any slack in the ropes. It seemed like we were there for a long time, and then it began to get lighter—around me and Kelly. The earth beneath us was glowing with that bluish-white light. She saw it too, it wasn't just in my mind. I expected to feel my skin burning or my brain to go tripping again, but that didn't happen. The luminescence grew stronger and brighter. My head felt empty.

Then the others came into view—I saw Billy Winthrop, grinning as if he had unexpectedly just won a spelling bee, Det. Miller, several other men I didn't know, and Father Jimmy, who came close, leaned over me and smiled. I tried to speak, but the tape completely muffled my words. He pointed toward Kelly, and I turned my head again to look at her. Jenny was there, kneeling beside Kelly, a long knife clasped in both hands. She raised it head high and plunged it into Kelly's chest. Once more, into her throat.

I spun my head away, trying not to hear the sounds.

"Everything that happens is God's will," the priest said.

Wrong, wrong, wrong.

"Everything."

I was shit, such shit.

"You are in a sacred place now."

Then Jenny stood over me, looking like a pale blue ghost in the persistent glow around us. I caught her eyes, but saw nothing recognizable there. As if she knew what I wanted to ask, what my mind was silently screaming, Jenny smiled almost sadly and said, "Why not?"

She knelt beside me.

The dripping blade streaked down toward my heart.

Paranoids are the only people who really get it.

SCRAMBURG, U.S.A.

For
Jack Ketchum
and
Dallas Mayr

Chapter One
What About the Boy?

Captain Frank Bell tossed his cigarette out the car window, pried a spearmint LifeSaver loose, and popped it in his mouth. He'd rather not have the Hacketts catch a whiff of the two double bourbons that he had downed at the Legion a few minutes ago. Reverend Joe Hackett was the pastor at Zion Lutheran and his wife Eileen ran the women's auxiliary. The Hacketts were fixtures in town—good people to be in good with.

And they had a problem. They needed his advice. Again. Capt. Bell smiled as he swung his car into Oak Lane, the short dead-end passage behind the church, where the Hacketts lived. He knew exactly what he was going to say. He'd be glad to give them his advice—but he could do better than that now. He could *help* them.

Capt. Bell parked in front of the trim white colonial at the end of the lane. It was one minute to four; he was right on time. A sun shower broke loose as he got out of the car, and he hurried up the gravel path to avoid the sudden rain. The minister's wife opened the front door about two seconds after he rang the bell. Middle-aged, short, and somewhat plump, she had strangely colorless hair.

"Mrs. Hackett."

She nodded at him without smiling. He noticed the way she held herself, her head and neck turned slightly away from him, her movements brief and stiff. It was a warm June day, but she was wearing a blouse with long sleeves.

"He's in his office," she said, gesturing to the first door on the right. "Go on in, he's expecting you."

"Thank you, ma'am."

She moved her head to keep the left side of her face from his view as he passed her. He knocked once and entered the office. Joe Hackett got up from the chair behind his blond wooden desk. He was tall and thin, but he had a paunch. He wore gray trousers, a white shirt, and necktie. He looked like a small-town insurance agent—which, in a way, he was.

"Good to see you." He shook hands with the cop and waved him to a brown Naugahyde armchair. "Thanks for coming by, Frank."

"Glad to."

"You want anything?" he asked as he returned to his seat behind the desk. "Lemonade? Glass of soda?"

"No thanks."

"So, how are you?"

"I'm fine, Joe. How are you?"

"Fine, thanks. Just fine."

The minister's hands fidgeted with some of the papers on his desk and his eyes avoided Bell's gaze. The cop knew what to expect. The poor helpless bastard would circle around for twenty minutes, like a dog looking for the exact right spot to dump his load.

"When did he hit her?"

Hackett was startled, but then his face crumpled and his hands fell flat on the desk. "The other night."

"Not the first time, was it?"

"No."

"He hit you?"

Hackett was breathing hard, still not looking at Bell. Finally, he nodded. "Yes."

"You ever hit him back?"

"Of course not." Hackett looked offended. "Fighting is wrong. It's no answer to his misbehavior."

Bell sighed. *Misbehavior.* A better reason was the kid was big and strong and would take the old man apart like a Tinkertoy.

"You ever spank him, over the years?"

"When he was a child, sure. God knows he needed it, he was such a handful. Right from the beginning."

"Joe, it's not your fault it didn't take."

"We've done everything we could for him."

"I know you did."

"Schramburg is a nice town," the minister continued, "a good town. We gave him a good home, all our love. We taught him right from wrong. We didn't spoil him with lots of toys and things, like other families, but he didn't go without. He wanted a train set, a bike, army men—he had those things. And vacations? We took him to—"

"You and your wife did your part," Bell interrupted. "He got it from his mother and father. Nothing you could ever do about that."

"That's why I don't like to blame him, not entirely. His father runs off, he and his mother end up in the Town Farm. And then . . . to live through that terrible tragedy. Dear God. None of that is Howie's fault."

Bell sighed again. "No, it isn't. But he is who he is, and that's what your problem is now. What else has he been up to lately?"

The rest spilled out quickly. The constant bullying and threats, the atmosphere of anxiety and fear that poisoned their home, the drunkenness, the cursing, the foul, vile language, the torrent of insults—all of that had been gradually increasing over the last couple of years. But now, in recent months, their adopted son had become physically violent.

"Who's he hang around with?"

"That's another thing. I don't even know their names. There's only three or four of them, but they're . . ."

"Just like him."

"Yes, that's right." The minister had a pleading look on his face. "Frank, there's nothing we can do with him. I'm afraid of where this might go, what might happen. You already gave him a couple of chances."

Bell nodded. "He was what, thirteen, fourteen? Shoplifting, minor vandalism. Most boys have a little of that to burn off. I'm always glad to give a kid another chance at that age. But some of them never straighten up and fly right, no matter how many chances you give them."

Hackett pulled himself together and sat up straight. "Frank, I have no doubt whatsoever that you should be the next chief. Larkin, God love him, he's a good man, but he's past it now. It's only a matter of time, and I believe you're clearly the best candidate to succeed him. Things will get better in Schramburg with you leading the force."

"Thanks, Joe." There were two Lutherans on the police board, the town's civilian committee that would cast the decisive vote.

"But, back to *this*. What can Eileen and I do about Howie? He is beyond our control. He is growing up to be . . ."

"A monster."

"That's what I'm afraid of."

"When is his birthday, Joe?"

"Last month, May Tenth."

"And how old is he now?"

"Eighteen."

Capt. Bell smiled. "I thought so, but I wasn't

sure. That's your answer, Joe. That's your answer, right there."

"What do you mean?"

"He's eighteen, he has no legal right to live here anymore," Bell explained patiently. "He's an adult. It's time for Howie to sink or swim on his own. He sure isn't going to college, but he can join the army, join the navy, or he can get a job and pay his own way. It's your decision to make, but believe me, the best thing you could do is put him out."

Rev. Joe Hackett sat back in his chair, startled. This was something that had never occurred to him. He thought about it for a few moments and then shook his head sadly.

"We couldn't do that."

"You can and you should."

"No, I mean we could never *do* that. It's beyond the point where we can tell him anything. Howie would . . . That would just touch him off again." He glanced away, shuddering at the thought.

"Nah, he'll go." Bell smiled again. "And he'll go quietly."

"What?" Hackett was puzzled, but hopeful. "How?"

"I'll be there to make sure he does."

Chapter Two
The End of June

Howie Hackett tottered slightly as he left Dr. Finsterwald's office on the third floor of the Greene Building. That hangover was still pounding in his head, *and* he'd just had a tooth yanked. There was a hole in his mouth that felt as big as Hilfer's gravel pit. It was plugged with a wad of cotton. The whole right side of his face felt like a pillow. The elevator finally arrived with a rumble and a loud clank. The old guy in the Phillip Morris costume tugged the gate open.

"Feel better yet?"

"Watch it, Dad. I'm not in the mood."

The elevator operator shut the gate, pulled the lever around to G and then sat back on his stool, smiling at the floor. Howie stood with his back against the wall of the carriage. The place stank, the whole damn building stank of cigars and old men.

Outside, it was still lightly raining. Howie stopped at Vic's Smoke Shop a little farther down East Main and bought a pack of Luckies. He cut through Kresge's and came out on Union Street. His blue '55 Chevy box was parked in the lot next to the Shamrock. Once he was inside the car, he reached under the seat, found the pint of Seagram's 7 and took a quick gulp. Some of it leaked through the cotton padding and stung like hell in spite of the novocaine. But the rest of it felt very good. He was about to turn the key when an older guy in a navy blue suit knocked on the window. Howie cranked it down a couple of inches.

"What?"

"You know me?"

"Nope."

"Captain Frank Bell." The man reached into his jacket pocket and came up with a badge. "Schramburg PD."

Howie blew air out of the left side of his mouth. "Okay, so?"

Bell pointed to the other door. "I want to talk to you."

Howie didn't move. "So talk."

The cop's eyes narrowed. "Open the door, Howie. It's raining out here. Don't piss me off."

Howie reached across the front seat and unlocked the door. The cop went around the car and got in. He smelled of Vitalis.

"Okay, what?"

"This your vehicle?"

"Yeah. You want to see the papers?"

"Your father give it to you?"

"No, my father never gave me anything," Howie said. "Joe Hackett gave it to me." He grinned. "Got tired of me using his car, I guess."

"Let's go for a drive."

"Hey, what the hell is this all about, anyhow? I just had a tooth out, my mouth is killing me, and I want to go home. You got a problem with me, tell me what it is right now."

"*Drive*. Otherwise, I'll haul your ass in to the station and put you in a tiny room with no windows, no sink, no toilet, and you can sit and wait for five or six hours, however long it takes, until I'm ready to talk to you again, like I am right now. I've got about three seconds of patience left."

"Okay, okay." Howie started the car. "Which way?"

"Get on South Main, heading out of town."

"Okay, but—"

"I'll tell you when to talk."

Howie drove. He had no idea what this was about. His anger was building quickly, but the thing that worried him and held him in check was that one word—captain. This guy was no ordinary cop. There were a lot of reasons why Howie could be in trouble, but he thought it was all nickel and dime stuff, minor violations—like the bottle of booze under the seat or the row of hedges he'd plowed through in somebody's front yard one night. But even if they knew about any of that, it wasn't the kind of stuff a police captain would come and talk to you about. Like this, with *you* driving *him* somewhere. Then Howie noticed the black-and-white in the rearview mirror, two uniformed cops in it. Shit.

"Cross the river up here and then get on 212 south."

That was the old turnpike in and out of Schramburg, now more of a secondary road. "Where we going?"

"I want to show you something."

"Show me what?"

"You'll see."

Ten minutes later they were on 212 and the houses fell behind and the countryside took over, rocky hills and a thick pine forest that was broken up now and then by weedy meadows or patches of swamp.

"You know that picnic area just ahead?" the cop said after they'd gone a few more miles. "Pull in there."

The rain was a little heavier now and the picnic area was deserted. Bell had Howie park near a wooden table at the far corner, screened from the road by trees. The black-and-white pulled up close behind them and the two cops got out.

"Come on."

Howie got out of his car and slowly followed the captain, walking off the dirt road into a grassy area beneath a huge maple where they were protected from the rain. One of the uniformed men was right behind them, and then Howie saw the other one—taking grocery bags from the cop car and putting them into Howie's.

He couldn't see what the bags were packed with, but they were full. Were they going to frame him with some stolen goods? He stopped and pointed back toward the cars.

"Hey, what's going on? What's he doing?"

"Putting your things in your car."

"My things?"

"Yep, your dirty underwear, crud like that."

"What for? What's—"

"Because you're leaving Schramburg. For good."

"Like hell I am!" Howie yelled. "I live here!"

"Not anymore, you don't."

The captain grabbed him by the arm and yanked him closer. Then he drove his fist into Howie's stomach so fast and hard that he didn't have time to react. The cotton wad flew out of his mouth. He doubled over in pain, gasping. The captain grabbed him by the ears, twisting them, and pulled his face forward as he slammed his knee into Howie's nose. Blood spurted and he screamed, dropping to the wet ground. Then the uniformed cop took over, stomping on Howie's hands and knees and ankles, kicking him in the stomach, ribs, and head.

"*You were in the goddamn poorhouse,*" the captain was saying as Howie moaned and writhed helplessly. "They gave you a good home, they gave you more than you ever would've had. And how did you repay them? Made their life a living hell. You piece of shit."

The other uniformed cop finished throwing

Howie's things into the Chevy. He came and stood over Howie. He unzipped his trousers, pulled his dick out, and began pissing down on Howie's face and head. The cop's partner started laughing.

"Man, how many coffees you have today?"

"Oh yeah, got a full tank."

"Jeez, I don't want to touch him now."

They grabbed Howie by his belt and his feet, and dragged him through the wet grass back to his car. They hauled him up and shoved him behind the steering wheel. He slid over on his side, the pain still so bad he could barely move. The passenger door opened and Capt. Bell leaned in, his face close to Howie's.

"You keep heading south and don't ever come back. I have twelve patrolmen and every one of them knows you on sight. You ever set foot in Schramburg again, I guarantee you'll drop off the face of earth. You hear me?" He slammed his fist into Howie's nose, mashing it even more. *Did you hear me, asshole?*

"Agghh-unhh . . ."

"Good. From now on it's *Scramburg* to you, bud. Now get the fuck out of here and don't even think of coming back. *Not ever.*"

Chapter Three
Ilona and the Elegant Twins

He drove south, holding a T-shirt to his bloody nose, breathing through his open mouth. There were lots of ways to get back into town and he took the one that seemed least likely, circling way around to the north, sticking to back roads and then quiet neighborhood streets.

His luck held; he didn't see a cop car, and eventually he made it to the Muellers's house. Howie pulled into the rutted driveway, away from the street, and hit the horn twice. Less than a minute later, Ilona came out the front door. He smiled and almost felt better. His bundle of love, she was all of 5'1" tall. Her blond hair was tied back in a ponytail. She wore tight blue jeans, a sleeveless white blouse, and penny loafers. He loved the way her curvy little body moved as she crossed the front yard, hurrying through the rain. Ilona hopped in the car—and screamed.

He winced. "Jesus, put a muffler on it."

"Oh my God, Howie, they killed you, baby."

"Damn near."

"What happened?" Ilona blinked back the tears, and then her face flushed with anger. "Who did it, baby? Who did this to you?"

He started to give her the bare details of it, but he had to cut it short. He quickly rolled down the window, leaned out and puked. His head was throbbing, his whole body ached, and he felt sick inside. He could still taste blood in his mouth and throat.

"I need to—"

"Come on inside," Ilona said. "You're all messed up. Don't worry, I'll take care of you, baby. You'll be all right. Just don't say anything about the cops, okay? My mother doesn't need to hear that."

"Those fuckin' bastards. . . ."

"They don't understand you, baby."

"Fuck them. Fuck fuck *fuck them all*."

"Come on, baby," Ilona said, helping him get out of the car. "You need first aid right now. I was a Girl Scout, you know."

"You were?"

"Three years. I learned first aid, all that stuff."

"Still got the uniform?"

"Probably. Why?"

"Jeez, I'd like to see you in that sometime."

"Yeah, you'll be all right."

Mrs. Mueller's hair was stringy, as usual, and she wore the same shapeless housedress she always had on when Howie came by. She was watching *Queen For A Day*. When she caught sight of his face, she blinked once and then started cackling.

"Somebody finally got you, huh?"

"Leave him alone," Ilona told her mother. "He's hurt."

"Boy, they sure made a meatloaf out of you."

"Mom, shut the hell up."

"*You* shut up."

"No, *you!*"

"I don't want him bleeding all over our things."

Ilona took Howie downstairs to the cellar. She had him sit in the old easychair next to her father's workbench. She disappeared for a couple of minutes—he heard her and her mother yelling at each other again—and she returned with some first aid supplies. She wrapped ice cubes in a washcloth and made him hold it against his lips, which were puffy and still bleeding a little. She got a basin of warm water from the sink in the laundry area and began to wash the cuts and scrapes on his face and arms.

"They can't do this to you, Howie. This is America. You can live anywhere you want."

"You got part of that right."

"There's a bump in your nose now."

"Yeah."

She gently cleaned away the clotted blood around the nostrils. "Can you breathe through it okay?"

Howie cautiously placed a finger on each side of his nose and tried to press and work it back into shape, a tiny bit at a time; otherwise the pain lit up his whole head. But he could feel something moving.

"Better now."

"That's good. Don't try to fix it all at once."

By the time she finished, much of the pain in his body had died down to a low ache. Howie could think clearly again, and the anger blazed inside. He was not going to let them do this to him. Joe and Eileen—they gave the cops his clothes, they were in on it. In fact, they must have come up with the idea in the first place. A fucking minister, a so-called man of God. Sorry, we're all tapped out of charity. Throw the bastard out, he isn't ours anyway. From now on it's *Scramburg* to you, bud.

Not that he hadn't given them good reason, but it still astonished and infuriated him that they'd do such a thing. *Well, think again, fuckers. I'm not ready to leave this little dump of yours. Not yet.*

Howie looked around the basement. "Say, your old man's got some workshop here. Got more tools than a hardware store. I bet I could borrow a couple of them and he wouldn't even notice they were gone."

"Howie."

He grinned at her. "Relax. It'll just be for a little while tomorrow. You'll bring them back before he even gets home from work."

"What're you going to do?"

"Make them sorry."

"Who?"

"All of them."

Ilona flashed a wide smile. "Oh baby, count me in."

"You sure? This could be the big flame-out. I've got nowhere to go and nothing to lose. But you—"

"Hey, remember me? I'm with you."

He smiled. "You're hot stuff, you are."

"Glad you noticed."

"Oh, yeah." He pulled her onto his lap. "I noticed."

Howie moved his car to the street around the corner from the Muellers's house and left it parked at the curb. If the cops spotted it, they might tow it in—he wouldn't put anything past them now. But he'd be taking a bigger risk if he drove it around town.

Howie used the Muellers's phone, and Vance and Vaughn picked him up about twenty minutes later. He often referred to them as the elegant twins, and sometimes he called one of them Cool and the other one Classy. They took it in stride. They had James Dean hair. They wore great shirts, never tucked in, collars turned up, sleeves folded back just twice—they had elegant wrists. When they were just standing around, they had a slouch that seemed like the most natural way to be. They gazed off into the distance in a way that showed how uninterested they were in whatever was around them—like the whole town. They said things like "I couldn't even work up contempt for the guy," or "That wouldn't sell in Paris," which had a magical ring to Howie. They would ride around for hours in their father's big old Hudson, sitting back, and it was like they owned Schramburg but regarded it as a minor burden and a disappointment.

Howie had known them since grammar school, but he never hung around with them until freshman year at Schramburg High. He'd been kept after in detention again, it was late winter, dark outside, and he decided to save time by cutting across the football field. Behind the Snack Shack, he saw the elegant twins getting pounded by four other kids. Howie didn't like the numbers and jumped right in. He was big then too, and he made all the difference in the fight. After that, he was in with the twins.

They had it made. Their mother had died of cancer a few years ago. Their father had his own business, a laundry. He used to beat them all the time when they were little kids, but then they got bigger and started to beat him instead. They owned the old man now. Whatever they wanted, fine. They believed he was going gaga from inhaling so much carbon tet over the years, and they were waiting him out. When he died, they intended to sell the business and move to Hawaii.

"You need a room?"

"We have a room you can use."

"Jeez, thanks. It won't be for long."

"Long as you want."

"Just don't make a mess, you know?"

"No, hey, I'm not a slob." He'd have to re-member that. Howie sat low in one corner of the backseat. He was trying to straighten out a Lucky bent almost in half—the goddamn cops had even kicked his smokes. "The other thing is, I need to put my car somewhere."

"The lot behind the laundry."

"You can't see it from the street."

"Man, you guys are the best."

"Hey." Dismissively.

"So, what do have in mind?"

"Kick some ass. All over this fuckin' town."

Vance and Vaughn glanced at each other, and then briefly back at Howie. They smiled, as near as they ever did. He'd never seen them look so in-terested in anything before.

Chapter Four
Shelter in the Grave

That night the elegant twins procured a case of Utica Club and sat up drinking with Howie in his new room. It was on the third floor over the laundry, at the back of the building. The old man lived on the second floor, so it would be easy to avoid him. The only drawback was that the room was stuffy and hot, even with the windows open. Vance and Vaughn shared the other room on the third floor, and there was a bathroom.

Howie had to call a few times, but he finally got in touch with his one other solid friend, Artie Boncal, who immediately came around to see him. Boncal was the only other surviving Town Farm child who still lived in Schramburg. He'd been taken in by a family that had three other kids of their own, who treated him as a resented outsider who didn't belong in their little nest. After fourteen years of that, Boncal stayed away from the house as much as possible. Now that he had just graduated from high school, he was try-

ing to figure out how to move out completely.
They tell you that you have to finish high school
in order to get a good job, so he did; he had
scraped through every damn year. And what did
that get him? He didn't know how to do much of
anything. The kind of jobs that he had a shot at
weren't even worth taking—they wouldn't pay
enough to cover a single room in the cheapest
boardinghouse in town, let alone an apartment
of his own. Boncal was trying to get a handle on
this situation.

"Man, they worked you over pretty good."

"They'll be sorry they didn't do a better job."

Boncal pulled the tab on a can of beer. Vance
and Vaughn were on the small sofa and there
were no other chairs in the room, so he perched
on the bed, a few feet away from Howie.

"Those brown spots mercurochrome?"

"No, iodine."

"How come you didn't use mercurochrome?"

"Ilona had iodine," Howie said.

"You guys use iodine or mercurochrome?"
Boncal asked the twins, who were slumped back,
smoking cigarettes and drinking beer. Their look
of shared boredom changed slightly to one of puz-
zlement.

"I never used either one."

"Me either."

"Good idea," Boncal said. "Don't get cut."

"You working yet?" Howie asked.

"Nah. The other day the old man told me he
heard there was a job going at Acey's, so I stop

by, thinking maybe they wanted somebody in the office, you know? Paperwork, writing up orders, that kind of thing? Turns out they need another tire changer. Fuck that."

"I could use some help," Howie said.

"Sure." Boncal nodded. "Like what?"

"I got to stay out of sight, at least for a few days," Howie explained. "So I need you to go sit in a car for me."

"Can do. Uh . . . is there more to it than just that?"

Howie gave a short laugh. "Well, yeah . . ."

At noon the next day, Ilona drove her '56 Ford into the parking lot behind the laundry. Howie quickly descended the back stairs and slipped in on the passenger side. He was wearing a baseball cap and sunglasses in an effort to make his face a little less recognizable. He gave Ilona a quick kiss and then sank down in the seat.

"How're you feeling today?"

"The hole from my tooth hurts and I'm still aching in about a dozen different places. Otherwise, okay."

"Oh, baby . . ."

"You bring the stuff?" he asked.

"Sure. It's on the backseat."

Howie glanced behind. "All of it?"

"Y-e-s spells yes."

"Good girl."

"Where to?"

"Get on Millville and head out of town."

"Okay. What's out there?"

"You'll see."

It took almost twenty minutes before they reached the eastern edge of the city, beyond residential neighborhoods, where houses were few and far between. Much of the remaining open land was undeveloped, because it was too rocky and hilly. Some of it was still on the books as the property of the town of Schramburg.

Howie reached behind him and picked up Mr. Mueller's bolt cutter. In the brown paper bag from Ray's Hardware was a hefty new padlock and two keys for it.

"Okay?"

"Perfect," Howie said. "Take the left, just ahead."

Ilona almost missed it because the entrance was surrounded on both sides by weeds and dense brush that stood eight or ten feet high. They were on a narrow gravel road, but had to stop almost immediately. Just ahead, a chain hung across the road from two wooden posts. A rusty NO TRESPASSING sign dangled from the middle of the chain and two others were nailed to the posts.

"Is this—"

"Right," Howie said. "The Town Farm."

Moving quickly, he got out of the car and went to the lock that held the chain in place. The bolt cutter easily sliced through it. Howie chucked the old lock into the woods, lowered the chain and waved Ilona on through. Then he pulled the chain back up in place and fastened it with the new lock. Ilona accelerated before he got the door completely shut.

"What do you think—one minute?"

"If that," she replied.

"Anybody drive by on the road out there?"

"Nope."

"Good."

The road soon swung to the right, and after another hundred yards they came out in a small clearing where the weeds only reached knee high. In the center stood the burned-out ruins of the Town Farm. Ilona parked a short distance away, and they sat staring at it for a moment.

"I never knew exactly where it was."

"You never been here before?"

"No."

"I used to come out here a lot when I was around twelve, thirteen," he said. "Looking for my mother's ghost."

"Ah, baby." Ilona put her hand on his arm. "Did you ever see or hear anything?"

"Nah."

"Why did you want to come here now?"

Howie took the other bag of things he'd asked Ilona to pick up and looked inside. Some bottles of soda and an opener, chocolate bars, potato chips, matches, and a pack of Luckies. Good. He opened the car door. "I'll show you. Let's go."

"Okay."

The Town Farm had been a long barn-like building, three stories tall. The exterior brick walls remained in place now, their windows vacant. Most of the roof and the upper two floors had collapsed during the fire, and the ground floor was still full of charred debris and crushed rooms. Years later, Howie heard the official version of what had happened—that late one night a fire had broken out in the small kitchen on the second floor, due to the inattention of somebody on the staff. The interior was a maze of boxy wooden rooms, so the fire very rapidly spread upward. It took a while for the fire trucks to get out there from downtown. The official death toll was twenty-two, but everybody assumed it was closer to forty, since it was no secret that the town unofficially housed some harmless local mental cases there along with the poor.

That was fourteen years ago, when Howie had just turned four. He couldn't remember much at all about that night. He had a sense of noise, of clamor and commotion and terrible screams, but they were more like dream images than memories of something real. What he knew for certain was that his mother had thrown him from their third floor window. They caught him in a blanket. Flying down three floors? It seemed like one more theft that he couldn't remember a bit of it. The smoke overcame his mother, or the floor collapsed first; either way, she was lost.

Same deal for Boncal, except that he claimed he could remember the entire fall to the ground, just like in a movie. He also claimed that he and Howie had been pals at the Town Farm, playing together outside, running up and down the long dark corridors, raising hell. Howie didn't remember any of that—as far as he knew, the first time he met Boncal was a couple of years later, at Twain Elementary—but he never contradicted him. Howie liked hearing those stories, whether they were true or not. There wasn't a whole helluva lot to like about Boncal, but that was one thing.

"Baby, I don't want to go inside."

"Don't worry, it's safe." He yanked several times on the sheet of corrugated metal that blocked the front door, prying it loose. "Come on, it's okay. You need to see this."

Ilona followed him, stooping slightly to squeeze through the tight opening. Inside, they edged along the wall, hemmed in by mounds of ash, broken and burned floor joists, and other debris. They went a short distance, and then Howie bent over and entered a dark tunnel-like passage.

"How-ie."

"Come on," his voice echoed out to her.

Carefully feeling her way, Ilona followed, and a few moments later she was able to stand up. It was still dark, but enough light filtered through and she saw Howie. There were in some enclosed space. The air was cool and damp, but had a bad musty taste.

"This was one of the offices," he said. "The fire was above, so it all fell down. You can see what it was like." He pointed. "That whole side of the office was crushed, but this part along the front of the building, it's still here. Look, you can see the edge of a desk sticking out there."

"Wow." She didn't know what else to say for a few moments. He seemed to be in such a strange, dreamy state of mind. "But baby, why did you want to come here now?"

"Okay." He turned to face her in the faint light. "I wanted you to see this place, so you know where it is and how to get here. I'm staying with Vance and Vaughn right now, but if things get too hot and I have to split real fast, and I can't get in touch with you and you don't know where I am, this is where you'll find me. You'll know I need you to come for me, and we can figure out what to do then. Okay?"

"Oh, okay."

Howie rolled the bag of supplies tight, found a place for it in one of the cluttered corners and covered it with debris. "In case I need it," he said, as if to himself. Then he took Ilona's hand and placed one of the keys in it. "You'll need this to get in. Make sure you put that chain back up right away. A cop probably drives by on the main road once or twice a day and looks to make sure the chain's in place."

"Okay."

"And don't tell anybody. 'Cause I'm not telling anybody else, not Vance and Vaughn, not Boncal. I want only you to know."

"Got it."

"I can trust them, but I don't know how far,

and I don't want to find out the hard way. You're the only person I trust totally."

Ilona almost leapt into his arms and kissed him. "Thanks, baby. I'll be here for you. Any time, any place."

He loved the way she clung to him, her body on his, her legs hooked around his hips, the way it felt to hold her like this with one arm under her sweet ass, the way her skin felt and smelled, her thick hair . . .

"But can we go now?" she said softly in his ear. "You don't want to make out here, do you? In this place? You got a room in town, remember? A room with a bed in it?"

"You're right, I do."

"Good. Let's go. I don't like it here."

Howie hugged her tighter. "Me either."

Chapter Five
Howard Doesn't Live Here Anymore

Vance and Vaughn moved Howie's car, as planned. They were out for most of the afternoon, picking up things that Howie wanted, and they returned to the third floor around eight in the evening with their girlfriends, the Apache sisters, Cindy and Cathy Grenier. The girls were one year apart in age. They both had long straight black hair and strange French-Canadian accents, which was why Howie had started calling them the Apache sisters a while back. They liked it.

Ilona had picked up some burgers and coleslaw at Duke's Drive-In. She and Howie ate the food back in his room. They made out some more and drank a few beers. When the twins arrived with the girls, Howie stood up, an eager look on his face.

"How'd you do?"

"No sweat."

"You got everything?"

"More than everything."

"Yeah, we had a couple of ideas of our own."

"Wow, that's great. Like what?"

"Tell you later," nodding toward the girls.

"Okay. Hey, I owe you guys."

"If you do, you do."

"The show must go on, right?"

"Damn right," Howie said.

Boncal turned up a little while later. He looked quite pleased with himself, and then even more pleased to see that he had a larger audience than he had expected.

"Any luck?" Howie asked.

"Jesus, what a day I had," Boncal began. He opened a can of beer and took a deep swallow. "Man, I needed that. Anyhow, I sat there for I don't know how long, and didn't see nobody, no cops, nobody."

"Where'd you park?"

"On Meadow, across from the entrance to Oak Lane."

"Okay, good."

"I went and got a cup of coffee, came back. Still nothing. Then I went and got a grinder and soda, came back. Still nothing, still nobody. I mean, some people did go in and out, the mailman, somebody else, one of the neighbors, I guess, but not your folks, and no cops."

"Man, they're really laying low," Howie said.

Boncal held a hand up, like he was stopping

traffic. "Maybe not. Because later this afternoon, he comes out."

"Joe?"

"Right, the minister. And he walks down the lane. He's got some papers in his hand, like folders? He walks out as calm as can be, turns on Meadow and heads down the street. I figured he's going to the church or maybe to see his lawyer—who knows? Something like that."

"Did you go to the house then?"

Boncal grinned. "That's exactly what I did."

"I told you to," Howie said, mildly annoyed.

"I know, I know," Boncal continued. "So I walk up the lane and go up to the front door. Before I knock, I'm tossing a coin in my hand, and I drop it, accidentally on purpose, right?"

The Apache sisters and Ilona giggled. That pleased Boncal. He smiled at them and became even more animated in his recitation.

"So I bend down to pick up the quarter, and while I'm down there I casually lift the milk box and take a quick look. Hey, you drink Brock Hall milk, huh? We drink Tranquility Farms. You really think Brock Hall tastes better, or what?"

"Was the fuckin' key there or not?"

"No, no key."

Howie frowned. "Figures. Then what'd you do?"

"I rang the doorbell. Nobody comes to answer. Now, the curtains are drawn, but the front window is open, with a screen on it, and I can hear somebody moving around inside. So I wait a couple, three minutes, and I ring the doorbell again. Another wait, nothing happening. So I ring it for the third time, and a minute later I hear somebody testing the locks on the other side of the door." The girls laughed. "So I go, 'Hello? Anybody home in there?' And this woman's voice says, 'Who is it?' I go, 'Is that you, Mrs. Hackett?' She says, 'Who is that?' I go, 'Mrs. Hackett, it's me, Arthur Boncal, I'm a friend of Howard's.' She says, 'What do you want?' I go, 'I'm looking for Howard. I haven't seen him in a while. Is he home?' And she doesn't say anything for a minute or so. Well, maybe less. Then she says, 'Howard doesn't live here anymore. He moved,' she says. So I go, 'Oh yeah? Where'd he move to?' Now, get this," Boncal alerted his audience. "She says, 'I don't know where. He didn't tell us'." Even the twins were laughing now. "So I go, 'Oh.' And she says, 'Please go now, I can't help you.' And I just get back to the sidewalk when this car comes screeching up, and who jumps out? None other than your old buddy, Capt. Frank Bell."

"Big Frank," Howie said quietly.

"Capt. Bell?" Cindy said.

"He's a friend of our old man," Cathy added.

"He is? How's your old man know him?" Howie asked.

"They drink together at the Legion."

"The American Legion club? Over on Crescent?"

"Yeah."

Howie nodded, then turned back to Boncal. "So, what'd big Frank say to you?"

"Oh man, it's, 'Who're you? Let's see some ID. What're you doing here?' I tell him I'm looking for you. He goes, 'Are you a friend of Howie Hackett's?' I tell him, 'Hell no, not anymore I'm not.' I go, 'He owes me ten dollars and I'm tired of waiting for it.' He says, 'Okay, beat it. And don't be coming around here and bothering the Hacketts no more, understand? Because you won't find Howie here anymore.' He's a meanlooking fucker but I'm cool, I tell him, 'Okay, okay.' And I walk down the lane and get in my car and get out of there."

"That was this afternoon? Where you been?"

Boncal shrugged. "I went back to the house and I sat down on my bed, and then I stretched out and fell asleep."

"You're okay, Boncal," Howie said. "Millions would disagree, but I think you're okay. Thanks."

"Hey, any time. So, what's next?"

Howie smiled. "I'm working on it."

Chapter Six
The Fourth of July

The telephone company substation in Schramburg was located on Franklin Avenue, in an area of tool shops, small factories, trucking depots, and other commercial enterprises. It was a very small brick building with a fenced-in parking area behind it. Howie knew it wasn't the place where the phone operators worked—Boncal's older stepsister worked at that place, on the other side of town. This was the junction box, connecting the town with everywhere else. Only one or two people usually worked there, maintenance men, fixing things when a problem arose. Today the lot was empty.

Ilona swung her car into the short driveway and went to the back lot. If anybody came out and asked, she was just turning around. But there was no one in sight. Beyond the chain-link fence was waste ground. On either side, brick walls. Howie pointed to the back corner, where a clutch of thick wires entered the building.

Ilona pulled up along the building and backed closer, so that her car was directly beneath the wires. Howie quickly got out, climbed onto the trunk and then the roof of the car, and began swinging the ax. He was a little surprised—each one was thicker than his wrist, and they were harder than he had expected. But the axe bit into them, and they fell to the ground, one after another. Three minutes, five? He was sweating and beginning to feel edgy, but still nobody appeared, and then the last wire snapped loose and flopped to the ground. He wanted to continue chopping, cutting the wires several more times, but he and Ilona had been there long enough. He dropped the ax on the floor of the backseat.

"Let's move."

Ilona was pale, her body rigid. It wasn't until they were nearly a mile away that she said, "What's that gonna do?"

Howie put his baseball cap and sunglasses on, and sank lower in the seat. He shrugged. "Piss off a bunch of people, I hope."

The parking lot at the high school filled up early. People walked the short distance from there to Church Street and the town Green to watch the parade. Howie and Ilona were parked on a verge of grass at the back end of the lot. They sat and waited. A few more cars came in, circled around and, finding no open space, left. They were alone. And then they could hear the martial music of the marching band as the parade approached the center of town, a couple of hundred yards away. Howie glanced around once more to make sure there was no one in the immediate area.

"Okay." He grabbed the gym bag on the backseat and then leaned across and kissed Ilona. "See you on Fairview."

"Okay, baby. Be careful."

Crouching low, Howie got out, hurried a few steps to the nearest car, got down on the ground, and then slid underneath. He waited a minute or so for Ilona to drive away. He'd thought about this, and he'd sat outside on the third floor back landing, lighting strips of cloth and counting the seconds to see how fast they burned. They didn't need to be soaked in gasoline.

He was careful and took his time, sliding on his back from one car to the next, reaching up to open the gas caps, using a bent coat hanger to push each long strip of the cloth down inside. Ten cars. Maybe that was pushing it. He had to get away. But ten—that'd sure get their attention.

Howie sat up and looked around. The only people he saw were two older folks some distance away. Their backs were to him as they walked down Hillside. He waited a few moments until they were out of sight. The band was loud now, the parade was in the center of town. Howie took his Zippo out, scooted from car to car, still keeping himself low, and he lit each piece of cloth. He walked briskly up Hillside.

Whoompf . . .

Whoompf . . . m-whoom-whoompf . . .

He lost track, but it sounded like most of them. Ilona was waiting where Hillside hit Fairview. He got in and she hit the gas.

"You got 'em, baby." She was more relaxed now.

"Yeah. Big trouble in a small town."

They had to hang around behind the laundry for nearly an hour before Boncal showed up. He was driving a powder blue '54 Chevy with a cream top.

"That's so cute," Ilona said.

Howie snorted. "Jeez, where'd you find that?"

"Hey, it wasn't easy. Lotta people out today."

"You hear anything?" Howie asked with a grin.

"Yeah, I heard the *boom boom booms*, and the sirens. Beautiful, man, I wish I saw it. No trouble, huh?"

"Nope. Okay, let's get going." He put the gym bag on the floor in the front seat of the car Boncal had stolen.

"Be careful with that," Ilona said.

Howie nodded. "See you at Palmieri's."

"You be there."

"We'll be there, don't worry." He got in the car. Boncal stared at him. "What's the matter?"

"I can't get used to seeing you wearing a baseball hat."

"Fuck you too."

"But the shades look cool."

"Shut up and drive."

"We're moving, we're moving."

Less than ten minutes later they cruised down Crescent and passed the Legion Hall. The meeting room and offices were on the right side of the long, low one-story building, the bar was in the annex to the left. The spaces in front were full of cars, and there were more in the side lot. Two fat older guys, one dressed in a military uniform, stood outside talking.

"Keep going," Howie said.

"Uh-huh."

"Thing I don't like about this car is, if they report it missing right away, you can't hide a car that looks like this."

"Hey, I did the best I could."

"I know, but . . . Jesus."

They turned around at a gas station about a quarter of a mile down the street and headed back. Howie reached into the gym bag and pulled out the two sticks of dynamite that were taped together. The twins knew a guy out of town who used the stuff the blow out stumps and ledge on his farm. Howie had been thinking about using three sticks, but then he figured three of them might roll easier, and he didn't want that.

"You test how fast that fuse is?"

"Yeah. Don't peel out, just accelerate. Once we're out on the street again, drive steady, not fast."

"Easy does it."

"Right."

"You figure a lot of . . . ?"

"Cuts and stuff. They'll get the shit scared out of them."

"Flag wavers piss me off. Dunno why, but they do."

" 'Cause you're not one of 'em."

"Right."

"And they're the first ones to tell you so."

"Damn, that's right."

"Well, Big Frank won't be drinking there tonight."

Boncal laughed. "Nobody will."

The two guys were gone; there was no one outside.

"Swing in."

"Yep."

Howie flicked open his lighter. As they came through the front lot and drove past the bar, he lit the fuse, held his arm out of the car window and heaved the dynamite.

"Keep going."

Howie glanced back. It must have landed on the roof, which is what he wanted. He didn't see it bounce down to the ground. Boncal had the car back out on the street. Howie twisted around in his seat just in time to see it go off, a big flash, the front window blowing out, the whole front part of the roof shredding, wood and shingles flying through the air. The blast shook the car as they drove away.

"I think we got bingo," Boncal said.

"Yeah. Whole lotta shakin' goin' on."

Howie pulled out a rag and began wiping down everything they might have touched in the front part of the car. A few minutes later Boncal pulled up and parked in front of Palmieri's Shoes, off East Main. The store was closed for the holiday and traffic was light on the street. Boncal took the loose wires he'd connected to start the car, and yanked them apart. He and Howie finished wiping off the steering wheel, the shift, the window and door handles. They got out and crossed the street to Ilona's car.

"You do it?" she asked.

"He's got a great hook shot," Boncal said.

"There's a hole in their roof."

Ilona's face lit up. "That is *so* boss."

"What next?" Boncal asked from the backseat.

"Nothing, for now," Howie replied. "What time is the fireworks show at Veterans Field tonight?"

"When it gets dark," Ilona said. "Nine, nine-thirty."

"Good."

"Drop me back where I live," Boncal said. "They're cooking dogs and burgers, and I'm hungry. You guys want to come in for some? It'll be okay. They're all assholes, more or less, but you don't actually have to talk to them."

"No," Howie said. "I'd better not. Can you come by around seven tonight?"

"Sure."

When Ilona and Howie got back to the laundry, she said, "They're cooking out at my house too this afternoon."

"That's okay. You go ahead."

"You can come."

"No." Howie shook his head. "Your folks aren't going to see me again. You tell them you broke up with me. You can tell them that it was because I'm always getting in trouble and fights. The last one was the final straw. Your mother saw me, they'll buy it, and that'll make it a lot easier at home for you, in case all this gets worse. Which it will."

"Okay."

"Listen, here's another thing. I want you to stay home tonight, or go to the fireworks with your family. I won't need you, and it's better if you're with them tonight."

Ilona wanted to protest. "You sure?"

"Positive. I'll have one of the twins call your house tomorrow, and when you get on the phone I'll get on and talk to you."

"Okay, baby." She smiled and kissed him. "Be careful, for me, and have a great Fourth of July. The rest of it."

"Oh yeah." Howie grinned. "There's a lot left to go."

At Howie's urging, the twins had spent the Fourth with their old man at a family gathering in Willow Falls, two towns south. Now the old man was up on the second floor, staring at the

TV with a bottle of Rheingold in his hand, and the twins were in the garage, pouring gasoline into quart bottles, while Howie cut more strips of cheesecloth. The Hudson had a big tank, and they must have siphoned off close to half of it. The three of them looked up sharply when the side door suddenly swung open, but then they relaxed as Boncal stepped inside. He grinned when he saw what they were doing.

"Oh good, the war's still on."

Chapter Seven
An Audience With
the Pope

"What the fuck is going on here?"

Police Chief Dickie Larkin winced. "Honest to God, Jimmy, it looks like random vandalism."

"Don't tell me that, we already wrote it." Jimmy Pope held up the morning edition of the *Schramburg Sentinel*, which carried a big headline: VIOLENCE MARS HOLIDAY FESTIVITIES. The sub-head: *Teenage Vandals Suspected.* A couple of photographs showed the damaged exterior of the Legion Hall and a line of blackened and burned-out cars in the high school parking lot on Hillside Avenue.

"You got it," Larkin said, his hands shaking.

"No, no," Pope said, seething. "The phones are knocked out for half the town for six hours, you have nine cars blown up at the high school and a lot of others damaged, you have the American Legion—*the Mother of God American Le-*

gion, for chrissake—blown up, *bombed,* with fourteen people injured. And then in the evening, nine stores and twelve more cars bombed. Fire-bombed. *Firebombed?* What the fuck is going on here? And exactly what the fuck are *you* doing about it?"

"When it rains it pours," Larkin said helplessly. "We'll run them down, Jimmy. No question about that."

Frank Bell sat quietly.

"And when we do," Larkin continued, "it'll be a nice little story for you. Couple of malcontents, mark my words."

Bell watched the Pope, as he was called. Medium height, fiftyish, slightly pudgy. Jimmy Pope was the owner and publisher of the *Sentinel*, which his family had owned since the year after the Civil War ended. He was more important than the mayor, three out of the last four of which he had pretty much elected by himself. If there was one person in Schramburg who could guarantee Bell the chief's job, it was Jimmy Pope. It was shortly after six in the morning, July 5th.

"Nice little story," Pope fumed. "Don't give me that shit. What do you have so far?"

Larkin turned and said, "Frank, what's the latest?"

Bell kept his eyes on Pope. "There are a few more incidents."

"What?" Larkin was surprised. "You didn't—"

"We were on the way in, a lot to talk about," Bell said.

"Right, right."

"Couple more cars, a liquor store."

"Jesus," Pope said. "Who *is* it?"

"Scum," Bell said. "Local scum, is my guess, and I've got a list of the most likely ones."

"You do?" Larkin put in.

"We're only twenty miles from the Canadian border," Pope ranted on. "How do you know this wasn't the work of skilled saboteurs? That's what it smells like to me. Phone lines? Since when do kids try to cut off a whole town? We're vulnerable out here."

Chief Larkin started to speak, but then hesitated, as if he didn't quite know what to say to that.

Bell jumped in. "Mr. Pope, that's exactly the angle I'd rather not see in the paper, at least not right now. I do think it's quite possible that local scum did this—with outside help."

"You do?" Larkin said.

"A-ha." Pope leaned forward on his desk, gazing intently at Frank Bell. "Go ahead, tell me more."

"But if that gets out, it'll probably scare them away. And we want to catch them—*all* of them. On the other hand, if they read the paper, and they think that we think it's just a little rash of vandalism, that could help us in two ways. First, it could make them relax, and get sloppy and careless, which could make it easier for us to trip them up and find them. Second, it gives us the necessary time to do the kind of behind-the-scenes work that will eventually crack this case."

"What kind of behind-the-scenes work?" Pope asked.

"Well, we may have to knock a few heads. Not that I want to, but sometimes you have to encourage people to talk."

"Heh-heh-heh," Larkin laughed weakly. "He just meant that in the figurative, Jimmy."

"No, I think he's got the right idea," Pope said.

"Well, sure, whatever it takes," Larkin added quickly.

"Okay," Pope said. "I'll hold off on that angle for now. But I want you to keep me informed on a daily basis of how you're progressing."

"I'll call you myself," Larkin replied.

"No, you've got enough to do, Dickie. You're the public face of the police department. Captain Bell here can call me. Say, between six and six-thirty in the evening?"

"I'll be glad to," Bell said.

Chapter Eight
In Response to
Your Editorial

"Did you read this?" Boncal asked, holding up the morning edition of the *Sentinel*. "You see what they're calling us?"

Howie nodded. "Yeah."

"'Cowards and bullies,'" Boncal recited. "What else? Oh yeah, 'Black-hearted scum . . . the lowest of the low . . . the kind of youth who decent kids loathe and avoid at high school.' Hey, that's us." Ilona laughed and the twins were smiling. "James J. Pope, Publisher," Boncal finished. He tossed the newspaper down on Howie's bed. "That guy must think he really is the Pope."

"The real Pope doesn't talk like that," Ilona said. "He's a sweet old guy, always smiling, like you wish your grandfather was."

"The Pope of Scramburg does," Howie said. "We were the scum of town at the Town Farm, and we still are. Right, Boncal?"

"Too fuckin' true."

Howie checked his watch. It was just past two in the afternoon. Even people who went to lunch at one would be back at work by now. Busy at their desks or counters, doing whatever crap they did.

"Let's go for a ride," he said. "I want to take a closer look at that newspaper building. I've seen it plenty of times, but never really paid any attention to it. Know what I mean?"

"What do you got in mind?" Boncal asked.

"What I got is one more stick of dynamite."

"Oh yeah, right."

"You ride with Vance and Vaughn, I'll ride with Ilona. You guys just pull up on the street, down a little ways. We're gonna drive past it a couple of times, swing in through the parking lot and take a look around, see if there's a doorman or a parking guard, anybody like that. That's a three-way junction there, so if we end up going one of the other ways, see you back here later."

"Okay."

The *Sentinel* building, which housed both the newspaper offices and the printing works, was located a couple of blocks from the Green. It was big and solid, old brick, with a lot of carefully trimmed ivy growing on it. There was a small parking area in front and a much larger one to the side. It was not as busy as a store, but somebody was going in or out of the building about every fifteen seconds.

"Okay, let's go in," Howie said after two

passes around the block. "Circle around slowly like you're looking for a space."

There was a reception desk inside, just visible through the glass entryway, but nobody at the door. Signs directed visitors and employees to the side parking lot, but there was no parking guard out front. The handful of parking spaces near the entrance had individual signs designating their exclusive use—MANAGING EDITOR, PRODUCTION MANAGER, etc.

"Whoa, *here*. Look at this."

Ilona braked. They were right beside the back end of a large, shiny Cadillac. It was royal blue and the rear license plate read JJPOPE. Howie laughed as he reached under his seat and pulled out the gym bag.

"Go around once more. I need a second."

He took out the stick of dynamite and quickly sorted through some pieces of cut fuse. He found one that looked like about two minutes, which he figured should be time enough.

"You sure about this?"

"Opportunity knocks," he replied. "Okay, stop."

"What if somebody's walking by when it . . . ?"

"Everybody has one really bad day," Howie told her. "We know not the day, nor the hour."

He glanced around. One person walking away from the building, turning onto Memorial Boulevard, another one on the way inside. Howie flicked his lighter and touched the end of the fuse. He got out of the car, holding the dynamite close to his leg, and walked alongside the Cadillac. He stopped and bent down, as if he'd dropped something, and shoved the stick under James J. Pope's beautiful car.

"Okay, we're done here."

They had to wait about thirty seconds for the light to change before they could get out of the lot and onto the street. Not bad.

"You want me to go around the block, come by again?"

"No. I'd love to see it, but the traffic's gonna get jammed up in a couple of minutes and there'll be cops all over the place. Let's just get out of here."

"Fine with me."

Howie laughed. "I'll read about it in the paper."

"We saw the flames shoot up in the air," Vance explained. "The car didn't go up that far, but it jumped."

"Yeah, we were just coming back around," Vaughn added. "There was no place to stop and traffic was steady."

"It was destroyed, right?" Howie asked.

"Oh god, yeah."

"Totally."

"Good."

"I thought the car'd flip up and fall over," Boncal said, sounding disappointed.

"Those Caddies are heavy," Howie said.

"One stick isn't going to do that. But they've got nice big gas tanks. Neither of the cars next to it went off?"

"No, but they got torched real good."

"Was anybody walking nearby?" Ilona asked.

"No."

"Oh, good," she said.

"But then lots of people came running out of the building, and the traffic slowed right down, everybody gawking and pointing. We just made it around the corner to Water Street, and we got the hell out of there."

Howie opened a beer and walked to the back window. He looked down at the parking lot and the garage. They'd moved his car inside, just to be extra careful. It was killing him not to be able to go anywhere with it. He felt mad and strong, happy about the way he'd struck back. But at the same time he was trapped, dependent on the others. He had almost no money left and it was too risky to keep breaking into joints like that liquor store, which anyhow had only been good for twenty-five dollars and a couple of bottles of Jack Daniels that he gave to the twins.

Ilona appeared at his side and put an arm around his waist. "What's the matter, baby?" she asked softly.

"Nothing. Just thinking."

"Thinking about what?"

"Thinking about what's next."

"What's next?"

"I don't know."

"We can leave. I'll go with you."

"Go where?"

"Anywhere away from here."

"And live on what?"

She shrugged. "We can both find work. Something. Who cares what, as long as we get out of here and can be together?"

"Yeah, maybe."

Howie put his arm around her and they walked back to sit with the others again.

"So, what's up next?" Boncal asked.

"You guys just go about your business," Howie said. "I'm going to sit tight for a few days. The cops'll be jumping around this town like fleas, day and night. Best thing is, we cool it for now."

The twins nodded.

"Okay by me," Boncal said.

Chapter Nine
You Know Me, Frank

"You feeling better?" Bell asked.

"Yeah, sure," Glen Fertig replied.

"Glad to hear it."

Bell sipped his drink and then took a long drag on his Chesterfield. Fertig was knocking back beers. They were in Sully's, a neighborhood bar at the foot of Crescent Avenue in the South End.

"All the same, it shakes you up."

"I'll bet it did."

"The sudden explosion, the screams, glass and wood chips flying through the air like bullets."

"Like war."

"That's exactly right," Fertig agreed. "Brought Korea right back to me, I can tell you. Jesus, it shakes you."

"Good thing people like you were there," Bell said. "You've been through lots worse. You know how to stay calm."

"Right, right."

"I'm sure that was a help to others there."

"Oh, sure, we pulled people out from under, got them outside where the ambulance boys could deal with them."

"Old man Pope is spitting fire about it."

"Oh yeah, they got his car a few days ago."

Bell shook his head. "Man, he was screaming."

Fertig gave a slight laugh. "Broad daylight, right in the middle of downtown. Pretty fucking bold, huh?"

"Bold is right," Bell agreed. "The bastards."

"We had to deal with that in Korea, in the cities and towns. Agents from the other side, planting bombs, sudden shootings. Like that."

"And they weren't wearing uniforms."

"Hell no. They were dressed like everybody else—that's why you never knew who they were until it was too late."

"That's what it's like here. It's like we got this little invisible army out there, driving us nuts."

"You going to run them down, Frank?"

"Yeah, and I have an idea who it might be."

Fertig perked up. "You do?"

"Yeah, but I need some help."

"What kind of help?"

"Strictly between you and me and nobody else," Bell said, leaning closer across the table.

"Sure. You know me."

"Okay. I'm too high profile, people know me, so I can't do the kind of intelligence work that needs to be done."

A faint smile appeared on Fertig's face. "Intelligence work?"

"Right, and shit, this isn't a big town, we don't have anybody else on the force who could handle that."

"Sure, of course not."

"On the other hand, nobody knows more about how to go about this sort of thing than you do."

Fertig nodded. He had a distant look in his eyes. "I could tell you some stories. I been through the book."

"Think you could . . . ?"

"What? Give you a hand?"

"Well, this conversation never—"

"No, never, come on. You know me, Frank. Of course I can."

" 'Cause I could sure use it."

"You got it."

"Thanks, Glen."

"No, really, glad to. If I could help put a stop to these creeps, I'd be only too happy. But I need to know where to start."

"I'm looking for a punk named Howie Hackett."

Fertig nodded. "Okay. Name means nothing to me."

"He's suddenly become impossible to find, but I'm pretty sure he's still around here."

"He's got to have a friend," Fertig said with growing enthusiasm. "A friend, somebody. And that's who we go through."

"Right. The one friend of his I'm sure about is another punk, name of Arthur Boncal."

"You're kidding."

"No, why?"

"Hell, I know the Boncals. I used to live across the street from them until I moved out on Cedar Hill a few years ago."

"They friends of yours?"

Fertig made a face. "Nope, not at all."

"Good."

"And I can tell you about Artie. Kid's a first-class jerk-off. He was drinking when he was thirteen. No respect for nothing. A regular little Mr. Tough Guy, as long as he could get away with it. But he's got no character inside him, if you know what I mean."

Bell nodded. "They're all the same."

"Get him boozed up and he'll be blabbing his mouth all over here and gone. Don't worry about that."

"Good. I hope so."

Fertig thought for a moment. "That all you want to know? Where this Howie Hackett guy is?"

"I want to know everything."

Fertig nodded. "In case it's not so easy . . ."

"Yeah?"

"Well, I'm just saying. It might get . . ."

"That's why I thought of you," Bell said. He smiled. "Glen, you know what you're doing, and you know what it takes to get a difficult job like this done. You've been through it. Personally, I don't care if I never hear of this Boncal again. All I'm interested in is results."

"Okay, Frank. I'm on it."

Chapter Ten
Just Curious

Boncal was sitting by himself at one of the picnic tables at Duke's Drive-In, across the street from Washington Park. He was nearly finished with his burger and birch beer when a wiry guy with a buzz cut came along and stopped abruptly. He sat down on the other side of the table.

"Hey, aren't you Artie Boncal?"

"Yeah." The guy looked familiar.

"I used to live across the street from you."

"Oh, yeah, Mr., uh—"

"Right. How you doing, Artie?"

"Not bad."

"Good. Everybody okay at home?"

"They're all the same as ever."

"Good. So, school's out, huh?"

Boncal laughed. "School's over, yeah."

"That right? You graduated?"

"Yeah, somehow."

"Don't matter how, long as you finished."

"So they tell me."

"Where you working?"

"I'm not, yet. Still looking."

"Oh. Well, good luck."

"Thanks."

"Say, Artie, you busy right now?"

"Nope. Why?"

"You want to make some money?"

Boncal straightened up. "Sure. I mean, doing what?"

"Since my wife died, I've got more darn things to do than I can ever catch up with around the house."

"Your wife died? Jeez."

"Thanks. Anyhow, I got a bunch of stuff up in the attic that I need to move down to the garage. Old stuff I'm going to give away or else take to the dump. Just boxes and bags, nothing too heavy."

"How long a job you think it is?" Artie asked.

Glen Fertig scratched the side of his jaw. "Oh, I'd say about four hours, maybe a little over. Figure the afternoon. But naturally I wouldn't be paying you by the hour. This ain't bagging groceries down at the Grand Union, where they pay you a buck-five an hour. This is more like a moving job or when the repair guy comes to fix your TV. You pay a flat fee for the whole job. See what I mean?"

"Uh, yeah. . . ."

"And to me this job is worth twenty-five dollars. What do you say?"

Boncal gulped. "Sure thing. Hey, thanks."

"Thank *you* for helping me out. You got a car?"

"No, I'm still trying to save for one."

"No problem," Glen told him. "I'll run you back into town when you're done."

It didn't go exactly as planned. Boncal gladly accepted a beer, then a second, then a third. He seemed happy to chat with Glen about anything, all thought of work forgotten. Glen would casually raise a subject, Boncal would start talking. In due course, Glen heard it all—about Boncal's home life, the kind of cars he liked, his high school years, his favorite football and baseball teams, and even about a couple of girls Boncal had dated. Only the last part was of particular interest to Glen.

"You're what, eighteen?"

"Yeah."

"Ever had a blow job, Artie?"

"Huh?"

"Don't worry, I ain't queer. Just curious."

"Oh, okay. Well, uh, sure."

"Yeah? How many?"

"A couple—a few. So far, that is," he added hastily.

Glen nodded. "Take my advice, get as many as you can. And never marry a woman who won't give you a good blow job. Otherwise, you'll be kicking yourself all the way to the grave."

"No, I wouldn't. I know."

"Ready for another?"

Boncal shook his beer can. "Sure."

The one thing Boncal wouldn't open up about was his friends. He never had that many, he said; he pretty much kept to himself. And since graduation, it seemed like hardly anybody was around. Glen gently pushed him, and Boncal finally mentioned occasionally hanging out with a couple of guys named Vance and Vaughn, and their girlfriends, Cindy and Cathy Grenier.

"Oh yeah? Frankie Grenier's girls?" Glen said.

"That's right. You know them?"

"I know Frankie from way back. Cute girls."

"Yeah, too bad they're taken."

"They're French, too. They'd know how to drain your pipe."

Boncal got a dreamy look on his face at that thought. Glen tried to draw him out more about his other friends, but it went nowhere. Finally, he got tired of it and stood up.

"Artie, give me a hand, will you? I got a case of Genny down in the basement. I want to put it in the icebox in the kitchen, but my back's been acting up lately. Some kind of twinge."

"Sure, I'll be glad to." Boncal tottered just a little when he got up. "Then you want me to start work on that job for you?"

"Or we can have another beer and you can come back tomorrow and take care of that stuff then. There's no rush."

"Hey, why not?"

Glen led Boncal down the narrow stairs to the basement, and then to an area on the right. A large square of linoleum had been laid down, there was an armchair, a side table, and a floor lamp.

"Hey, you fixed this up nice," Boncal said.

"Yeah, I needed a place to get away from the wife sometimes. Yak, yak, yak, you know? This way, I could sit back, have a few beers, and listen to the ballgame on the radio."

"Yeah, I get you. Now, where's that beer?"

Glen pointed to a case of Genny sitting on the floor across the room. Boncal started toward it, stepping past Glen—who took a sock full of ball bearings out of his pocket, swung it hard and caught Boncal just behind the right ear. The kid went down and didn't move.

By the time Boncal came to, Glen had him stripped naked and tied with metal wire to a straight wooden chair in the middle of the linoleum. The armchair and side table had been pushed farther away. The wire bound Boncal's hands to the arms of the chair, his ankles to the legs, and several more strands across his stomach were lashed tightly to the back slats. The wire was sharp and had already drawn trickles of blood. There was a rope around Boncal's throat, tied in a slip knot and stretched taut to a hook in the ceiling above. Boncal could not move without hurting or choking himself. Fear and panic filled his eyes as he grasped the situation.

"Oh, no . . . Hey . . . please. . . ."

Glen stood at the workbench on the other side

of the basement. He turned and walked slowly toward Boncal. He had his army bayonet in one hand and large grooved pliers in the other.

"Artie, listen carefully now. We can do this neat and easy, or we can do it messy. Don't fuck around with me, you hear? Because I don't like it when people fuck around with me. I ask you a question, you answer me right away, and it better be the truth. You got that?"

"Y-yeah."

"Okay, good. Now, where's your pal Howie Hackett?"

"Howie Hackett? I ain't seen Howie in weeks," Boncal said in a rush. "He's not my pal, he owes me money. Somebody told me he left town not long after graduation—his mother, his mother told me. I went to the house looking for him. I—"

Glen frowned. "Artie, you're just not taking me seriously, and you should, because I'm *very* serious. Let me give you an example."

Glen clamped the pliers on Boncal's right nipple and pulled it, stretching the skin and flesh. Boncal screamed. Glen flicked the bayonet once, slicing the nipple off. He dropped it in a bucket on the floor and went to get himself another beer. He knew it'd be a minute or two before the kid got back to where he could talk again.

"Frank? Glen."

"Hi. Any luck?"

"You bet."

"Yeah? What'd you get?"

"Everything. The whole ball of wax."

A sharp intake of breath. "How soon can you be at Sully's?"

"Better give me an hour."

Glen walked up behind Boncal, raised his pistol, and fired once at the base of his skull. He got it right—instantaneous, with hardly any blood coming out. He smiled. He hadn't lost it; he still had that touch.

Chapter Eleven
Same Goes for You

"Hey, Ma, somebody's looking for Artie," the kid in the doorway hollered over his shoulder. *"And it's a girl."*

"A girl?" an adult voice called back. "Our Artie?"

"Yeah."

Mrs. Boncal appeared on the other side of the screen door a few seconds later. She was wiping her hands with a dishrag and she nudged the boy aside with her hip.

"Can I help you?"

"Hi, Mrs. Boncal," Ilona said. "I'm a friend of Artie's from school. Is he around?"

"Nope. Artie hasn't been home the last two nights."

"Oh. Do you know where he is?"

"Nope. But he's done this before."

"He has?"

The woman nodded. "He and some of his

buddies go on a beer binge and don't sober up for three or fours days. He'll be back."

"Maybe he went away for good," the kid yelled.

"Don't count on it, Jess. Artie's always talking about leaving home for good," she explained to Ilona, "but he never does."

"Okay. Well, thanks."

"If you see him . . ."

"Yeah?"

"Oh, never mind."

Ilona returned to her car and got in. It didn't make a lot of sense. If Boncal was on a beer binge, it'd most likely be with Howie. Maybe Boncal had some other friends she didn't know about.

She'd brought Howie some donuts that morning. He was starting to get a little stir-crazy up in that third-floor room, so they decided to spend the afternoon at Gorge Lake, twenty miles from Schramburg. Since she had to go back home for her swimsuit and a few things, Howie asked her to stop by Boncal's house on the way to see if he was around.

Oh well.

Ilona was about to turn onto her street, but then she saw the police car parked outside her house. She killed the turn and drove on, somehow resisting the urge to floor it. Fear swirled inside her. Okay—maybe they only wanted to ask her some questions. But she wasn't going to face that unless she had no choice. She'd thought about it. Sometimes she thought she could be cool and would have no problem, but other times she was sure that she'd be so nervous she'd give something away.

She parked behind the laundry and ran all the way up the back stairs to the top floor. Breathless, her heart pounding, she got to the open door of Howie's room and saw him shoving some of his clothes in a bag. Vance and Vaughn stood nearby, looking anxious.

"What's going on?" Ilona asked.

"The cops were here," Howie said.

Vance: "Not two minutes after you left."

Vaughn: "We talked to them downstairs."

Ilona looked at Howie. "But you're still here, thank God. What did they say, what happened?"

"I gotta split. Fast," Howie told her.

Vance: "They're looking for Howie, all right."

Vaughn: "They said they're coming back with a warrant."

"How did all this happen," Ilona said. "The cops were at my house just now too. I saw their car and I kept driving. I drove right back here."

"The cops at your house too?" Howie echoed.

"And another thing, Boncal hasn't been home for two days."

Howie and the twins stood looking at each other.

Vance: "Boncal?"

Vaughn: "Could it be Boncal?"

"No, Boncal wouldn't squeal," Howie said after a moment. "He's in this as much as the rest of us. You don't know—it might be those Apache sisters, if they got talking to somebody."

Vance: "No, no. They're our chicks, man."

Vaughn: "They're gonna get us in trouble? No chance."

"Shit, I don't know," Howie said. "We'll figure it out later. Let's go. I gotta split this place now."

The twins helped Howie carry some bags down and put them in the back of Ilona's car. Howie handed his car keys to Vance.

"I'll give you a call in a day or two," he said. "We'll figure out a place where we can meet, and you guys can bring my car."

"You know where you're going?"

"Only that it's out of town. Thanks, both of you."

Vance: "Hey, any time."

Vaughn: "It's been a kick."

"Yeah." Howie grinned. "I think we made our point."

"I told you so," Frank Bell said, turning the key in the ignition of the unmarked police car.

"Damn, they really are stupid," Glen said.

"Very stupid, and predictable."

"Yeah, but how can anybody be *that* stupid?"

"They've had practice."

"You going to pick up those twins later?"

"I don't know," Bell said. "I don't really care

about them right now. It's just a matter of time before they get themselves in some kind of trouble bigger than this, anyway."

"What about the Mueller girl?"

"She's in it as much as Howie."

Bell followed them across town. He knew how to fade back one or two cars and still keep the Ford in sight. They were on Millville, heading out of Schramburg, when it hit him.

"Well, fuck me pink."

"What?"

"I know where he's going."

"You think it was Boncal?" Howie asked.

"No," Ilona replied.

"Me either."

They were sitting back, resting against the trunk of a large maple tree, drinking warm beer. An empty Milk Duds box and an Almond Joy wrapper were on the ground beside them. Howie had an arm around Ilona's shoulder, his hand lightly touching her breast. He loved the way she felt, the way her body nestled against his. All the worry and fear had vanished once they got to the Town Farm.

"He likes you too much to do that."

"We were there together," Howie said, flicking his thumb toward the ruins. "That's why."

"How bad was it living here?"

"I don't remember any one terrible thing, other than the fire. But it was sweltering hot in the summer, drafty and cold in the winter. The rooms were so small. I remember being scared of other people all the time. Most of 'em just sat around or stood around or walked around going nowhere. It was like they were zombies."

"What was your mother like? You never told me."

"Beautiful, like you. Fell for a loser, like you did."

"Howie, don't say things like that."

He laughed. "I don't know. She was my mom, and at that age that was good enough for me. I still miss her, so . . ."

"That's answer enough."

"You going home?" he asked a minute later.

"Nuh-uh."

"You'll just get in more trouble if you don't."

"Like I care. How much more trouble can it be, after the cops have been at my parents' house looking for me?"

"Oh yeah."

"Besides, if I go home, you'll just crawl into that rat hole and sleep in there. This way, at least you can sleep in the car."

"You're sleeping in the car too, right?"

"Well, of course I am."

"It'll be like the drive-in, but without the movies."

"No," Ilona said. "The one thing you never did at the drive-in was fall asleep. Not that I noticed."

"Sit in the backseat with me?"

"Y-e-s spells yes."

Bell pulled the car up close to the chain, wondering if he had made a mistake and enabled them to get away. He was so sure they were headed for the Town Farm that he'd deliberately dropped farther back and let them get out of sight, so there'd be no chance Howie could spot them.

But now he wasn't so sure. He didn't expect the chain to be up. He figured Howie would pop it and just keep going. Bell got out of the car and examined the padlock. Oh yeah. It was shiny, practically brand new, and it was cheaper and a little smaller than the locks the town used in its parks and properties, as Bell knew from years of checking them on patrol.

"We're hoofing it from here."

"Okay," Glen Fertig said.

They quietly closed the car doors and started up the dirt road. When they got to the bend, they moved into the woods. It was slow going because the brush was thick and the ground was soggy. They were out of the direct sun, but the air was full of gnats. When it felt like they were near the crest, where the land would then begin to dip down into the meadow where the crumbling Town Farm ruins stood, they worked back toward the edge of the road. They moved very slowly and quietly now.

"There's the car," Bell said softly, pointing.

"Yeah, and there they are."

"Where?"

"The big tree, over to the right."

Bell spotted them. "Good eye, Glen."

"Looks like they're having a picnic, fer cryin' out loud."

"They almost have their backs to us. What is that, forty yards, would you say? Fifty?"

"Closer to fifty. You want to rush 'em from here? We can do that," Glen said with a crisp new air of authority. "The breeze is coming this way. Take off, keep to the right, widen their field of blindness, keep the distance, then we come up straight behind them. We fork off the last ten yards, you take one, I'll take the other."

"Right," Bell said. "I'll take him, you cover the girl. If she starts acting up or screaming, give her some knucklewurst."

Glen nodded. "Run soft, don't thump your feet."

"Yeah, and don't trip and shoot your balls off."

"Ha ha. I forgot, you were in the army too."

Guns in hand, they stepped out of the brush and trotted along the edge of the meadow. It was easy, the movement was good, and Bell felt a burst of exhilaration inside—he hadn't run across a meadow like this since he was a kid. Glen looked fierce, crouching low, never taking his eyes off the couple beneath the tree. At ten yards they slowed to a walk, since it was obvious they were undetected. They split off, circling around either side of the tree, arms extended, guns pointed. Howie and Ilona were locked in a long, passionate kiss.

"He's armed with a handful of tit," Glen said.

"Hands up, Howie. *Now*."

Howie and Ilona spun up off the ground in shock.

"Okay, okay," Howie said, raising his arms.

"You bastards!" Ilona wailed in despair.

Glen grabbed her arm and pulled her a couple of steps away. "Put your hands on your head and kneel down," he told her.

"Fuck you." But Ilona obeyed.

"Same goes for you," Bell said to Howie. "Put your hands on your head, kneel on the ground."

"Okay, okay. You got me, big fuckin' deal."

"You have a gun or knife?" Bell demanded.

"No," Howie replied. "Just a buck knife in the car."

"Let me ask you, miss," Glen said politely. "Do you blow him?"

"Two or three times a day," Ilona snarled. "And we fuck once or twice a day too."

"Glen."

"Just curious, Frank."

"Okay, Howie," Bell said. "Face down on the ground. Nice and slow. That's it. Good boy. You should've been this obedient the last time we met."

"I live here," Howie said. "I got nowhere else to go."

Bell came around behind, still holding his gun

to Howie's head. He straddled Howie's hips and crouched down. He switched the gun to his left hand and reached toward his back pocket.

"Before I put the cuffs on you, Howie, tell me, are you right-handed or left-handed?"

"Right."

"Same as me."

Bell took a smaller pistol from his back pocket, leaned forward and put the barrel close to the right side of Howie's head. He pulled the trigger and the kid jerked once.

Ilona jumped, screaming, her face contorted, tears washing across her cheeks. Glen clipped her across the jaw. It wasn't enough to stop her noise, but it knocked her to one knee. Bell swung his arm slightly and shot her three times in the chest. She fell right back and didn't move.

Glen shook his head. "Damn. I liked her."

Bell stood up. He holstered his own pistol, took a handkerchief out of his pocket and carefully wiped the other gun. Still using the cloth, he bent over and placed the gun in Howie's hand, pressing Howie's fingers to the grip, touching the index finger firmly to the trigger. Just to be sure, he checked Howie's pulse, and it was gone. Bell stood up again. He went and checked Ilona's pulse. He moved back a few paces and stared at the scene, and finally he was satisfied.

"Murder-suicide," Bell said as he and Glen walked back down the dirt road. "Same old thing. Good-bye, cruel world."

"I could see why he liked her so much."

Before he backed out onto the main road and they left, Bell gave the gas a sharp hit. The car shot forward, the cheap lock snapped and flew off, and the chain fell to the ground.

Chapter Twelve
It Was in That October

The Legion bar was packed and there was a current of anticipation in the air. Everybody was waiting to see what Kennedy would say and do about the missiles in Cuba. Voices grew louder and had more of an edge in them. There was a sense of gathering darkness—unfamiliar but inviting, soft and silky to touch, its flavor elusive but sweet.

"They fixed this place up real nice," Pope said.

"Yeah, they did a good job," Bell agreed.

"Who got the contract?"

"Buddy Malone."

"That right? His old man was a Democrat."

"I know, but Buddy's okay."

"Good. I haven't been here in a while."

"Yeah, you ought to come in more often, Mr. Pope."

"I'll try. I've got to get back to the office now. This is one of those big front-page nights."

"Sure is. Say, what's your guess?"

Pope frowned. "This guy doesn't have the balls to go right in and get rid of Castro, but that's what he ought to do. Solve the problem once and for all. And if the boys in the Kremlin so much as twitch, take them out too. That day is coming sooner or later, so we might as well get it over with while we've still got the clear edge in firepower."

"Right."

"Nice talking with you, Frank."

"You too, Mr. Pope."

The publisher was gone less than a minute when Glen Fertig came and stood beside Bell.

"Hey, Frank."

"Glen. How's it going?"

"Not too bad. You?"

"Fine."

"Good, good." Glen sipped his beer and said nothing for a moment. "Frank, about that day."

"Yeah?"

"What if somebody saw us?"

"Like who?"

"I don't know. Anybody."

Bell sighed. "It's out in the middle of nowhere."

"Yeah, but it's a big open area, and you got all the woods around it. Somebody out hiking, going fishing, kids. Like that."

"Jeez, Glen, if anybody saw anything, don't you think we'd have heard about it by now? It's been about three months."

"Yeah . . . Yeah, I guess."

"It's over. Forget it."

"You don't have anybody following me, do you, Frank?"

"Following you? No. Why the hell would I do that?"

"No reason, that's why I asked."

"You think somebody's following you around?"

"I can't go so far as to say that," Glen said. "I haven't seen anybody on my tail. But lately I've had this feeling that somebody is watching me, keeping tabs on me."

"A feeling." Bell lit a cigarette.

"Right. You know how you think you're alone, but then you get a feeling that somebody's there, and you turn around and see somebody you know coming? Or you notice that somebody across the room is staring at you at just that particular moment?"

Bell nodded tolerantly. "That's what it's like?"

"That's what it's like, right."

"Otherwise, you feeling okay lately?"

"In the pink."

"Look, Glen, you want my honest opinion?"

"Yeah, of course."

"I think maybe you're spending too much time alone at that house. Anybody's alone too much, they start seeing and hearing things. Imagining things. It's not healthy. I know you miss your wife. . . ."

"No, not really."

"Okay, regardless. It's been a while since she died. You need to get out more, see some women again. Get laid."

"You could be right," Glen said. "I've had some dreams about that girl. I got her hair wrapped in my hand, I'm holding her head down—"

"What girl?"

"The one . . . you know . . . Town Farm."

"Jesus, Glen, I don't want to hear that. Get your head aired out and your feet back on the ground, okay?"

The place fell quiet as Kennedy appeared on the TV mounted high on the wall behind the bar. When he finished, the air filled with an instant buzz of talk and there were a lot of boos around the room.

"Gotta run, Glen," Bell said quickly. "See ya."

"Yeah, okay."

Glen Fertig stood alone. He looked around.

Chapter Thirteen
All Hallow's Eve

James J. Pope left the *Sentinel* building a little after seven that night. The weather had been quite mild the last few days, and still was, but some rain clouds had drifted into the region that afternoon, and now the air was thick with a wet mist.

He had never much cared for Halloween, even as a kid. He always felt uncomfortable dressing up in any costume, except a suit. Now it made him smile every year to publish Joe Hackett's slightly revised opinion piece on the pagan origins of Halloween and why it ought to be abolished. That was not going to happen, of course, because Halloween was also a business event. The only business Pope opposed was smut.

The last few years, he and his wife had worked out a handy way of getting through Halloween. Pope never knew exactly when he'd be able to leave the office; it depended entirely on the news of the day. He didn't like to have his wife home alone, kids coming to the door every five minutes. You can't be sure who's out there on Halloween, so Louise would spend the evening at their son Jay's house, with him and his family. If Pope got away early enough, he'd join them there; otherwise he would see Louise later, at their own house. It had been a quiet day, so he still had plenty of time to go to Jay's and visit for a while.

Pope quickly stepped along the sidewalk in front of the building and unlocked the door of his new ivory and gold Cadillac. He turned the key in the ignition, pulled the headlight switch, and was startled to see a girl in front of his car. She sat on the low brick wall between the sidewalk and the flower and shrub bed along the front of the building. She was bent over, her face in her hands. How could he have passed so close to her and not seen her? Pope opened the door and got out of the car.

"Excuse me. Are you all right?" He couldn't tell if she nodded or was just crying, or both. "Listen, you can't stay here. Can I help you? Do you need to use a phone?"

The girl looked up at him, her face shockingly pretty in the glare of the headlights. "My father threw me out."

"Threw you out? Of the house? How old are you?"

"Seventeen."

"He can't do that," Pope said briskly. "Come on, I'll take you home and make sure he understands."

"No, he'll just get madder."

"It's the law," Pope said dismissively. "Don't you worry, when I get through with him, he'll understand."

"But then you'll leave, and he'll beat me."

"Oh no he won't. He'll never beat you again."

The girl wiped her tears, smiled, and stood up. She got in the car. She sat with her hands clasped between her legs, which pulled her skirt up a little above her knees.

"Have you been out here long?"

"A few minutes," she said. "I was walking around. I didn't know where to go or what to do."

Pope nodded. "Are you very wet? There's a blanket in the trunk, if you'd like."

"No, that's all right."

"What's your name?"

"I don't want to say yet."

"Well, your first name?"

"My first name is Betsy, for short."

"Okay. What did you do that got your father so upset?"

"That's kind of personal," she said.

"I need to know, if I'm going to talk to him."

Tears welled up in her eyes again and she looked distraught. Then she slid quickly across the seat and leaned against him, resting her cheek on his chest.

"I'm sorry," she said. "I'm so scared."

Pope awkwardly patted her shoulder a couple of times, and let his arm remain there.

"That's all right," he said. "You don't have to be afraid."

She took his left hand and squeezed it. Then she pressed his hand over her breast. "He touched me—here." For a few moments neither of them moved or said anything. Then she took his hand a put it between her legs. "And here." She left his hand there and put hers on his thigh, sliding it up. "And he made me touch him here, and he said, 'See how you make me feel?' And he was hard, like you are. And the thing is, I liked it. I liked being touched. I liked touching." She pulled his zipper down and got his cock out of his boxer shorts, stroking it. "Like this. And then he said, 'Go on, go on, take it.' So I did."

She took the tip in her mouth, her lips warm and wet. Pope sat frozen in arousal and anxiety. His eyes glanced around, but it was dark and misty out, and the night-shift people were all inside, working.

"And I liked it. Like this."

"Ohhhhh . . ."

His head tilted back and his eyelids fluttered, half closed. Then she moved her body slightly, and Pope had a brief uncomprehending glimpse of her hand coming up toward his face, as if to caress him.

The blade slid easily into his throat and punctured an artery. She held him tightly until his body stopped shuddering.

Before she vanished into the night, she pressed the fingertips of his right hand on the handle in

several places. Then she let the knife drop naturally onto his lap.

Glen didn't like Halloween. He had to go out
and buy a bunch of candy, otherwise the neighbors would all think he was a creep. He wished
he could turn off all the lights and make them
think nobody was home, but he couldn't do that.

Frank Bell was stopping by. It wasn't easy getting Frank to agree. He said he had a number of
things he was doing that night, so he couldn't
promise to meet Glen at any one place at any certain time. Finally he gave in and said he'd swing
by at some point.

Kids came as ghosts and witches, cowboys and
baseball players, and Glen would say, "Yeah,
yeah, very nice," give them each a candy bar and
usher them out as quickly as he could. The only
good moment came when two teenaged girls
dressed as cheerleaders arrived at the door.

"Lemme see you do a cheer," he said.

They waved their pom-poms and yelled "Rah-
rah, sis boom-bah!"

Somehow it was disappointing, but he gave
them each three candy bars. "If you girls need
any part-time work, I could use some help
around here. Dusting, vacuuming, like that."

Their giggles turned to laughter as they hurried away.

"No, I mean it."

When he shut the door and turned around, he

thought he saw the kid again—standing at the top of the stairs to the second floor. But then he was gone again. This had been going on, a glimpse here, a glance there, always out of focus, out of the corner of his eye. At first he thought—hoped—that it was the girl, but it wasn't. Glen had one clear look a few days ago, just for an instant, and it was that Boncal kid.

"You're flirting with Bellevue," Glen muttered.

He opened another can of Rheingold and sat down, trying to think it out. He had to talk to somebody, and Frank was the only person who would understand from whence this came. But how could he tell Frank? In a way that would make any kind of sense, that is.

Was he going queer? Does it happen like this? He had to wonder. Because he'd been through war, and the dirtiest, ugliest part of war at that. And Glen hadn't flinched or wavered—he did what he had to do and got through it. Of course, you never forget, but life goes on. Compared to that, the thing with the kids was a day at the beach. But he couldn't shake it and he kept seeing something and feeling what-the . . .

Frank didn't arrive until almost ten o'clock. He bustled past Glen and sat down in the living room.

"Thanks for coming. What can I get you?"

"Nothing, thanks. I can't stay long."

"Okay, I won't keep you. How're you doing?"

"Did you have kids coming in here and getting candy tonight?"

"Sure, it's Halloween. Why?"

"With that gun out on the coffee table?"

"Oh, well, mostly they just stayed in the doorway."

"That the gun you had that day?"

"Yeah. I meant to clean it tonight."

"You ought to just get rid of it," Bell said. "Treat yourself to a new one, dump this one in a lake."

"That's a thought."

"So, what's up?"

"Well, Frank . . ."

The girl was sitting on the floor between his legs, smiling up at him. She rested her head on his crotch, her hair fanned out along his thigh. She kind of nestled her face against him, and he was hard right away.

"Yeah, what?" Bell said.

"He killed me," the girl said to Glen. "I could see that you were the good person there. I liked you. I knew that I could talk to you. If only we got the chance."

"Come on, Glen," Bell said with annoyance. "You just going to sit there staring at your fly?"

Glen looked up for a second. "Well, Frank . . ."

"But he killed me."

"You killed her," Glen said.

"Killed who? That girl?"

"Yeah."

"Damn right I killed her. And him. So what?

Jesus, Glen, what the hell are you still bringing that up for?"

"See?" she said. She pressed her lips around the bulge in his khaki pants. "He did it, but you can save me."

The Boncal kid was beside Glen's chair. He nodded at Glen and took his hand. He moved it toward the coffee table. He smiled. Glen took the gun in his hand.

Frank Bell started to jump up and reach for his own gun, but a hand on his chest slammed him back in the chair. There was no hand, but that's what it felt like. He was confused for a moment.

"Glen, put that down and listen to me. You—"

"You killed her," Glen said.

"Yeah, and you killed that other kid. Who the fuck cares?"

The girl smiled up at him as she rubbed and nuzzled him with her face and mouth. Boncal was smiling, nodding yes yes *yes*. And without even looking, Glen turned the gun toward Frank and fired three times.

"Thank you, baby," she said.

Boncal winked. At least Glen thought he winked, but the kid was gone as soon as it happened. He looked down again and felt a great sense of relief. She was still there, still smiling up at him.

"You do care," she said. "Don't you?"

"You saw. For you."

"You want to come with me."

"Yeah. . . ."

"You want to taste me?"

"Yeah. . . ."

"Want me to taste you?"

"Oh, yeah. . . ."

"Lift me up, baby," she said. "Take me to you."

Glen swung his arm up and gazed down the barrel.

"Mmmmm . . . hit me *hard* . . . *now*."

He did.

Joe Hackett's unofficial anti-Halloween ziti dinner was a lost cause, but he held it every year nonetheless. It was a good thing to do. Some folks came, mostly the ones whose kids were grown and out of the house. A few others straggled in later, after they'd taken their kids on the rounds. But Joe didn't mind. He'd put on a couple of records—maybe some oompah music, a polka band—and there were door prizes, a funny quiz and some jokes that he found in an old volume of humorous anecdotes at the town library. God always noticed and cared, even if few others did.

Back at the house, Eileen went into the kitchen to make them both a mug of hot chocolate. It wasn't winter yet, not by a long shot, but they both liked hot chocolate before bed, even in warm weather. With a marshmallow floating in it, melting slowly.

Joe went into the living room and sat down in his chair. He picked up the Bible. This was the one book in the whole history of the world that you could read forever, and never be finished with. He opened it and found that he was reading the story of the prodigal son. He felt a slight pang, but the words rolled on, pulling him in, as they always did whenever he turned to any passage of this book.

He tore the page out, stuffed it in his mouth and began to chew. He tore another page out, shoved it between his lips and bit into it. He felt like he was in a dreamy state—the paper and ink tasted so good; he had no idea. Now Joe was yanking off thicker clutches of pages and cramming them into his mouth, animal noises escaping in short bursts. He used his fingers and pushed, shoving the paper down.

Eileen came into the room. The tray flew through the air and made a terrible racket as it crashed to the floor. She clutched her hands together at her throat. Joe's face was purple, turning black, and his hands moved in a stiff, robotic fashion, ripping pages from their family Bible and shoving them down his throat. She could hardly think, let alone grasp what she was seeing. She tried to cry out to Joe, but it was as if a hand was clamped to her throat. She tried to rush to him, but the hand pressed her back against the wall and held her there.

Joe moved like a windup toy that was near the end. He could only tear off parts of pages and push them at his mouth—most of the paper now fell away to the floor. A strangled sound of bottomless need emanated from him, an unbearable strangled grunting. Then he keeled over on the floor and, after a few spasmodic hand twitches, stopped moving.

Eileen struggled, but couldn't move. The invisible hand still held her by the throat against the wall. She whimpered, and it turned into a long hopeless wail—but it was cut off sharply when she felt warm breath on her cheek.

"*He* hit you."

She knew that voice.

The hand disappeared—she was free. For a moment she couldn't move, she just stood there shaking. The voice whispered in her ear, in a voice that shocked her because she knew it so well.

"*You* explain it."

FINISHING TOUCHES
THOMAS TESSIER

INCLUDES THE BONUS NOVELLA
FATHER PANIC'S OPERA MACABRE!

On an extended holiday in London, Dr. Tom Sutherland befriends a mysterious surgeon named Nordhagen and begins a wild affair with the doctor's exotic assistant, Lina. Seduced and completely enthralled by Lina, Tom can think only of being with her, following her deeper into forbidden fantasies and dark pleasures. But fantasy turns to nightmare when Tom discovers the basement laboratory of Dr. Nordhagen, a secret chamber where cruelty, desire and madness combine to form the ultimate evil.

OFFSPRING

JACK KETCHUM

The local sheriff of Dead River, Maine, thought he had killed them off ten years ago—a primitive, cave-dwelling tribe of cannibalistic savages. But somehow the clan survived. To breed. To hunt. To kill and eat. And now the peaceful residents of this isolated town are fighting for their lives....

ISBN 10: 0-8439-5864-2
ISBN 13: 978-0-8439-5864-5 $7.99 US/$9.99 CAN

EDGEWISE

GRAHAM MASTERTON

Lily Blake's first mistake is getting involved with dangerous forces she doesn't understand. But she is desperate. Her children have been taken. The police are no help. And George Iron Walker claims he can summon the Wendigo, a Native American spirit that can hunt anyone…anywhere…forever. She doesn't think he can really do it.

Then the man who took Lily's children is found— ripped to pieces. Lily's second mistake: she tells George Iron Walker that she can't keep her part of the bargain. Now she has become the prey, hunted by a spirit that will never rest until Lily is dead.

THE TAKEN

SARAH PINBOROUGH

She's a beautiful little girl, only ten years old with pretty blond curls. Why, then, does she strike such terror into all who see her? Because she died thirty years ago—a horrible, agonizing death in the middle of a raging thunderstorm. Tonight the storm has returned…and so has she.

She has returned from a shadowy realm unseen by the living to exact revenge on those responsible for her death. One by one she will make them pay. There is nowhere to hide, no way to escape. It is only a matter of time before her ghastly vengeance is complete….
